# MISSING MAN

A THRILLER

BEYOND THE BRIDGE SERIES
BOOK 2

## SUSAN SPECHT ORAM

SOS COMMUNICATIONS

Published by SOS Communications LLC in 2024

www.susanspechtoram.com

First Edition

ISBN: 979-8-9891982-3-8 (paperback)

ISBN: 979-8-9891982-4-5 (e-book)

**PREVIOUSLY** (in Under Jackson Bridge, Book 1):

When Irena Fishbone and her friends take a boat trip, a rogue wave washes Irena and her ex-husband Jack overboard. He is missing, leaving behind clues to a secret life. Irena suspects a friend of foul play.

 Formatted with Vellum

# A STAR WITNESS IS MISSING

Frankie McNalley paced by her car at the designated meeting spot. Briny air drifted past, coming from the Salish Sea, and she frowned. Her star witness in an upcoming fraud trial was an hour late. The plan was for Jack Fishbone to fall overboard, swim to shore, and meet her at the mile nine marker on the old highway into Millersville.

She gripped her phone tight and called his cell for the third time, but it rang and rang. An owl swooped overhead, wings flapping, and she ducked. A ship horn blasted five times, warning of danger. A squirrel chattered on a perch in a nearby tree.

Her partner, Special Agent Mark Brick, cleared his throat. "Looks like he's a no-show."

Her hands clenched. "Let's check his place before heading to the office. I hope he isn't dead."

At the apartment house, they stomped up a stairway permeated with stale cooking smells, and she knocked on Jack's door. "FBI. Open up, we need to talk."

She was about to kick the door down when a gray-haired neighbor stepped into the hall. "He's not home."

She flashed her identification. "Agents McNalley and Brick. We need to enter his apartment."

The older man pulled a key from his pocket. "I'll let you in. He told me he was leaving town and mentioned the FBI, but he said to keep it quiet."

She said, "Did he say where he was going?"

He unlocked the door and fiddled with his glasses. "No, but I got the impression he was going away for a while. I'll lock up after you leave."

"Thanks."

They moved through the apartment, inspecting rooms. She opened a door and flicked on overhead lights highlighting a display of expensive sneakers. She said, "Brick, get a load of this."

He came in and beamed. "Nice collection. I like the orange ones."

They hurried out and hopped in the car. On the freeway heading south to Seattle, she braked as red tail-lights lit up and traffic came to a halt. Her stomach soured. Jack's going missing would scuttle her sought after promotion. If she didn't find Jack Fishbone, she could be made a pariah or booted out of the Bureau. Her father was proud of her work with the FBI, and she couldn't let him down.

She gritted her teeth. Jack was out there somewhere. In the office, they'd check surveillance cameras and match facial recognition. He might be boarding a plane at SeaTac airport or crossing the border into Canada in a boat. He could be dead in a ditch, murdered by loan sharks. She shook her head, wondering why he couldn't stop buying those limited-edition high-end sneakers.

When the car in front moved ahead, she pushed on the accelerator. Like her car, she had to roll with what was going on around her. She said to Brick, who was riding shotgun, "Fishbone was ready to leave the area and start over, but now he's in the wind. Wonder what changed."

Brick's jaw tensed. "Maybe the crooks he owed money to got to him first."

She wiped a sweaty palm on her pants. "That's a possibility. For now, let's assume he's alive and make every effort to bring him in. He'll regret his decision to disappear on us."

He gazed out the side window. "He won't slip through our fingers. But what a hassle it'll be finding him."

She said, "I don't look forward to telling the boss about this development. She's going to be ticked off."

## 1

### IRENA

I glance at my best friend, Abby Love, who I've known since high school. We're sitting at a two-top in Gigi's Café, and the place is packed. The smell of fresh-baked scones wafts through the room, making my mouth water.

I stifle a yawn. Abby was out of town for work when my ex-husband Jack disappeared, so I say, "How was the convention?"

Abby sets her coffee cup down. "We won a blue ribbon for the Best Vanilla flavored ice cream. But tell me about Jack. I can't believe he's missing."

I draw a shaky breath and say, "Jack and I were on the bow of Craig's boat, and a rogue wave swept us overboard. I made it back to the boat, but he didn't. The Coast Guard and other boaters searched but haven't found him yet." I brush a tear from my eye.

Abby bites her lip. "Everyone loves Jack. He can't be gone. I don't know what we'll do without him."

Thinking of my daughter, I say, "Kelly is devastated. But he might have disappeared on purpose because he was deep in debt and involved in a scam Craig was running until the FBI shut it down."

Abby nods. "I feel for Kelly, with her dad going missing. But Jack was helping older people invest their money. That's what he told me."

I raise my eyebrows. It's just like Jack to spin different tales, depending on his audience. "He was an FBI informant, and Craig's in jail."

She blinks. "Wow, that's a lot to take in. What's going on with Jack's debts?"

"I plan to sell his prized shoes to pay off his debts. Maybe then he'll come back."

She cringes. "He loves his sneaker-head collection. Is there any other way?"

I grip the table edge. "He owes money from a bet on the stock market. He borrowed from a thug who threatened us. And he owes me ten years of back child support. It's no wonder he set up a disappearing act."

She says, "He's not good with money, that's for sure."

My pulse picks up. "I have so much to do, and I'm not sure how to get it all done. Jack's landlord wants the place cleared out in five days."

Abby reaches out and squeezes my hand. "Take a deep

breath. Being this stressed out isn't good for you, and Kelly is smart. She'll know you're upset."

I whoosh out a breath. "You're right."

"You shouldn't have to deal with this all by yourself. Is Buzz helping you clean the place and sell the shoes?"

I massage my temples. "I found out Buzz lied to me, so I broke up with him. It turns out he helped Jack disappear. Kelly needs her dad around, so I don't know what Buzz was thinking. He put his best friend first and ended up breaking Kelly's heart."

Abby opens her hands and says, "I'm sure Buzz meant well. I was married to him, and I should know. He wouldn't do anything to hurt Kelly. He was probably doing what Jack asked him to do."

Karina, the new owner of the café, sets down plates with slices of quiche and warm scones in front of us. She returns with a coffee pot and refills our coffees. "Anything else?"

"No, thanks," I say.

Karina pats my arm. "I'm so sorry to hear Jack is still missing. He's such a great guy. We're sending positive thoughts that he'll be found."

I nod and pick up my scone, taking a bite and moaning. To my surprise, Abby is wiping her eyes. She blows her nose on a tissue. I say, "Everything okay?"

She shrugs and picks up her fork. "Got something in my eye."

We eat in silence for a few minutes. I take a bite of

quiche, and the crunchy bacon crumbles contrast with the creamy egg and cheese mixture. The flaky, buttery crust melts in my mouth. Soon, our plates are empty.

Abby says, "Buzz loves you. He's been stuck on you since grade school. When you broke up with Jack years ago, Buzz asked me for a divorce, and I was devastated. But you guys get along great, so you should keep an open mind about getting back together with him."

"I dumped his things by the curb in the rain, so I doubt that'll happen."

Her eyes grow wide. "A lot happened while I was out of town."

I shrug. "Our friends' group is gone. Nothing's left except for you and me."

Karina, the café owner, comes by with a pot of coffee. "Refills?"

I check the time and say, "No, thanks, I've got to run. I have a violin lesson." I slap a twenty-dollar bill on the table and pull a violin case from under the table.

Karina says, "I didn't know you played violin."

"Jack left it behind for me to find. He knew I've always wanted to play."

Abby looks down at the table. "I wish he left me something."

# ABBY

Irena strides out the door, and a cool breeze blows in, carrying dry leaves.

Karina watches her go. "She's been different since she and Jack fell overboard."

I say, "She's not herself."

Karina pours coffee and says, "She said the experience shook her up."

"Facing death would do that." I inhale the aroma of fresh brewed coffee and lean back in my seat. "She sounded more upset about Jack going missing than about breaking up with Buzz."

"Maybe she still loves him," Karina says and moves on to another table.

I sip hot coffee and mull over the news. This might be a wrinkle in the fabric of our group of friends, or it could be the death knell.

2

---

## IRENA

I pull off and make a quick stop at Jack's apartment on my way to my first violin lesson. I tromp up the stairs to the second floor and use the key I've had for years. This was where we lived after we were first married. Our thirteen-year-old daughter took her first steps here. I step inside and lock the door. This place was as busy as a fishing derby the other day because my ex-husband gave out keys to friends. Everyone had a reason for sniffing around, even criminals in town.

I glance around the living room. File drawers are open, papers are strewn across the floor, and sofa cushions are slashed, tossed aside. Someone was here looking for clues to Jack's secret life and his finances. But I was the one who found the number and password to his offshore bank account, and the thugs who trashed the place didn't.

The air is still and smells musty. I stride to the nerve

center of where our marriage melted down, the second bedroom. I open the door and flip on the overhead lights, illuminating pairs of sneakers on their own special wood shelves.

I shake my head and say, "This marks the end of your hoarding sneakers, Jack. How could you buy more when you owed people money? You set a horrible example for Kelly."

I count the shoes, flick off the lights and close the door to Jack's shrine to shoes. Going down the hall, I frown because he was addicted to buying the best collectible sneakers and didn't stop, even when he couldn't hold down a job. I'll pack them up in the next day or two and take them to my house to sell online.

I lock his apartment, wave to a retired neighbor who I've known for years and hurry to my car. The violin maker's studio is located near Cedar Channel, and I wonder once again where Jack is. I have a sneaking suspicion my former boyfriend Bud Wiser, who goes by Buzz, did something to Jack so he won't be returning to town. I last saw him laughing in the rain after we parted ways. In the coming days, I intend to find out if my hunch is right, and he hurt Jack.

I park by a one-story white wooden building. Long planks of lumber are stored in stacks in a carport. I glance around, looking for the entrance to the violin maker's studio. A tall front door shows a carved lion's head and a sign in the window says "Closed."

The violin maker told me by phone to come into the workshop, where he'll meet me. I walk around the side to another door and grasp a metal knob, pushing open a heavy wooden door. My stomach flutters. I have never had a music lesson, and I wanted to, but growing up poor meant that wasn't an option.

I call, "Hello?" My footsteps echo on the cement floor in a large room. Workbenches by tall windows let in filtered light. The space is immaculate, not a speck of dust in sight.

A tall man in his seventies comes out of a side room and extends his hand. His gray hair touches his shoulders, and a long pointed gray beard reaches his belt buckle. A red and white polka dot bow tie is clipped to his beard below his chin. He smiles, and I try not to stare when his thick mustache moves.

He says, "Welcome. I'm Mercury Thunder."

We shake hands, and I say, "I'm Irena Fishbone, and my ex-husband left me a violin with a note that said to see you for lessons, and you had all the answers? I got the feeling he was talking about more than music. Do you know anything about Jack and the situation he was wrapped up in?"

His thick brows arch, and he looks at me with gray eyes. "I'm not at liberty to share information at this time. I'll have to get to know you better. Perhaps after you learn to play the violin as well as a high school student bound for Juliard, we'll have a frank talk," he says with a twinkle in his eye. He gestures to a door. "Right this way."

He turns and goes through a door, and I follow behind. I'm finding since Jack fell overboard, every task has been difficult. I want my old life back, where my friends hung out together and laughed. Our shared history of knowing each other since high school bound us together. Until it didn't, when Jack went missing.

We enter a wood-paneled room with thick red velvet curtains over the windows. The small space holds a desk and three straight-backed chairs. In a corner is a three-drawer file cabinet with sheet music stacked on top.

Mercury puts his hands on his hips. "By the way, I'm just a small part of your progress. Ninety-nine percent is the work you do on your own at home and one percent me. I can be your guide but you have to carry your own luggage. I have to be honest and tell you it's best to learn to play the violin when you're young. Are you sure you want to go ahead with lessons?"

I say, "I'm sure. Jack wanted me to meet you, and I've always wanted to learn how to play the violin."

He tilts his head. "Saxophone might be easier to learn at your age. Or the bell choir at church?"

I smile. "It's the violin and nothing else will do. When I was young, I listened to a classical music station out of Seattle when my mom wasn't home. I fell in love with the sound of the violin."

He claps his hands. "Let's get started. Did you get the workbook I mentioned?"

I shake my head. "No, the music store was closed. They're moving to a new location."

He opens a file drawer and pulls out a blue workbook, handing it to me. "Here, it's on the house with the first lesson because Jack is such a great guy."

My eyes grow wide. "How well do you know him?"

He tucks a strand of gray hair behind his ear, saying, "Go ahead, get your violin out."

I open the case and pull out the violin, holding it in my arms like a baby. Just like I held my daughter, who is now thirteen years old, but I still remember when she was born. Jack and I were close, but he never mentioned Mercury Thunder until his last note he left with the violin I'd always wanted. I say, "How did you two meet?"

He eyes me. "You have a lot of questions, don't you? Let's stop talking about this. It's touchy, and I can't get into it. Do you know how to hold a violin?"

I put the base of the violin to my neck. "Like this?"

"No, no." He picks up his violin and begins to play with fluid motions. Beautiful music fills the room. He stops and says, "Now you try."

"Okay." I move the bow, and a horrible sound comes out, making me cringe.

He waves a hand. "Don't worry. With practice, you'll improve. It'll sound better."

"How long will that take? A few months? The last time I was a student, I took diesel engine repair classes."

He laughs. "You've come to the wrong place if you want quick results. Music is not for the faint of heart. You've got to be tough. You've got to be strong, and you've got to work past the notes that sound like a bird squawking. If you practice every day for five or ten years, you might be able to play in an amateur community orchestra. Practicing an instrument builds character." He beams.

I wince and wonder if I'm up for learning an instrument at forty years old. This isn't the best time to take up a new hobby. I'm in the middle of a midlife crisis, with my ex going missing, my daughter being distraught about his disappearance, and my recent break up with my boyfriend. But chaos, like divorce, hasn't stopped me from moving ahead in the past, so I might as well dive into music lessons and hope Mercury Thunder will tell me what he knows about the violin and Jack. Maybe his information will help me find Jack.

Mercury demonstrates the technique for playing the violin and has me repeat it. We go over the first lesson in the blue book, and I play along with him. At this rate, I'll be ruining nursery rhymes for anyone in hearing range for the next six months or more.

He says, "Go home and practice every day for an hour. Do you want to schedule your next lesson in a week or call me when you're ready?"

"I've got a lot going on with Jack missing. I need to

clean out his place and work my regular job, so I'll call you to set up a time."

He wipes his eyes. "Such a shame what happened to him."

I put the violin in the case and am about to ask him what he knows when my phone rings with a call for my boat rescue business. My pulse quickens, and I say, "I've got to take this. Thanks for the lesson."

I answer the phone. "Nimbus Boat Rescue."

"We ran out of fuel," a man says, "and we're drifting near Cedar Island. Can you help us?"

I nod to the violin maker, who adjusts his bow tie affixed to his long beard, and I head outside carrying the violin case. A breeze brushes past my cheeks. I stride to my car, stow the violin, and hop in. "Give me your position. I'll be right there."

# JACK

My eyelids are heavy. My skull throbs. People are talking near me, and soles of shoes squeak on the floor. My eyes fly open, and I blink in the glare, wondering what brand of sneakers they're wearing.

My throat is dry. I croak, "Where are my shoes?"

A woman in a white lab coat with a stethoscope around her neck says, "I'm Doctor Ward. You weren't wearing shoes when the ambulance brought you in."

I grasp the bedrails to sit up, but the room spins. My head hurts. I groan and lie back in bed. My mind drifts back to when I woke up in an ambulance taking me to the hospital. Bright lights flashed, and ice picks of pain hammered at the back of my head. I clamped my eyes closed and groaned. Arms lifted my aching body onto a stretcher and loaded me into an ambulance. The doors slammed shut.

A needle pierced my skin, and I moaned. The ambulance moved ahead, and the stretcher holding me shuddered in a bumpy ride.

A man said, "What's your name?"

I swallowed. "I don't know."

He patted my shoulder. "Relax, we'll be there soon."

Now, I blink and say to the doctor, "What's wrong with me?"

She pats my arm with a warm hand. "You have a head injury. An aid car brought you in. Someone called and reported they found you and you were injured."

A thought tickles at the back of my mind, but I can't grasp it. "They found me? Where?"

"Don't worry about that. Just focus on your recovery."

I say, "Recovery from what?"

"We'll talk later when you're fully awake."

I sigh. Machines beep around me. "Am I in Costa Rica?"

"You're in a hospital in Mt. Vernon, Washington."

"I want my shoes."

She leaves and says to a nurse dressed in blue, "John Doe is asking about his shoes."

The nurse says in a low voice, "He has bigger concerns than footwear right now."

I close my eyes and sleep overcomes me as I try to remember my name.

# CRAIG

I sit in a cell and think of the many ways I'll get back at Jack for my being stuck in here. I expected my parents to bail me out, and they have the money for it, but that hasn't happened. They're loaded but letting me rot in jail. I can't believe I was charged for running a scam. I don't deserve to be thrown in a cell behind bars. Jack is the one who should be locked up, not me, because he was in charge of the operation. My buddy Jack turned me in, and I'll never forgive him for that.

A guard pushes a cart past. The grub here might as well be dog food. I'll get back at Jack for framing me, and he'll regret the day he met me.

# KELLY

I glance over the letters I wrote to my dad. They all say the same thing. I'll never forgive you for abandoning me, but I love you and miss you. I miss you so much. Come home, so I can get angry to your face and hug you and never let go. In the meantime, Mom is planning to sell your precious shoes. She's been busy and ignoring me. I feel like you're the only one who cares about me. She won't look me in the eyes since you disappeared. When I asked what was wrong, she said, "I'm pre-occupied is all." But I suspect something bigger is bothering her than she's letting on. Come home, Dad, I need you. How could you leave me behind?

**3**

---

**BUZZ**

I'm checking for a book on the shelves in my bookstore but stop when I hear a woman speaking in a quiet voice in the next aisle. Her voice is familiar, and I bend so I can see between the book shelves. Irena is browsing in the music section. I duck down to stay out of sight, straightening shelves while I lean in and listen.

She speaks into her phone in a low voice, "No one knows about the gold shoes. How did you find out? Did Buzz tell you?"

A female voice comes through the phone. I strain to hear, and it sounds like our friend and my former wife Abby Love. Abby says, "Jack told me about them. He promised to give me the gold leather shoes."

My eyes open wide. Jack sent those shoes to me at Irena's

when I was living there. How did Abby find out about the expensive sneakers? I didn't tell her. I hold my breath and stand still, not making a sound. I want to find out what Abby is up to. She has a habit of whining about not having enough money. She comes off as innocent, but during the time we were married, I learned Abby is a pathological liar. She has no remorse over fibbing to get what she wants.

Irena says, "Jack didn't send the shoes to you, he sent them to Buzz, so you're not getting them, even if you are my best friend. I have a feeling when I settle his debts, he'll come back to town. Kelly needs him, and I like having him around."

She pulls out a book about how to master playing the violin and opens it. I peek between the shelves and hope she won't spot me spying on her. I have loved her since grade school when we bonded over being teased about our names, Bud Wiser and Irena Pickle. I told kids teasing her to stop, and I've been her protector on the playground of life ever since. She booted me out of her house the other day, but she'll change her mind. I'm waiting for the right time to approach her about getting back together, but everyone in town is tense with Craig being thrown in jail and Jack going missing.

Irena says in a harsh whisper, "You're wrong. Jack sent those shoes to Buzz for safe keeping. The note said for Buzz to keep them until he returned. But that won't happen because I'm selling them to pay off his debts, which include the ten years of back child support he owes me."

Abby says in a loud voice, "That's not fair."

Irena says, "Nothing is fair. When you were out of town, everything changed."

"You need a day off and some pampering. Let's get massages and pedicures."

I roll my eyes. Irena works with her hands fixing boat engines. She doesn't wear nail polish and would rather get a tooth extracted than spend a few hours at a spa.

Irena says, "I've got to go. A distress call's coming in."

I duck my head as she turns. My heart pounds. I kneel on one knee, the way I imagined I'd propose to her for the second time before everything fell apart.

"Buzz, is that you?" Irena says.

I look up, and my face heats. "I didn't see you there. Next time you're in my store, say hi. I was looking for a book."

She crosses her arms. "Were you listening to my conversation?"

I wipe sweat from my brow. I've never been good at deception, but I've been practicing so I can achieve my relationship goals with Irena. With Jack out of the picture, I'll finally have her to myself.

I clear my throat. "Who were you talking to?" My right eye twitches.

She stares at my tell and says, "Abby says Jack promised to give her the gold leather shoes."

I say, "No way. We're keeping them for Jack until he gets back."

She shakes her head. "There is no we anymore. You lied to me, and I don't trust you."

I move around the stacks and stand in front of her, looking into her eyes and giving her a concerned look. I'll never tell her that I left Jack dead on the dirt road by the old cannery. "I helped Jack leave as a way to protect him. The people he owes money to are after him and want to hurt him. Babe, we can work this out. This is a tiny wrinkle in the universe of you and me. I know you want us to get back together as much as I do."

She blinks back tears. "It's over. Anyone who takes Jack away from his daughter can't be close to me. What we had is rotting under water with no chance of recovery."

I open my arms. I've got to turn the situation around because she means business when she hauls out the boating metaphors. "Hon, it's been a stressful time. Let's not throw away our relationship over one incident that was a misunderstanding. I was keeping Jack alive, so he could come back to Kelly one day. But you and I, we have something good going between us. Let's forget what happened and start over. I love you."

She steps away. "I don't know what's true or not anymore. I need time to sort this out on my own, so don't text me or call. I've got way too much going on with cleaning out Jack's place, selling his shoes and answering distress calls."

I say, "I can help you with all that. You don't have to do it alone."

"Thanks for the offer, but I need to handle this on my own and clear my head. And don't try to come in my place, because I'm changing the locks. I'll see you around."

My heart sinks, and I watch as she strides away, in a perpetual hurry like she always is when going to the rescue of a boat or a friend in need. She stops at the cash register and buys the book on playing the violin. She'd be better off spending the time practicing than reading about it, but I won't tell her that, after she just shut me out of her life. I'll wait to give her pointers when we are living together again and engaged. When we're married, we'll spend evenings together, side by side, the way it should be.

Bells jingle when she walks out the door with the book under her arm. I rub my chin, concocting a plan. Before she changes the locks, I'll let myself into her house, take the gold sneakers and sell them, keeping the money. Jack won't be coming back due to my regrettable outburst of temper that fateful night by the cannery. On his permanent vacation, he doesn't need shoes or cash, so I'll buy a beautiful engagement ring for Irena. She'll love me again and cry with joy when I present a sparkling ring to her. With Jack gone, I will finally have my one true love all to myself.

# 4

## ABBY

I hang up after talking to Irena and consider my options. Jack joked about giving me the gold leather sneakers with a red star sewn on the side. When our friends were at work and my shift at the ice cream factory ended, he and I would hang out.

I think back to one afternoon when we were sitting on bar stools at the Brown Lantern, and I ordered a pint of Guinness. Jack raised his hand and said, "Make that two." He grinned at me and said, "You're buying, right? I'm waiting to hear back about a new job."

I groaned and smacked a palm on the bar counter. "How do you do it?"

He cocked his head. "What?"

"You get out of paying and come up with an excuse every time. And I fall for it, like an idiot."

He shrugged and gazed into my eyes, giving me butterflies. Magnetism wafted off the man, and I leaned closer to him. He said, "What can I say? I haven't found the right job yet. My passion project is building my sneaker collection, but no one appreciates how important that is, except for you, that is." He grinned at me.

I smiled, hooked by his kind words. He had a way of making me feel special, like I was his only friend in the world. In high school, he was the leader of the group he hung out with. I looked on, watching them in the cafeteria during lunch or out on the grass before school. One day, he called me over to their spot by the flagpole and asked me to join them. I've been friends with Jack, Irena, Craig, and Buzz ever since then.

In the bar, he said, "I'm working up to buying a pair of Double Guard Half Spin Super Splat signed sneakers. That pair of shoes will be the crown jewel in my collection. But I need fifty grand more to win the auction."

I shook my head. "Don't look at me for money. With the cost of groceries going up, I may need to get a second job."

He patted my shoulder. "I bet you've got good credit. You could take out a loan, and lend me the money without interest because we're friends. I'll pay it back. You know I'm good for it. I'm just short of funds for the time being. My new credit cards are maxed out."

"I'm not going into debt for you."

He lifted my chin and looked into my eyes. My pulse picked up. He said, "Come on, pretty lady, help a guy out.

You know, it's too bad you and I didn't get together in high school. We would've made sweet babies and had a good life."

I was sitting close, so close I could smell his citrus aftershave. If only I had met him first. If only he had picked me over my best friend. My heart hammered. I smiled and said, "Let's give it a try now. It might work out."

His eyes grew wide, and he shoved his hands in his pockets. Clearing his throat, he stared at a blue bottle of gin on the back of the bar and said, "Sorry if I misled you. I was just joking. This isn't a good time, and I don't want to ruin our friendship."

A stab of jealousy speared my chest, and I hunched forward, studying my chilled glass. Condensation dripped down onto the coaster, and I wished I could become invisible and stride out the door with my dignity intact. I knew better than to open myself up and get hurt. He was stuck on Irena, making him a love wasteland for any who followed in her wake.

I choked out a forced chuckle. "Don't play with my feelings like that and pretend you don't love Irena. And no, I won't get a loan to help you buy crazy expensive sneakers for your collection."

I gave him a good hard glare and reminded myself not to fall for his fancy talk in the future. He wanted free meals and banter, but he didn't want me. I said, "Besides, what good are shoes if they're sitting in your second bedroom and never worn? Your daughter needs her own room when she stays with you. You should sell them, get out of debt, and give her a better place to sleep than on the couch." I blew out a breath, proud of myself for rousing from a knock down in the dating department. He was the only guy I knew who wasn't in a relationship. Some nights, it seemed like I was the only single person under eighty years old in town.

He waved a hand, swatting away my suggestion. "Kelly doesn't mind. She's fine sleeping on the sofa. She told me so."

I arched an eyebrow. "I bet she's saying that to please you. A girl that age wants her own room, and you have one, but it's devoted to shoes. Why don't you sleep on the couch and give her the bedroom when she stays with you?"

I crossed my arms and smiled, pleased I got in a conversational jab. I was angry as a hornet for how he brushed me off, and the sting of revenge was satisfying. I gritted my teeth. Compared to self-confident Irena, I felt I was a drab wallflower working at a factory instead of running my own business and rescuing boaters in trouble. For years when our group got together, she would regale our crowd with riveting stories of boating escapades. I was tired of being in the audience, clapping for her. I wanted to be the one getting the applause.

He drank his beer. "I'll give what you said some thought. Right now, my priority is to get the gold sneakers, and then I want an early pair of Bill Bowerman running shoes, the ones with the original soles made in a waffle iron." He hooted and pounded the bar with a fist. "That will be the ultimate find."

I drained my glass and set it down. The beer was sweet and rich, just how I liked it, but sitting with him was souring my stomach. He sounded like a zealot who wouldn't listen to reason. He was in debt. Why did he keep buying more shoes?

Zerk, the bartender, came by and touched the dragon tattoo on his neck. "Another round?"

Jack said, "Sure, and two bacon burgers with fries." He turned to me. "Right?"

I shook my head and stood up. "You know what, I've had it for tonight. See you later." I shrugged on my coat and slung my purse over my shoulder.

Jack laughed. "Come on, stick around. We'll laugh like we always do. And listen, if anything happens to me, the gold shoes are yours, if I get them. It'll be pay back for all the drinks and dinners you've bought me."

I bit my lip and deliberated. Zerk fingered the dragon tattoo on his neck while he waited. Jack reached out, squeezed my hand, and said, "I'm lonely and could use some company. Please stay?"

I sat back down on the bar stool and hung my purse on a hook in front of my knees. "Fine, but just this once. I can't keep paying for you. And you've got to get out of debt, find a job, and sell those shoes."

His sudden smile didn't reach his brown eyes.

Zerk patted the bar. "Two beers and two burgers with fries, coming right up."

My mind snaps back to the present when a chill blows past in the breakroom. I tap my fingers on the windowsill, staring out at a gray rainy day and a paved parking lot. My break is about to end, and I'd better go back in. If Jack had chosen me over Irena that day we talked at the bar, I would have helped him escape his money problems. If he was mine, he would have been with me at the ice cream convention south of Seattle, and he wouldn't be missing. But I was out of town the day of the boat trip, when he was swept overboard.

I pocket my phone. Jack wanted me to have the gold shoes, and I feel I deserve something after being taken for granted all those years. Resentment bubbles up in a toxic stew. Jack is missing, and Irena doesn't sound sad about it. As usual, she is focused on straightening out the situation. She might not miss Jack, but I do. I long to hear his laugh and hope to share many more beers with him in the future.

A door to the ice cream factory opens. Machines hum. After work, I'll get the sneakers. I can't wait to track down Jack, and I hope he'll be happy to see me, but I know I can't force it. If wishing could turn dreams into reality, I wouldn't be standing in the middle of an ice cream factory, but on a beach in Mexico sipping a beer.

I head to my work station in a football field-sized manufacturing room and pull a quart of mocha ice cream off the assembly line. Dipping in a spoon, I perform my job of quality control testing. Cold ice cream melts in my mouth. I nod to myself and check off a box on the computer in front of me. The flavors of deep, rich chocolate paired with coffee ice cream come through loud and clear. There's a hint of crunch from bits of ground coffee beans. I grin because that was my contribution to the recipe. It was a group effort, and I'm proud of my part.

I chew on a chunk of dark chocolate and sigh as a feeling that all is right with the world spreads throughout my body. This is how I feel when I'm around Jack. A tiny thought flits past, telling me I should feel good about myself no matter what. My well-being shouldn't depend on someone else. With a shrug, I decide to mull that over later. Right now, I need to taste test the latest batch of vanilla ice cream with hints of ground nutmeg.

**5**

———

## JACK

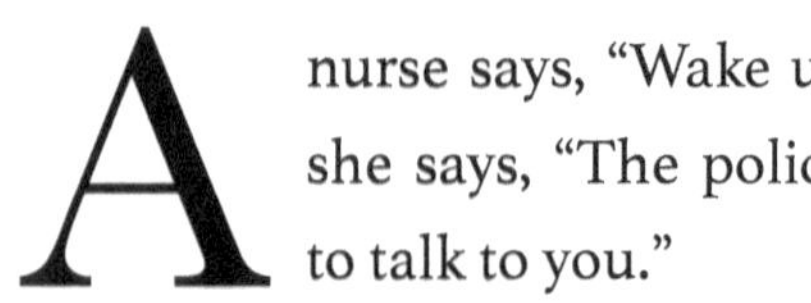

nurse says, "Wake up." When I open my eyes, she says, "The police are here, and they want to talk to you."

My skin breaks out in a cold sweat for some reason. "Make them go away."

She touches her yellow framed glasses. "Our administrator had to report you to the authorities because you don't remember who you are. We do this with all John Does. The police have to see you."

"The back of my head hurts, and I have a horrible headache. Can they come back another time?"

"It won't take long. I'll bring them in."

"Maybe they'll tell me who I am."

She goes out to the hall and ushers in two police officers in blue, a woman in her thirties and a man in his forties. The woman says, "Hello, I'm Officer Kelenick, and this is Officer Anderson."

I nod, and a wave of fear rushes through me, making my pulse pick up. Apparently, I'm afraid of cops. His face is weathered, and he looks like he's been out on boats. So, I must know some people who go boating. Maybe after I get out of here, I can walk around a marina to see if anyone recognizes me. The female officer has a heart-shaped face, which reminds me of someone, but I can't place the name or how I know her.

He says, "We understand you were picked up by the old wharf and brought here with a head injury. Do you remember what you were doing there?"

I clear my throat. "I don't know. I've tried, but nothing comes to me."

The woman says, "What about your name? Do you remember that?"

With a sigh, I say, "I don't, but I wish I did."

She pats the bed rail. "Maybe in time, you'll recall who you are. Do you think you're from this area or from Seattle?"

"Seattle sounds familiar. I might be from there. And I think I know people who go boating, and a woman with a heart-shaped face. Maybe I'm married, and she's my wife. Look for a woman with a face like that and ask her who I am."

The man motions for her to step aside and says in a

low voice, "Kind of hard to find out who he is by checking every woman's face in the state. This is pretty hopeless."

She nods. "He's loopy, probably from medications and the injury. We'll have to come back another time."

# 6

## IRENA

I wave goodbye to the skipper in distress and leave his white wedding cake of a boat behind. His power boat ran out of fuel, and I towed it to the fuel dock. It's all in a day's work and how I keep a roof over my daughter's head. When a boater in trouble calls, I hurry from the dinner table and leave Kelly on her own, now that she's a teenager. I know from experience how that can lead to loneliness, so I keep a close eye on her moods and make sure I'm around otherwise. But despite my best efforts to care for her, nothing can fill the hole in her heart caused by her dad's disappearance.

I nose my boat into my marina slip, secure the lines, and hurry to my car. My friend Abby has been acting different and distanced since she returned from her conference. We're all upset that Jack is missing, but when I first told Abby over the phone that he was gone, she burst into buckets of tears as if she was the one who had been married to him. I had no idea they were that close. And when I told her he owed a major amount of money to a lot of people, she didn't seem surprised.

A pang of jealousy stabs me. I secretly hoped Jack wouldn't fall for anyone after we divorced, but that was ten years ago, and it was unlikely he'd stay single. That was as foolhardy as wishing the briny blue ocean would turn into fresh water. He wasn't the husband I wanted him to be, but I was surprised I didn't want anyone else to have him. It would twist my gut if Abby and Jack fell for each other. I couldn't deal with that.

I hop in my car and head home. Because there was a chance Jack was working undercover for the Feds before he went missing, I called the FBI yesterday and asked for the whereabouts of Jack Fishbone. But they wouldn't divulge any information. I may never know where he's stashed away, or if he's alive, until our former friend Craig comes to trial.

I chew on the inside of my cheek and form a plan. After the trial, Jack could come live with us, and I hope we wouldn't argue about money like we used to. We could be carefree, like when we were first married.

I park in the driveway and frown, because our front door is ajar. I'm sure I locked it when I left, and Kelly is at school, so she didn't do this. I hop out of the car, scan the street for unfamiliar cars and push the door open. The hinges creak.

My hands tremble, and my heart pounds. All is quiet inside. A tsunami of unknowns about where my ex-husband is hovers, keeping me on edge. Perhaps the door wasn't closed properly, and a breeze blew it open. I cringe when I hear footsteps in the kitchen. My pulse quickens, and I pick up the fireplace poker.

Abby sashays into the living room with an open shoe box. She stares at the gold leather limited edition sneakers as she walks.

I purse my lips. Those pricey sneakers will make a world of difference in eliminating Jack's debt and bring him one step closer to coming home to me. I clear my throat, and she jerks.

She looks at me, and her mouth falls open. Her brown shoulder length hair has been recently cut, framing her heart-shaped face. Her complexion is smooth, but mine is lined from working outside in all kinds of weather.

She swallows and says, "I didn't expect you home for a while. Mike at the marina said you were out on a call."

I cross my arms. In our small town, we know each other's comings and goings. When I gave her a key to my house in case of emergencies, I never thought she'd creep in and steal from me. "What're you doing with those shoes?"

"They're mine. I told you that."

"They're not yours. Give them to me."

I march over to grab the box as she wraps her arms

around it. I say, "How could you do this to me? Come in my house and steal? I thought we were friends."

Her dark eyes glint, and she stares directly into my eyes. "I'm not stealing. Jack said he'd give them to me."

My hands clench. "Jack had the shoes delivered here. I have to sell them to pay off his debts."

She pulls a piece of paper from her jeans pocket and hands it to me. "I thought you might say that, so I brought the note where he promised he'd give them to me."

I unfold the paper, and my eyes open wide. Before me is a letter giving Abby the precious shoes that will help pay off Jack's debts, including some of the child support he owes me. I rub my aching neck. "This can't be real."

Clutching the shoe box, she says, "Do you see where he signed it?"

I nod. It looks like his signature, but I wouldn't put it past her to fake it. She likes to weave a web from fragments of the truth and sweet talk her way into freebies, like at the local beer festival last summer when she strode in without paying the entrance fee.

I frown. All these years, she's been my sidekick and supporter, no matter what I was going through, and now, with Jack gone, we're fighting over footwear. "Did you forge this note?"

She shakes her head. "I wouldn't do that. We're best friends. You can trust me."

Just then, Kelly bursts in and tosses her school backpack on the sofa. She grabs the shoe box and takes it from

Abby. "Oh, good, I've been looking for these. I want to see how much we can get for them online."

I give my daughter a quick hug. The days of holding her in my arms are gone, but I'll take the meager seconds I can get. I say, "I hid the shoes, but not well enough, I guess."

Kelly rolls her eyes, "Yeah, I never would've thought to look on top of the fridge." She smiles at Abby.

A headache throbs, and I rub my temples, sending Jack a million dagger thoughts for leaving me with a mess. When he pulled a disappearing act, he left a trail of chaos in his wake. If I didn't still love him, dealing with his disappearance wouldn't hurt so much.

Abby reaches for the shoes. "Those are mine. I have a letter that proves it."

Kelly grabs the letter and studies it. "This isn't Dad's signature. See the way the J is crooked? He doesn't sign it that way anymore. He stopped doing that years ago. I know because we used to sit after dinner practicing writing our signatures."

A tear runs down Kelly's cheek. "He's coming back for me. I know it." She turns to Abby, "Where did you get this note?"

Abby's face flushes, and she says, "All I know is your dad gave me this letter."

Kelly says, "Well, I know that's not his signature." She turns to me, "Did you learn anything about where he is?"

Abby's eyebrows shoot up. "Do you know where he is?"

Something about the way Abby is fixated on this fragment of information makes me suspicious. Why is she so intent on finding Jack? He's my former husband but just a friend to her. I say, "We don't know where he is. The authorities might be hiding him until Craig's trial."

Abby makes to take the shoe box, but Kelly stuffs it in the hall coat closet and stands with her back to it.

Abby says to me, "Seriously, do you have any idea where Jack is?"

I blow out a breath. "I wish I did, but I have no idea. He must be in witness protection." I don't mention my hunch that Buzz hurt Jack because it's based on suspicions, and I can't prove anything. I want to track down where Buzz left Jack and in what shape he left him. But selling the shoes and clearing out the apartment comes first, before Jack's landlord hires junk collectors to clear it out.

Abby sizes me up. "You look like you know more than you're letting on. You've always been an open book."

I open my hands. "That's all I know. Now, give me the house key back. I don't trust you anymore. You tried to take the shoes, and you should be ashamed of yourself."

She digs in her pocket, drops a gold key in my hand and says, "If someone comes in and steals the sneakers after this, you'll know it wasn't me. Hey, want to go for pizza?"

I arch an eyebrow. We aren't friends. We're finished. But apparently, she doesn't see it that way.

Kelly's face brightens, but I say, "We've got too much to do. We're making it an early night, aren't we?" I give Kelly a meaningful gaze, and she nods. The words early night are a signal we worked out for when one of us doesn't want to go somewhere.

I walk Abby to the door and hold it open, waiting for my former friend to leave.

She gives me a one-armed hug, but I'm stiff as a board. She was stealing from my home. The best she deserves is a boot in the butt and a fast farewell.

She says, "Let's get together sometime."

I give a weak smile and suppress a groan, closing the door and locking it. I lean against it and say, "I thought I knew her. I'll have to be more careful about who I give our house keys to."

Kelly pulls the shoe box out of the hall closet and hugs it. "I can't believe she tried to steal our shoes."

"I know." I head to the kitchen to make dinner. A car door slams outside, and I hurry over to glance out the front window. Abby is walking down the sidewalk with my violin. I run outside and race after her, grabbing the violin case from her hands.

My body trembles. I say, "Have you no shame, stealing from friends?"

She stares at the pavement. Wind plays with a strand

of her hair and brings the scent of fall. "Stress brings it on. I've told you that."

I say, "Keep away from us from now on. This is beyond the breaking point. We're officially broken up as best friends."

I turn and leave her weeping on the sidewalk. I don't care if she is stressed. I stop on the doorstep and yell, "Stay away and don't come here again."

I go inside and slam the door, locking it. I set the violin down gently on the coffee table. But as I stride into the kitchen to make dinner, a knot in my chest reminds me that I'll miss my good friend Abby Love and perhaps I shouldn't have been as hard on her. I'll think about it after the shoes are sold and Jack's apartment is cleaned out. I'm too busy to be pulled into other people's personal drama now.

Kelly comes in the kitchen and sinks into a chair. "That was pretty harsh, what you said to her. We should've been kinder to her. She's admitted she has a problem with taking things."

I whoosh out a breath. My thirteen-year-old daughter is wiser than I am. "Maybe you're right, but I can't think about it with everything else going on."

Kelly gets up and opens the fridge. "Being busy is no excuse for being mean." My face heats with shame because she's right. She says, "Besides, you're too stressed. Why don't you let Buzz sell the shoes?"

My hands fly to my hips. "I don't trust him or anyone else to handle it. I need to do it myself."

She puts a jar of pasta sauce on the counter. "You aren't super woman. Let others help you for once."

I blow out a breath. "I'll think about it. We'll have pasta with veggies for dinner and see how much the gold sneakers are worth online."

"I think we should keep them for Dad. He specifically told Buzz to keep them until he comes back. He won't be happy when he hears what we did."

I fill a pot with water and place it on the stove top. "He should've thought about that before he got so deep in debt. Selling them is the only way to rescue him."

She pats my arm. "You know you don't have to rescue everyone. It's okay if some of us learn by sinking."

I turn the burner on under the pot of water and hug my dear daughter. "I don't think you realize how far he has to sink, but I'm listening and taking what you say to heart."

She nods. "Good. Maybe if you do, you'll be happier. You know I skipped dance class this afternoon to come home and check on you. You've been so worried since Dad disappeared."

I clap a hand over my mouth. I forgot about her dance class, the one she loves. What kind of person am I turning into?

7

———

**ABBY**

Out in front of Irena's place, I slump behind the wheel of my car, sobbing until my eyes ache. She accused me of stealing from her, but the shoes were meant for me. Jack said so. I have trouble controlling my habit of taking items from people's homes, and I wish Irena was more understanding after being friends for so long. No wonder she and Jack didn't get along and broke up. She thinks she's always right.

I blow my nose and drive to my apartment, hands trembling on the steering wheel. All these years, I've envied Irena but never told her. She owns a cozy home on the sunny side of the street, while I rent a dark studio apartment. She obsesses about being the best at repairing boat engines, but I make ice cream. She fixes boats and sends skippers on their way, performing dramatic rescues, while I adhere to manufacturing quality control standards and perform taste-testing. It's my job to deliver what the customer expects in a frozen treat, and that was enough for me. But in the wake of Jack's loss, I want more out of life.

If I went missing today, what would people say about me? "She made sure the vanilla ice cream was rich and creamy." They could put in my obit, "She was a saver. Just look at her bank account." But now I want to laugh more and share love, which is why I need to find Jack.

I park on the street, lock my car, and mosey under a bunch of tall brooding trees with low-hanging branches. A dangling twig scratches my neck, and I shriek and scoot away. The way Irena turned on me and accused me of stealing is making me jumpy. I was taking the violin to my car so no one would come by, open her car and steal it. She left her car unlocked, and I was protecting her, but she didn't give me time to explain.

I come to a locked gate and badge my way in the apartment complex. The heavy gate groans with a complaint when I push it open. I make my way to my apartment along a dark path. The outdoor lights are off. I need to call the building manager to fix those. A breeze sweeps by, and a chill runs up my spine. Someone is out here. I can feel it. Goosebumps prick my flesh, and I pick up my pace.

I approach my apartment with my keys in hand and am about to unlock the door when someone steps out of the bushes. My heart thuds, and I clench my fists, ready to defend myself. Unlike Irena, I'm not brave. I'm an ordinary woman trying to live my best life, despite harboring grave regrets about my sticky fingers habit.

A man appears out of the darkness, and I can't see his face. I clench my house key between my index and middle fingers, making a fist, ready to protect myself. He clears his throat. My hands turn cold. I'm trapped by my apartment door.

I'm about to run when Buzz says, "Hey, it's me. I thought you'd recognize me."

I shake out my hands. "You gave me a scare. Next time, text me before you stop by."

He hugs me, and I recall why I enjoyed being married to him. He is kind. He is generous with his time and money. We watch the same shows and read mysteries and thrillers. We even made up a menu for the days of the week. Meatball Mondays was my favorite. He liked Spaghetti Sundays best.

For old time's sake, I say, "You might as well come in now that you're here."

He follows me inside, and I look into his eyes, speaking my truth. "I wish I could forgive you for leaving me back then. You made me promise to tell everyone the divorce was my idea. But you wanted out of our marriage the minute Irena broke up with Jack. I hated you for ditching me and chasing after her so fast."

He cocks his head. "It's not my fault. I was following my heart."

I make a choked sound and turn my back on him,

swallowing tears. What a fool I was in high school to fall for a man who loved someone else. But when Buzz proposed after graduation, I threw away my fears and embraced a new life. I thought he had grown out of what he called his "Irena obsession." But it turned out he hadn't. His longing for her was a silent partner lurking, crouched in every corner of our lives, during our marriage. I loved him, but my husband loved my best friend.

Some nights, he would call Irena and talk instead of coming to bed with me. I would lie on the firm mattress he insisted we buy with my eyes open, hearing him laugh in the other room. Even though I live alone now, I have never been as lonely as when Buzz and I were married.

Buzz says, "Do you have any ice cream?"

I flick on the lights and scan the room, imagining how I'll leave this place behind. My possessions don't mean much, compared to my freedom. But I won't tell Buzz about my plan to sell some sneakers and escape my boring life. Maybe I can manipulate him into unknowingly helping me. He owes me that much after leaving me and running after Irena. Time hasn't healed the wounds of being dropped on a moment's notice and divorced. Even though it was years ago, I haven't forgotten how I was hurt, and I might joke with Buzz, but the scars in my wounded heart remind me of how it felt to be betrayed by my beloved. We'll always be friends, but I don't trust him.

8
___________

## BUZZ

I walk into Abby's apartment and sit in an easy chair, wanting to learn what Irena might be saying about me. Abby perches on a straight-backed wooden chair. Her face is pinched, and her arms are folded. I can only guess how much she misses Jack now that he's gone. She's always had a thing for Jack, even when we were married. It used to drive me crazy. One time, she said his name in bed, and that moment crushed my dreams of sharing a life together. Our marriage would have lasted if not for her eyes for Jack, my best friend.

I say, "How're you holding up with Jack gone?"

Abby pulls out a tissue and dabs at her eyes. "I miss him so much."

I run a hand through my hair. "We all do. I'm devastated. He's my best friend. What's Irena up to? Did she say anything about me?"

She shakes her head. "She's taking violin lessons. Isn't that strange?"

I sit back. "A lot of what's happening is strange, like the scam Craig was running. Did you know about that?"

Her shoulders soften. "Craig asked me for two-thousand dollars for an investment he was making, but I said no. Every dime matters to me."

I nod because Abby isn't the best with money, and her studio apartment looks like it with two mismatched chairs, a bed in the corner, and a tiny kitchenette with a hot plate and mini-fridge. I was lucky to attend college, and I own a used book store. She works at an ice cream factory and is just getting by. "You dodged a bullet by not going in on their scheme."

She says, "What do you know about the gold sneakers? Are they valuable?"

"They are. The shoes were delivered to me at Irena's, but she kicked me out. She was furious I lied to her about helping Jack disappear, but I was keeping a promise to him, and he told me not to tell anyone."

"You helped him disappear?"

"I did, because he wanted to get out of town. I guess some bill collectors were after him."

She says, "Can you get those gold shoes from her?"

I shrug and pretend I didn't go into Irena's house and take them, leaving behind a pair of knock-offs. If Abby heard that, she'd tell Irena, and we'd never get back together. I say, "She won't let me back in the house. She dumped my stuff on the curb in the rain. I even had to beg to get my dog back."

Abby says, "She's angry, and we're all upset Jack is gone. She must be taking her frustrations out on you. Don't tell her we talked about the gold sneakers. She's determined to sell them to pay off a chunk of Jack's debts."

My stomach churns. The hot dog I ate earlier threatens to come up, but I swallow and force my features to appear placid. No one can suspect the truth about my creeping into Irena's house while she was out and taking the gold leather sneakers. She hasn't changed the locks yet or asked for my key back, which is giving me hope that she still loves me and wants me back.

My mouth forms a thin line. "Did you know Jack's debts includes ten years of child support he owes her? She's not rich, and she needs the money. How could Jack do that to her?"

She says, "Jack just hit a hard patch, but maybe his luck is about to change."

I choke down a chortle. She's lying to herself if she thinks his being a leech since high school is due to a string of back luck. "Let's be honest. Jack doesn't like to work."

Her face flushes, and her jaw tenses. "Nobody does, except for you and Irena. Here's an idea. Why don't you take the shoes and give them to me to sell? We'll split the proceeds."

The corners of my mouth quirk, and she catches it. "What's so funny, Bud Wiser?"

I wince when she calls me by my given name, which is why I was teased on the playground. Irena and I bonded over being bullied when she moved to town. Back then, before she married Jack, her name was Irena Pickle, and kids picked on her. Adults did nothing to stop it, so I became her protector and never stopped.

Abby focuses her gaze on me, and I examine the worn tan carpet. She says, "You look like you know more than you're letting on. What is it?"

I wave my hands in surrender. "You know as much as I do. She thinks when his debts are settled, Jack will come back to town. The ghost of Jack haunts us."

Abby narrows her eyes. "Jack didn't give her permission to sell his sneakers. He'd be devastated if he knew what she was doing, liquidating his life's work."

I say, "She has to. No one's paying Jack's rent, with Craig in jail. Life moves on."

Abby says, "Let's work together. You take the shoes, and I'll sell them, and we'll both benefit."

"Sorry, but it's not my style to do that."

She frowns and folds her arms. "Fine, but don't tell Irena I suggested that."

I shove my hands in my pockets. "That's a deal. Man, I miss Jack. Don't you?"

Her eyes fill with tears. "I had a secret crush on him when I was married to you."

I chuckle. "It was no secret. You looked at him like he was a hunk of chocolate cake, and you wanted a bite of him. What else is Irena saying about me? Anything?"

"Just that she's ticked off at you."

My heart sinks, and I stand, ready to go. Abby gives me a hug, and I pat her back in a brotherly way and say, "I'm sorry I had eyes for Irena when we were married, because look where that got us. Nowhere but trouble."

"And now you and I are the best of friends."

Holding her in my arms and smelling the scent of her shampoo brings back memories of when we were married and showered together. But I only have one true love, and she runs a boat rescue business. I bet she is waiting for me to come back and counting the minutes and hours until we're together again.

I step toward the door, resting my hand on the metal knob. I clamp my mouth shut and don't mention how I plan to buy a ring for Irena. No one can know, or it'll spoil the surprise. I say goodbye and turn away with a smile, imagining the look of joy I'll see on Irena's face when I propose. My fingers tingle with anticipation. But first I need to sell the sneakers.

9

## JACK

I release a ragged breath. The man in the next bed moans, and a fabric curtain separates us. He coughs and hacks, and I wince, wondering how I landed in a hospital ward. A clock on the wall ticks as the seconds of my life slowly pass. My head throbs with pain, and I squint, trying to remember my name and the life I led. I must be a loner, because if I had friends, they'd be here by my bedside helping me figure this out. But I'm on my own, biding time with my injured brain and missing memory.

My bladder is bursting, and I hit the red call button for the nurse. She appears and says, "You called?"

"I need to use the bathroom."

"You're not allowed to get out of bed. We're worried you'll fall because of your head injury. I'll get you a urinal."

I sigh. Images of a carefree life in Costs Rica flit through my mind. Sunshine and sandy beaches sound good to me now in this stark room.

The nurse hands me a plastic jug with a handle. "Call me when you finish using it, and I'll measure the amount." She closes the curtain and leaves.

I finish my business and push the red button. She takes the urinal, which is a third full, and says, "Any luck remembering your name?"

"Nothing yet."

"Brace yourself for if and when your memory comes back. You might not like recalling what led to your head injury, and your world may change while you're away."

I slump back on the pillow. "If I had friends who cared, wouldn't they look and find me here?"

She nods. "They're probably looking for you now."

My stomach rumbles. "Can I get some food? I'm hungry. And something for the pain?"

She points to a white board at the foot of my bed. "You're NPO or nothing by mouth, doctor's orders. They'll need to conduct tests, and you'll likely need surgery."

I wince. "What kind of tests and surgery?"

"The doctor will fill you in."

I squirm on the thin mattress. "Is someone coming to take me to a hotel?"

She furrows her brow. "Would you repeat that for me? I'm not sure I understand. You're in the hospital, and you're not going to a hotel. You're not well enough to be discharged."

I clear my throat and wonder where my wife is, if I have one. Shouldn't she be here with me, by my bedside? I say, "I have a foggy memory of maybe being married. Was my wife here?"

"So far, no one has called or come looking for you. Do you know her name?"

My head aches. Jolts of pain shoot through my skull. I touch a thick bandage on my head and moan. "I don't know."

The nurse says, "I'll see if I can give you something for the pain."

She leaves, shoes squeaking on the floor, and I swallow hard. Why haven't my friends found me? Tears trickle down my cheeks. I'm alone.

## 10

### IRENA

I swallow a bite of noodles drenched in marinara sauce and say to Kelly, sitting across from me at the kitchen table, "After we eat, let's go to your dad's and take his sneakers home with us."

She frowns. "We've been rushing around since Dad disappeared. Can't we hang out here like we used to, just for this one night? Besides, I have homework to do."

I get up and kiss the top of her head. Her hair gives off a pleasant smell that reminds me of bubblegum. "Homework comes first," I say. "We'll stay home, and I'll tackle it tomorrow."

I wash the dishes and grit my teeth. I can't wait until the shoes are sold, Jack's apartment will be empty, and we'll move on with our lives. I fall asleep on the sofa watching the news but wake when Kelly shakes my shoulder.

"I'm going to bed," she says, clicking off the television. "And you should too."

I stand and give my daughter a hug. "Night, sweet dreams."

She says in a trembling voice, "Do you think we'll ever see Dad again?"

I suck in a deep breath. "I hope so, sweetie. I've tried to track him down, but no luck so far."

I turn off the living room light and am about to follow her down the hall to bed. But a sense of being watched prickles at the back of my neck, and I turn to peer out the front window into the dark night.

Buzz is leaning against his car parked in front of my house. He's watching me through binoculars. I lower the blinds and pace, debating whether to confront him.

I pick up my phone and text him. "You're giving me cringy stalker vibes. Don't hang around staring inside. You're creeping me out."

Seconds later, my phone dings. "I know you love me. Let me in and we'll talk."

Footsteps approach the front door, and my stomach knots. Until Jack took off, I trusted Buzz and loved being around him, and I saw a future for us. I put my ear against the door and hear him breathing on the other side. Was I too quick to push him away over one lie?

I frown, feeling like he picked Jack over me when he kept Jack's secret about how he disappeared. Shouldn't I come first, before his best friend? On the other hand, Buzz gave Jack his word, and Buzz doesn't break promises, like the one he made to love me through thick and thin. When I said I wasn't ready, he stood up, brushed off the knees of his tuxedo and said, "I guess the honeymoon will have to wait a little longer. I'm here for the long haul."

I kissed him and said, "I just need a little more time. It's a big change."

Outside, a dog barks. It sounds like his dog Happy, who is the best dog ever. I miss having Buzz and Happy in my house, and I think Kelly feels the same way. Buzz deserves a full-throttled two-way top speed love, holding nothing back, and if I can recover from being lied to, maybe I could give him that. By being stubborn, am I denying myself what I want, which is to be loved and trust another person with my life?

I say through the door, "Hey, I miss you."

Buzz says, "I love you, Irena. I always will."

"Let's talk in a few days, okay?"

"You know where to find me."

The sound of him running makes me move to the window and peek through a gap in the blinds. He starts his car and drives off with his dog barking out the window.

Kelly steps softly into the room. "Is everything okay?"

I blow out a shaky breath. "Yeah, it's fine. Buzz was outside, but he left. If he comes by when I'm not here, call me and don't let him in. We have unresolved issues."

"Okay, but I don't think he's as bad as you're making

him out to be. He was protecting Dad from people who wanted to hurt him, and that was the right thing to do."

I nod. "I'm sure Buzz thought he had the best intentions when he picked up your dad from under Jackson Bridge and helped him disappear. I just wish he'd been honest and told me what he did."

Kelly says, "It feels like there are shades of right and wrong. Buzz lied to us because he made a secret pact with Dad. Is it really that bad?"

I ruffle her hair. "When you put it that way, maybe not. I guess it's good someone was looking out for your father, because he must have been scared. The law was bearing down on him, loan sharks were after him, and he was talking to the Feds about what Craig was doing."

"I miss him."

I kiss her cheek, and the part of my heart that pines for Jack, the life of the party, is full of sorrow. "I do too, and we'll get through this together. Maybe he'll walk through the door tomorrow."

Kelly wipes her eyes. "Don't get my hopes up for no good reason."

"Sweet girl, wherever he is, he's thinking of you and sending you balloon bouquets of love."

She sniffs and smiles. "That's corny, but I like it. I'm going to bed. I'm tired."

# BUZZ

I drive home from Irena's and my hands shake as I grip the steering wheel. How could so much have gone wrong in such a short time? Irena and I were living happily together a few days ago, and now she won't let me in her house to talk. My new reality boggles my mind.

I reach over and pat my dog. "We'll get through this. Don't worry. She loves us. It won't be long before she invites us back. Kelly loves you, old boy."

At my house, I step past books stacked on the floor. I kick off my shoes, leaving them where they land. Irena was always after me to leave my shoes by the door, so that's the only benefit of us not living together.

I dig in my pocket and pull out a metal key. A cloud of guilt hangs over me about my losing my temper and hitting Jack at the wharf, but solace is footsteps away. I walk to the closet in the second bedroom, unlock the door and flick on the light.

Gazing at the framed photo of Irena taken in grade school, I send up a prayer that she will be my wife. Sometimes one person in a relationship can see into the future, and right now, that's me. It may take more time than I'd like, but I'll wait. When her world crumbles without Jack, I'll rescue the woman who races to help boaters in distress, and she'll be forever grateful.

"You're mine, and you always will be. It's just a matter of time."

I take a pen and paper and scribble out a love poem in a white leather notebook with others waiting for the day I'll show them to her.

**11**

---

**IRENA**

When Kelly leaves for school in the morning, I pull out the violin to practice, sounding like a cat wailing, and fifty minutes later, I stop and stow the instrument in the velvet case. I hop in the car and head to Jack's apartment. Going up the stairs, steps groan underfoot and stale cooking smells fill my nostrils.

I unlock the door and go in, locking the door behind me. I don't want someone walking in, not after a fake pizza delivery guy with a gun tried to break in the other day. A mouse skitters across the floor and disappears in a crack below the kitchen cabinets. Jack didn't want to set out traps and hurt his resident rodent.

I stride to the second bedroom and flip on the overhead lights. Jack's sneaker collection is spotlighted, and each pair is displayed on a separate wood shelf he built with loving care. I cross my arms and glare at the shoes that caused our divorce.

When Kelly was little, Jack lost his job. But instead of going out and finding work, he bought another pair of expensive limited-edition sneakers. That led to a raging argument in this very apartment, from which he never moved, and our marriage didn't survive. Before that, we exchanged tense words about his addiction to buying shoes and over-spending, but the last pair of sneakers was what sunk our ship.

I frown at a pair of black canvas shoes worn by a basketball star. Jack installed track lighting in the room that is a shrine to sneakers, with one bulb aimed at the pair that broke the back of our relationship. We divorced when Kelly was three, which was ten years ago, but the day those shoes entered this apartment is fresh in my mind.

Jack opened a package and beamed. "They're here. The shoes are finally mine."

I turned from cooking dinner in the kitchen after a long day of learning to fix diesel boat engines. Spaghetti was the easiest choice, I figured. My fingers were stiff and cold from work but steam from the boiling pot of water warmed them as I dropped in the pasta to cook. My stomach soured when he mentioned shoes. I thought after our last talk that he had agreed to stop collecting sneakers and be satisfied with what he had. I figured I must have misheard him, so I said, "What did you say?"

He held up the box and showed me. There were the black sneakers that he promised he wouldn't buy. He smiled at me, and a tear rolled down my cheek. I had warned him if he bought another pair of shoes, that would be it for me.

I said in a choked voice, "Hon, I love you, but your habit is dangerous. We can't live together or share a checking account anymore. You hoarding shoes and not controlling your spending is tearing us apart."

He came over and tried to hug me, but I stepped away and held out the wooden spoon to keep him from coming closer. He said, "Come on, do you really mean that? You know I love you, and I also love my shoes. Both of you make my life worth living."

I swallowed tears and said in a quiet voice, "I'm sorry you feel that way, because I told you it was either the shoes or me. And you picked the sneakers. I'll pack tomorrow and take Kelly with me. I'll rent a place in town."

"Don't do this to us. We love each other. We have a wonderful daughter. Stay with me. I'll try to change."

I shook my head. "Trying isn't enough. This is final. You can have Kelly here on Wednesday nights and every other weekend."

Jack dropped to one knee and held out a hand. "Don't do this to us."

The pasta on the stove bubbled and boiled over, hissing on the burner.

Kelly came into the room, picked up our vibe, and burst into tears. Jack picked her up and gave me a sad look. "See what you're doing? You're destroying our family." Kelly whimpered, nuzzling his neck.

I turned the heat off under the spaghetti pot and rubbed Kelly's back. In a low voice, I said to the man I had loved since I met him in high school, "We're over our heads in debt. You keep taking out credit cards. We can't keep going like this."

He half-smiled. "It'll all work out."

"Banks don't operate that way. We can't repay our mountain of debt with coupons of hope. I'll file the papers for separation and work on paying off our debt. But after that, you're on your own."

Kelly squirmed in his arms, and he set her down. "I don't feel it's an addiction. It's a passion project that deserves respect. I guess this means I'll have to hold off buying the pair of early Bill Bowerman running shoes I've wanted. This sucks."

Tears clouded my vision. I dropped the wooden spoon in the sink. "You can eat if you want. I just lost my appetite." I fled to the bathroom, locked the door and leaned against the wall sobbing quietly for all we had lost.

Remembering all that, I heave a sorry sigh and pull out my phone, taking photos of the black sneakers in Jack's apartment. "Those should bring in a lot of money, if what Jack said was right." I'm snapping pictures of the shoe collection when a loud knock on the door makes me flinch.

I stride to Jack's door and say in a loud voice, "Who is there?"

"Mr. Abernathy, the neighbor."

I open the door, and the hinges creak. I always knew when Jack was sneaking in late when we were married, after going out drinking with Craig and Buzz. I could have asked the building manager to oil the hinges or done it myself, but I wanted the old-style alert system to Jack's comings and goings.

"Come in and sit down," I say and give him a quick hug. Mr. Abernathy smells of aftershave and old books with a hint of floral dryer sheet in the mix. "Would you like a glass of water? That's all I can offer. Jack didn't leave much in the way of food or drinks when he disappeared."

Mr. Abernathy sits in a straight-backed wooden chair that Jack and I picked out when we were married. The chair groans under his weight. He leans his elbows on the table and it rocks. He says, "It's been a whirlwind last few days. How are you holding up?"

I drop into a chair and blow out a breath. "I've been running ever since Jack left, so I haven't had time to think about it."

"How's Kelly? She must miss her father something fierce."

I nod, but an arrow of guilt pierces my heart. I clear my throat and say to the man who became a father figure over the last thirteen years, "I admit I've been preoccupied working and sorting out who Jack owed money to. I know I need to spend more time with Kelly, and I'm going to do that."

He drums his fingers on the table, and it wobbles. "Irena, I've known you and we've been close for years. Is it all right if I tell you something that might hurt your feelings?"

I swallow and cross my legs, pretending not to be worried about what he might say. "Sure. It's been a crazy time, and I'd like to hear anything you have to say. Go ahead and tell me. You won't hurt my feelings because I'll know it'll be said out of caring."

He adjusts his glasses and gives me a gentle smile. "I've noticed you tend to rush around doing tasks. You accomplish a lot, more than the average person by midday. But sometimes you might forget about feelings in the process of checking things off your to-do list. And right now, your daughter needs you more than ever. Don't leave her behind while you hurry to clean out Jack's apartment."

I open my hands. "But I only have five days to clear the place out."

He reaches over and pats the table. "Slow down and pay attention to Kelly during this whirlwind time. If you don't, she'll never forgive you. Take my word for it. I know the look on the face of a forgotten child. And she's changed since Jack disappeared. She is lost and needs you as a stabilizing force. We're all at sea with Jack gone, and you're her emotional rescue boat until he returns, if he does."

I sit back and nod. "You're right, and I'll do better. I should've seen it myself."

"Don't blame yourself. You would've realized it in time. But by then it might have been too late to regain her trust. Inside she's probably a mess but putting on a brave front for you and to get through school."

I pull my hair back in a ponytail. "How do you know so much about this? I thought you worked on tugboats."

"I wanted to be an elementary school teacher, but my parents said that wasn't work fit for a man. They pushed me to pick another career. But I've always wanted to work with kids, and I've read about emotional intelligence and topics like that."

"I'm impressed. Whatever your other insights are, please share them."

He sits back and rubs his chin. "I have advice, if you'd like it, about how to get this place cleaned out."

I lean forward. "Please, tell me what you'd do in this situation."

"Here's the plan. First, haul the sneakers out of here. If you don't, someone is likely to steal them. I bet word is spreading like wildfire around town that the place is vacant. Those shoes are valuable."

I pull out my phone and take notes. My mind is swirling with details, given all that's going on, and I might forget a critical part of what he's saying. "Makes sense."

"Bring Kelly by to pick out what she wants to take to your house."

I make a face. "I don't really want anything of Jack's at my place."

He points at me. "Remember, it's not about you. It's about Kelly and memories of her father. If she wants the ugly dresser in the bedroom, let her take it to remember him by. After all, he might not be coming back."

"You're right. I don't if he'll ever be back."

He pats the table. "He's a great guy. I'd hear his laugh across the hall in my apartment. I loved to hear you two laughing when you were married."

I bite my lip. "The early days were the best."

He straightens up. "Okay, so now you've cleared out the valuables and let Kelly pick items with precious memories. By the way, in my line of work, we lost people at sea, and I learned it's best if you're honest and tell Kelly her dad might not be coming back."

I nod and wish my last words to Jack had been kind. Instead, I sniped at him about his increasing debts. I wish I let him know how much I loved him and how great a father he was. I hope he knows that without my saying it to his face, if he's alive.

Mr. Abernathy fiddles with the frames of his glasses. "He knew so much about shoes and the history of jogging."

I tilt my head. "Jogging? He never talked to me about that."

"He was working on a book about it. Last time I saw him he asked me what I thought of several titles he was considering using. His favorite was A Runner's History of the World. I told him it was an ambitious project, but he said he was already halfway through."

I purse my lips. I guess there are things I didn't know about Jack, but that might be true about people in general. My friends who I thought I knew were hiding secrets, and I had no idea. I say, "He never talked about writing a book."

Mr. Abernathy says, "It's human nature not to trust others or accept the totality of who we are."

I think of how Buzz lied to me and say, "But do we really know anyone, or ourselves, through and through for that matter?"

He shrugs. "Maybe not. But we can try to get a better understanding of ourselves as time marches on. I know Jack tried to stop the demons tormenting him that were telling him to buy more shoes. He went to an addiction group but left after one meeting and said they didn't understand where he was coming from. He swore he saw a few of them smirk when he said he was addicted to collecting sneakers."

I put my head in my hands. "I wish he would've told me this. I might've been more understanding." I gulp down tears. "Poor Jack, wrestling with beasts on his own."

Mr. Abernathy taps the table. "When you've taken the valuables and Kelly's items, then you're left with stuff that doesn't matter to you. Like this table and these chairs, the bed, the sofa that someone slashed when they were tossing the place after Jack disappeared. But I suppose you'll take his computer and the filing cabinet?"

"I will, although I don't know where I'll put them. It'll be fascinating to read his book."

"He never let me read it. With the stuff left in the apartment, you could pay someone to haul it to the curb and post it online as free. Or call the local thrift store and see if they want to take anything. If it was me, I'd call the one that benefits cats."

I say, "That's a good idea. I'll bring Kelly over, and she can pick things out. I'll take the computer and filing cabinet to my place. Then I'll call Feisty Cat Thrift Store and the junk haulers for the rest."

My phone dings with a text from Kelly asking where I am. I had promised to pick her up after school. My face turns hot, and I stand. "It's a half day at school, and I'm supposed to pick Kelly up. I've got to run."

## 12

### IRENA

Mr. Abernathy says a quick goodbye and lets himself out. I rush into Jack's second bedroom and put four pairs of sneakers with their boxes in a black plastic garbage bag. My pulse pounds in my ears. I've got to get going. I glance at the remaining nine pairs and flick off the lights. I'll come back later for the rest.

I lock the apartment door, set the bag in the trunk of my car and drive to school, scolding myself for failing my daughter and being an inadequate parent. There are many mistakes to be made as a mother, and I had no idea what lay ahead when Jack and I decided to conceive. Every day I spend with Kelly brings oceans of joy and zings of self-recrimination for my not being the perfect parent she deserves.

I chew on the inside of my cheek and drive. Jack is a go with the flow kind of guy, but I like to be in control and doing my best every minute of the day, which is exhausting at times. I approach the school, but no kids are in sight. My stomach plummets. Kelly will never forgive me for this. She is my most important loved one, and I've got to do a better job. If this was my paid gig, I'd be fired for how I've acted since Jack left town.

Down the street, two teenagers walking side by side catch my eye, and I drive closer. A girl Kelly's age plays with her long braid and bumps Kelly's shoulder, and they laugh. My chest loosens a little bit. I'm still an awful mother, but at least Kelly is okay.

I pull up, roll down the window and say, "You girls want a ride?"

Kelly turns to her friend. "Want to come to my house?"

I almost blurt out something about how I wanted to go to Jack's to take the rest of the sneakers and have Kelly pick a few things out. But I keep my lips sealed and wait.

"Sure. I have to tell my mom, but I'm sure it will be fine." She texts something, and we wait. A message comes in with a ding, and she says, "Okay, let's go. I need to be home by six. We're having Thai take out for dinner."

Kelly looks at me and says, "My favorite."

They climb in the car and sit in the back. "Hi Mrs. Fishbone, I'm Plum. I'm in Kelly's class and new to town."

I nod and glance in the rearview mirror. "You can call

me Irena. I was new to town once too. Kids used to make fun of my name."

Kelly giggles. "My mom's last name then was Pickle."

They erupt into laughter, and I feel forgiven for being late. I desperately want to be a good mother during this difficult time. She deserves that after Jack ran away from his problems, leaving her traumatized by his disappearance. But to his credit, Jack did help the authorities shut down Craig's scam that was preying on the elderly. I wonder if I'll ever see Jack again.

I swallow a lump in my throat and swerve to avoid a squirrel running into the road. To help Kelly get through this tough time, I want to be less selfish and more giving. She needs me to be present and not distracted by a million things on my to-do list, like paying quarterly taxes and refueling the boat so I'm ready for the next distress call.

Kelly says, "By the way, we're not girls. We're young women. Just so you know."

They laugh and point at someone as I drive past. Kelly says, "That's my Aunt Abby. I wonder where she's going? Slow down, Mom. I want to talk with her." She rolls down the window, and Abby turns to us with a smile. Kelly says, "Where are you going? Come home with us."

Abby glances at me. "I was just going for a walk. But sure, I can stop by." She trots over to the car and slides in the front passenger seat.

"Hey, you," she says, patting my shoulder. "We haven't seen much of each other lately. This will be good to catch up."

"Yeah," I say. I give her a quick flash of a fake smile. Driving away, I clamp my jaw shut and wish my former best friend wasn't going home with us.

## 13

### ABBY

I glance over at Irena and wonder what is bugging her. Her jaw is clenched, and her mouth looks like she ate something sour. My taking the violin out of her car wasn't that big a deal. If a friend can't forgive you, they aren't a real friend. When I can get her alone, I'll apologize again.

I say, "I've missed talking with you. We've been busy since Jack disappeared."

A teenager in the back seat says, "Who disappeared?"

Irena gives me an ice-cold glare, and I cringe. I guess I shouldn't have brought it up. Irena is defensive about Jack being gone, and she has turned into a mother bear for Kelly's sake.

In the back seat, Kelly says to her friend, "That's my dad. He fell off a boat with my mom, and she was rescued, but he disappeared. I don't know if I'll ever see him again."

Her friend says, "That sucks. I don't know what I'd do if that happened to me. I'd probably stay home and cry in bed all day."

"That would just make me feel worse. The hard part is, I can't do a thing to bring him back."

Irena says, "We're doing all we can. I wish we knew where he was so we could go see him. I'd scold him for giving us a scare."

Kelly blinks, and a tear trickles down her cheek. Her friend holds her hand. In the quiet of the car, I hold my breath and feel Kelly's pain. When I was ten, my dad died. He fell off a ladder working on the gutters above the driveway. I was the last one to see him alive. I heard a clatter and a yell. As I looked out my second-floor bedroom window, my dad floated past, his mouth open in surprise, arms flailing, legs kicking, going down. But it was too late for me to save him.

My mother ran outside and screamed. Neighbors came running. I called 911 for an ambulance. When the EMTs in the red truck arrived, I hid inside and shivered by the front window. An EMT stepped back and shook his head. He was pronounced dead, and it wasn't until they hauled his body away that I cried. I'll never forget that day.

After that was when I started taking little things when I visited people's homes. Small things they wouldn't miss, like a paper clip or a round refrigerator magnet slipped in my pockets. But the compulsion grew stronger with each passing month and year. A hair brush or a piece of costume jewelry, like a tourist pin with a Hula girl from Hawaii, made me feel better for a few hours. But then my fingers itched for something more substantial.

Jack and I bonded over our addictions. He hoarded sneakers, and I took items from people's homes. We went to a group counselling session with other addicts, but he made me promise never to mention it to anyone. I confessed to being a thief and felt better for it, lifting my hidden veil of shame. He told the others in the group he was hooked on buying sneakers for his collection. He thought a few people snickered at what he said, but I didn't see that reaction.

I purse my lips and gaze out the window as we pass a park with a stone bandstand. It's a shame Irena is going to sell the shoes that he worked so hard to get. Jack told me she never understood how much the shoes meant to him and that collecting was an art form for him. Before she sells them, I might as well help myself to a few pair from his apartment.

Buzz drives past. He is hunkered over the wheel, staring ahead and looking intense. I wonder what he's up to.

14
___

## BUZZ

Something is pulling me back to the place where I left Jack. I've heard perpetrators return to the scene of the crime, lurking in the crowd, and now I understand the draw. I want to see the wharf where I dropped Jack off to start his new life. Irena knows that much by now. But what she doesn't know is how I left him, dead and bleeding. I told my staff at the bookstore I'd be right back and hopped in my car. Driving down the road, I clench my teeth and wonder what I'll find at the wharf. Will his body still be there?

I turn off at Martin Road making my way to the waterfront. Jackson Bridge looms in the distance, with a steady hum of car tires coming from vehicles crossing. I drive down a dead-end dirt road and pull to a stop.

The old wooden Martin Wharf once held a thriving cannery, but now the building is rotting and leaning, as if about to fall. That will be my life, falling down and collapsing, if I don't keep my mouth shut about what I did to Jack. It was a mistake, and I'm not proud about how I lost my temper and went into a rage when he said he was going to take Irena and Kelly with him and never come back. What kind of best friend wants to steal your girlfriend and take your future? Jack was focused on what was best for him, and he took it to a level of Olympic sport.

I climb out of my car and stretch my legs, doing my best to look casual as I scan the area for onlookers. But there's no one in sight. It was dark, and I didn't get a good look at how much damage I inflicted when my fist connected with his jaw and he fell back, his head connecting with the ground with a crack.

Before I left him that night, I emptied his pockets of identification. He didn't even moan as I pulled out his wallet. He was that far gone. I've been thinking about what to do with his wallet and haven't decided on a good place to put it.

I approach the spot by the wharf where I left Jack dead, and my jaw falls open. There's a brownish-red stain on the dirt and a jagged-edged rock. He must have fallen and hit his head on that, but his body is missing. I glance around and don't see him. Someone hauled him away. I could call and check funeral homes to see which one has him, but that would look suspicious. It doesn't matter, anyway, because he's gone.

Windows of a car parked behind some bushes glint in

the sun. Who cares if anyone sees me? I'm just a guy looking at an old building beside beautiful blue water, where sunlight dances and dazzles.

With a shrug, I walk to my car and head back to my empire of books. As I approach town, I pat Jack's wallet in my jacket pocket. I might be foolish, but I'm keeping it with me as a reminder of what I did.

## 15

## IRENA

Buzz drives by as we pass a stone bandstand in a park. He's driving the speed limit, like he always does, being the law-abiding guy he is. I recall how he supposedly helped Jack disappear, and a wave of suspicion sweeps over me. I must find out what he's up to.

I turn the wheel to follow him, and Kelly says, "Where are you going? I thought we were going home."

I nod. "We are, but I have a quick stop to make first."

Kelly leans back and says, "Okay." She talks with her friend in the backseat.

Abby whispers, "I saw Buzz go by. You're following him, aren't you?"

I nod. "It won't take long. I want to see where he's going. I have a hunch, and I want to check it out."

Abby pokes me in the side playfully. "You and your hunches. Remember when Jack told you he was going on a spiritual retreat, and you tracked him down at a sneaker convention?"

That's her version of what happened, but I remember it differently. I glance in the rear-view mirror. I don't want Kelly learning about the lies Jack told me because that would ruin her perception of him. Abby shoots me a smile, but it's not a laughing matter. Deceit in a marriage is deadly.

Back then, Jack had said, "I want to go to a self-help retreat. It's three days and they charge a fee, so I'll take it from our savings. I want to do this to help our relationship."

I crossed my arms. I wasn't sure if he was truly going off on a spiritual journey that would remake his life or if he was fibbing to get out of the house. In the end, I shrugged and said, "I hope you come back with whatever it is you hope to find."

While he was in the bathroom before he left, I tucked a note under his socks in his canvas duffel bag. It said, "I hope you're having a good time at the retreat. Love, Irena."

He kissed Kelly and me and said, "I'll be out of touch at a mountain retreat with no cell phone reception, so don't try to reach me. I'll hopefully be back a new man in a few days. Wish me luck." With a grin, he waved goodbye and walked out.

Hearing his happy feet skip down the steps, I nodded to myself. Something was up, and I had a hunch he wasn't telling me the truth. I knew the sound of his footsteps when he was off on a lark, hiding something from me.

I went to the window and we waved. Kelly said, "Bye, Daddy."

Jack shoved the duffel in the backseat, glanced up and threw us a kiss, and drove off. I hurried to the computer and checked online. Sure enough, there was a sneaker head convention in Seattle that weekend. He came home a few days later with rosy cheeks, grinning from ear to ear. His mohawk hair was gelled to perfection on the top of his head. The brown braid in back was tidy.

I gave him a welcome home hug and kissed him before stepping back and waiting for what he might say. "Babe," he said, smiling, "you'll never guess what I found on the way home."

I held my breath. He reached out in the hall and brought in a shoe box. I clamped my jaw shut, counted to five to calm myself and said, "What did you do?"

He opened the box and thrust it toward me. The orange sneakers smelled new and looked expensive. He smiled. "I bought them before anyone else could. They'll only go up in value. I'll make a special shelf for them in my trophy room."

I staggered back against the dining table. It toppled over with a thump, and I landed on my butt. Kelly woke from napping on the couch and cried.

He offered me a hand, but I shook my head and got up on my own. Tears streamed down my cheeks. "I guess that supposed retreat in the mountains didn't help you at all. You lied to me. How could you do that?"

He put the new sneakers down and picked Kelly up, soothing her, rocking her back and forth in his arms. He smiled, but I wanted to march over and slap his face.

He said, "I guess I can't break the habit, so why try? Think of it as an investment. In a few years, you'll thank me and say you're glad I bought them."

I clenched my fists. "I'll be back when I cool down. I need a time out."

Kelly giggled. "Mommy needs a time out."

I stomped to the bedroom, closed the door and wept on the bed. My shoulders shook and my heart broke because shoes mattered more to him than telling me the truth. But I told myself it would pass. A sneaker addiction wouldn't last for a lifetime. Surely, his lust for shoes would fade in time. I told myself the words every spouse says to themselves when they're beyond irritated. "It'll get better. He'll change. He'll outgrow the habit."

Abby speaks up, breaking into my thoughts. "How are violin lessons going?"

I follow Buzz's car to a deserted area along the waterfront, keeping my distance so he won't spot me. I say, "It sounds like a cat howling in pain. It's not the best time to pick up a new hobby, but Jack's note was mysterious and said something like, 'Ask the violin maker. He knows.' So, I'm giving it a try."

Buzz parks and climbs out, looking around. I turn into

a pull off surrounded by a clump of bushes and pull ahead so he won't see me. I turn off the engine, and it pings.

Kelly leans forward and says, "What're we doing here? Why are we hiding? Isn't that Buzz over there by the water?"

I put a finger to my lips. "Keep it down, in case he can hear us. I want to see what he's up to. He's been acting suspicious."

Kelly snickers. "You've been watching too many spy shows. Let's go home."

Her friend says, "But look, he's walking around, looking at the ground. What's over there anyway?"

Abby says, "Yeah, what is he doing over there? It's just an old empty wharf."

I say in a quiet voice, "When he leaves, we'll check it out."

Buzz hops in his car and drives by, not slowing when he passes us. I breathe out a sigh of relief and, after a few moments, start the car. Why was Buzz at this outpost away from town? Heading for the wharf on the bumpy dirt road, I wonder what we'll find.

## 16

## IRENA

The girls tumble out of the car. Abby and I get out and stride over to where Buzz was staring at the ground. He walked in circles and squinted into the sun. But nothing is here at the end of a dirt road except an old wharf and an abandoned salmon cannery.

The wooden building leans, like it's about to fall over, which is a lot like my life in its current shape. I want to sleep a solid eight hours, and I crave a break from dealing with the mess Jack left behind. Timber groans and creaks. A shiver runs up my spine, and I rub my arms. This is the place where Buzz saw Jack last. I swallow a lump in my throat and wonder if Kelly will ever see her father again.

The girls point at a brownish-red stain in the dirt and on a jagged-edged rock. "Why was he looking at that?"

My stomach knots. Buzz said he dropped Jack off here

on a secret mission. What if Buzz hurt Jack that night? But they're best friends, so he wouldn't do that.

I turn and scan the area, seeing no signs of Jack. Dread fills me, and I say, "Stay back. That could be blood, and this may be a crime scene. We can't contaminate evidence."

Abby looks at me and nods. "Got it, Sherlock."

Kelly says to her friend, "This comes from watching too many mysteries."

Plum nods. "My mom is like that too."

I say, "Make fun of me all you like. But you never know, I could be right. I'm calling the police." I pull out my phone, but Kelly says, "Can't you do that at home? I'm hungry."

I blow out a breath. Guilty as charged for forgetting about my daughter and her friend's needs. I say, "Sure, let's go home, and I'll make you a snack. I'll call the police from there."

Abby says, "Aren't you Suzy Homemaker." I roll my eyes, and she says, "You're a good mom. Don't be so hard on yourself. No one's perfect."

A breeze blows past, caressing my cheek. I hope no boating distress calls come in today. I'd like to spend time with my daughter.

Kelly glances at the wharf. "Creepy place, but I like it."

Her friend says, "Me too." She whispers, "A murder could happen here."

They laugh, but I cringe as we climb in the car. Plum's

statement might not be so far off because Jack might have been hurt here. But I might be paranoid from not getting enough sleep and rushing around in a confused state. I give Abby the side eye and realize if I ditched her for stealing, I'd be totally without friends, now that Craig's in jail, Jack's gone, and Buzz is ousted from my life for lying to my face.

On the way to town, Abby says, "If I were you, I wouldn't call the police. Sure, we saw Buzz staring at the ground, but that doesn't prove anything. And you said Jack was going off to start a new life. So, he's alive and well somewhere. Aren't the authorities putting him in witness protection or something like that?"

I suppress a groan and glance in the rear-view mirror. Kelly wipes her eyes, and her friend pats her arm. I say to Abby in a low voice, "You might want to think before you blurt something out. Her dad just disappeared. She doesn't need to be reminded."

Her hands fly up in the air. "I was just saying what everybody knows, that's all. Nothing's wrong with that."

I bite my lip. I love her like a sister, but sometimes she drives me crazy.

## ABBY

Irena slams the car door and motions to the house. "Come inside. I'll fix us something to eat. Then I'll call the police and go to Jack's place to start clearing it out."

I nod, surprised she invited me in after her tantrum earlier about the violin and the gold sneakers. I follow Kelly, her friend and Irena inside. In the house, I glance at the closet where the gold shoes were hidden the last time I was here. Irena is wired hot and ready to break. Her hands were trembling at the wharf. All I saw was a smudge in the dirt, and that's nothing to alert law enforcement about. I think she's imagining things.

I want to get to Jack's place before Irena does. I'll leave here after a quick visit and get a pair of shoes or two at his place before she turns up. It'll be a slam dunk. She'll never suspect I was up to anything. Jack owned so many shoes, no one will notice two missing pair.

I follow Irena into the kitchen and say, "How can I help?"

Irena says, "Make yourself at home and take a seat. I'll take care of it."

I pour myself a glass of water from the tap and ask the others if they want any. Kelly and Plum take glasses of water, and I bring mine to the table. Putting my feet up on a chair, I muse that if Irena knew what I was planning, she'd blow her stack and have a heart attack.

## 17

### KELLY

My mom cooks cocoa in the kitchen, just like when I was little and skinned my knee. I hand Plum a warm mug. "Come on, let's go in my room."

She leans in and whispers, "I can't drink this. I'm lactose intolerant."

I bite my lip and set the mugs in the sink. "Sorry, we should've asked. Do you want a peanut butter sandwich?"

She says in a quiet voice, "I'm allergic to peanuts, so no thanks."

Mom comes over. "I'm sorry I didn't ask if you have dietary restrictions. How rude for me to make assumptions. How does a bowl of pasta with olive oil sound? Can you eat that?"

Plum shakes her head. "I'm gluten intolerant."

My eyebrows go up. I wonder what we can give her. It sounds like cheese won't work.

Mom pats our backs. "I can run to the store and get something you can eat. And I apologize for not having more choices here. What would you two like?"

I say to Plum, "Can you eat scrambled eggs?"

She smiles. "That works, as long as you don't use milk or butter to make them. I can have salsa on the side, if you have that. Do you have any fruit?"

Mom counts on her fingers. "We have apples, oranges and bananas."

Plum says, "I'd like scrambled eggs and an apple."

Mom says, "We have figs too."

We wrinkle our noses at the idea of eating figs.

Mom says, "Take the water and apples in your room, and I'll call when the eggs are ready."

We grab two apples and head down the hall, but Plum says, "Are these washed? My mother says I should wash them before eating them."

Back in the kitchen, we go to the sink and turn on the faucet.

"Back already?" Mom says. My cheeks grow hot. She has such a big personality, sometimes it's difficult to be around her. That's why I like to dance, to be in a creative space where no one is talking to me and telling me what to do. My dad understands that. But she means well, and I love her.

We wash the apples under running water, and Mom says, "Getting rid of the pesticides and all that, eh?"

Abby sits at the kitchen table holding a mug of cocoa, but she isn't drinking it. She stares out the window, not saying anything. Maybe she misses my dad almost as much as I do. They did get along and laugh a lot.

Mom glances at Abby as we dry the apples with paper towels. Something is going on between them. They're avoiding looking at each other and not talking much.

Mom pulls out a metal mixing bowl, and it clangs against the counter when she sets it down. Her jaw is tight. Abby sits up straight. My father's leaving us left a disaster in his wake, and my heart is ripped open.

"Let's go," I say to Plum.

In my bedroom, I close the door and turn on music to take my mind off of my dad deserting me. Plum glances at a Ouija board on the floor by the bookshelf. My mom gave it to me and said it was from when she was a kid.

Plum says, "Do you want to ask it if your dad's coming back?"

I swallow salty tears and shake my head. "What if the answer is no? I couldn't take that. It's better not to know."

She says, "Yeah, I get it. You said your dad had a sneaker collection, but where is it?"

"He didn't live here. They're at his apartment."

Mom knocks on the door. "Scrambled eggs are ready. Come and get it."

I roll my eyes because she sounds like she's acting. I

hope she stops trying so hard to please me. My dad isn't dead, he's just gone. But he didn't take me with him, and for that, I don't think I can ever forgive him.

As we come into the kitchen, my mom says, "I need to go to your father's place and collect some things to sell. Do you want to come with me?"

I look at Plum, and we nod to each other.

Plum says, "I'll have to check with my mom, but I'd like to see the sneaker collection Kelly talked about."

Mom sets golden scrambled eggs on white plates on the table. "Good, we'll all pitch in and get it done."

I glance around the kitchen. "Where's Abby? I wanted to talk to her."

Mom shrugs. "She barely drank her hot chocolate and said she remembered she had an important errand to run."

"I wish she'd said goodbye to me."

"We'll see her another time."

From the way my mother says it, I get the feeling she'd rather not see Abby for a long while. Sure, Abby was in our house and tried to take the gold sneakers and the violin. But she's one of my parents' oldest friends. I hope their group won't stay broken up over my dad's disappearance. If that happens, my mom will hover over me more and watch my every move. I'll do anything to prevent that.

18

## ABBY

I jog to my car, hop in and drive to Jack's apartment. Running upstairs to the second floor, my armpits prickle with sweat. Before I go in Jack's place, I stop to knock on a neighbor's door across the hall to ask him not to mention to Irena that I was here.

Mr. Abernathy opens the door and breaks into a broad smile. "Abby, I haven't seen you for a week or so. Have you been out of town?"

I smile at the man who joined Jack and I at his place when I brought over groceries and Jack cooked pizza or pasta or a tater tot casserole. The man could cook hearty meals, I'll give him that. We often invited Mr. Abernathy over. He liked to laugh and had interesting stories to tell about when he worked on tugboats.

I say, "I was at an ice cream convention, so I wasn't here when Jack went missing. It must've been crazy, until people realized he planned to disappear. But I'm worried about him."

Mr. Abernathy says, "I am too. And now that Jack is gone, the landlord told Irena to clear out the place so a new tenant can move in. Would you like to come in for a cup of coffee?"

"I wish I could, but I'm pressed for time. Thanks though. I hope Jack will come back."

"I do too. Have you heard where he is?"

I shake my head. "I have no idea. I'd like to track him down just to see him again. We're close and have a lot in common."

He glances down the hall with a worried look. "Are you alone? Did anyone see you come in the building?"

"Yes, I'm alone and as far as I know, no one saw me enter the building. What's going on?"

He holds up an index finger. "Wait here, I'll check something and be right back." He goes over to a window overlooking the street and scans the road. Coming back to me, he says, "I was worried the guy with the gun might come back. He belted me in the gut when you were out of town. He was angry, and I think it had to do with what Jack and Craig were up to."

I grimace. "That's awful you were hit. Sorry, but I have to get going."

He rubs his stomach. "You'd better do what you came here for." He cocks his head. "Did you forget something at Jack's? What are you looking for?"

I shrug. "Just something I left when I was over hanging out." I hold up my key. "I'm helping Irena clean the place, even though she didn't ask. Will you keep it a secret between the two of us that I was here?"

"You're such a tight group of friends from way back. I envy that." He starts to close his door. "Come by sometime for that cup of coffee, won't you?"

"I will. Please don't tell anyone I was here. I want my cleaning the place to be a surprise."

He nods. "This'll be our secret. You can count on that." He closes and locks the door. I hurry to Jack's door and unlock it. The hinges creak as I open it. The place has been tossed. Couch cushions are slit with stuffing on the floor. A file drawer is open, and papers are strewn around the room.

I close and lock the door behind me. My pulse picks up as I go down the hall to the second bedroom. I flip on the overhead track lights Jack installed and cross my arms, staring at four blank spaces on the display shelves he built for his rare collectible sneakers. He was so proud of himself for installing the lighting and shelving.

"Where are the other four pairs?" I say to myself and frown. "Someone was already here and took them. Maybe Irena did it. I'd better get busy and take what I want before it's too late."

I open the bedroom closet door and pull out a big duffel bag Jack kept there. I was the one who stood by his side when a new pair of shoes arrived. Humming to myself, I take two pairs of sneakers, put them in their boxes and set them in the bag. Then I hurry out to my car and hide them in the trunk. My white sedan blends in and looks like every other car in the lot, which is fine with me.

I slam the trunk shut and spot Irena's car coming down the street. My heart thumps. My palms turn moist. I could drive away and hope she won't see me, or I could run back upstairs and pretend to be cleaning as a favor to a friend.

I run into the apartment building, my feet pounding up the steps. I'm out of breath and panting when I enter Jack's place. I close and lock the door behind me and race to the kitchen and grab a broom. But then I remember I left the bedroom lights on, so I run in there, turn off the lights and pull the vacuum out of the hall closet.

By the time Irena walks in with Kelly and Plum following behind her, I'm halfway down the hall, vacuuming my heart out.

Irena comes over to me. "What're you doing here?"

I flick off the noise-maker and say, "I decided to surprise you and help clean the place. You're too busy to do this all by yourself."

She squints at me, as if doubting my sincerity, and a wave of acceptance washes over her face. "Thanks," she says. "I didn't think anyone would understand. I have way too much to do and not enough time to handle this."

I smile. "That's what friends are for, right?"

Kelly gives me a hug. "Right." Her friend looks on and smiles.

Irena goes into the second bedroom and shrieks. The girls run in after her, and I follow.

Irena points to the two spots on shelves where the shoes I took are missing. She says, "They're gone. I was just here, right before I picked Kelly up after school."

She rounds on me with a glazed look in her eyes. If she had a butcher's knife in her hands, she'd look like a murderer now, and I don't think she'd hesitate to hurt me. She says, "What did you do with them?"

My mouth drops open. "I came here to do you a favor and clean. Is this how you treat a friend? If so, I'm out of here. I don't need this. I have better things to do with my time than be blamed for what I didn't do."

She looks me in the eyes. "Did you see anyone here?"

"No, but a car took off when I turned into the parking lot. The guy was big and had a beard. Do you think he might've done this?"

She sighs and leans against the wall. Rubbing her temples, she says, "I have no idea what's going on, and I've had a splitting headache ever since Jack and I fell overboard. I can't wait for this to be over."

# KELLY

I point out the sneakers my dad collected to Plum. He spent hours describing them to me before he bought each pair, so I can recite the details of who wore what pair and how they won which championship game by heart. Plum nods and stares at the shoes. The lighting makes it feel like we're in a special place, a shrine to foolishness as my mother calls it. But I admired my dad for following his passion. At least he had an interest and knew a lot about sneakers.

Plum murmurs, "So many sneakers."

I turn to my mom. "Are you sure you're doing the right thing by selling them? Dad would want you to keep them for him, in case he comes back."

I notice Abby nod, watching for my mother's response.

Mom says, "I'm not sure about anything anymore. But your dad owed a lot of money to a lot of people, so I need to sell them to pay off his debts. I wish I didn't have to, but I must. It's the right thing to do."

Abby says, "I could take them off your hands and sell them. That would save you time. You have better things to do than clean up the mess Jack left behind."

Mom rubs her index finger over her bottom lip. The room is silent. I'm not sure if it would be the best thing to trust Abby with the shoes. She might keep part of the money. I overheard my mom once say to Buzz when she thought I wasn't listening that Abby was light-fingered. Things do occasionally disappear from our house when she pays a visit.

Mom says, "Thanks, but no. I'll sell them and be the one Jack blames when he comes back. Okay, let's put the shoes in their boxes and take them to my car. And Kelly, if there's anything you want to take home, let's do it now if we have space. Abby, can we load stuff in your car?"

Abby says, "The back seat is fine. But the trunk is full of stuff I need to take to the thrift store."

I smile. "Can I look at it? Maybe I'll want something you're giving away."

"Sorry, it's just nothing good, so no need to look at it. I might even drop it off at the dump instead."

I shrug and walk over to my mom. If I didn't know Abby so well, I'd suspect she was up to something. I say, "Okay, what do we do first? Match the shoes with the right boxes?"

# 19

## IRENA

We pack up the sneakers, matching each pair with the right box, and take them out to my car and Abby's back seat. She seems super uptight, so maybe she has more going on than I realized. I know she and Jack were close, and she must be missing him almost as much as I am. Maybe that's why she's acting odd.

We tromp back up the stairs from our cars, and Mr. Abernathy pokes his head out of his apartment. I wave, say hi, and continue on our way, but I catch the neighbor giving Abby a quick wink, which strikes me as odd because they barely know each other.

Back in Jack's place, Abby says, "I'll keep cleaning." She turns on the vacuum and moves into the second bedroom.

Plum stares at the living room. "Why did someone wreck the furniture?"

I say, "We're not sure. Maybe they were looking for something."

Plum frowned. "What if they come back?"

Kelly says, "Mom?"

I pat her shoulder and say, "We're pretty sure they won't come back, but we won't stay long. Kelly, what do you want to take home with you before we go?"

"I'm not sure. Can I decide later?"

I move to give her a hug, but she squirms out of my arms and stands by her friend. I say, "Sure, and I'll tell Abby we're leaving."

I find Abby vacuuming the sneakerhead room. I tap her shoulder, and she jumps, letting out a squeal. "Thanks for doing this. You can call it quits. Let's go to my place and you can drop the shoes off."

She turns off the vacuum and leaves it. "I'll come back tomorrow to finish the job. Did you call the police?"

"No, I don't think Buzz staring at a road is a good enough reason to call. But I do wonder what he was doing out there."

She says, "You know Buzz. He likes to explore historic sites. He used to drag me around to look at old buildings and blather on about who built what. Talk about boring."

I tilt my head. "He never struck me as boring. Each to their own, I guess."

We file out, and I lock Jack's door. I wince as a twinge of missing Buzz stirs inside.

As we go down the stairs, it strikes me as unusual for Abby to be here helping. She hates to clean. But I may have underestimated her generosity and how good a friend she is. The girls jabber ahead of us.

Abby says, "When I was married to Buzz, I envied how well you two connected. Now you guys can be together."

I say, "I'm not sure. Everything is upside down since Jack disappeared."

We step outside, and I clear my throat, swallowing an ache from facing unknowns. Do I want to marry Buzz? I thought I did before all this blew up, but I hadn't told him yet. It's as if the pieces on the board game were knocked to the floor, and I need to find each one and figure out where they go.

I unlock the car and say to Abby, "See you at my place."

I get in the car, and the girls tumble in back. I narrow my eyes as we pass near Buzz's bookstore. It bothers me that he drove to the wharf where he left Jack the night he disappeared. But perhaps I'm making too much of it. Facts and unformed theories swirl in my head, but the story is straightforward. Buzz misses his best friend, and that's why he went back to the last place he saw him.

I pull up at my house and turn off the car, thinking about how Jack was deep in debt. Our group of friends should have done an intervention, but we didn't. Why were we so passive when our friend burned and crashed?

The girls spring out of the car and carry shoes in the house. I pick up a box and scan the street, looking for Abby's car. She should be here by now. A cool breeze blows past, and a feeling of dread seeps into my bones. A dry leaf skitters on the sidewalk. Crows caw.

I bite my lip. It's not like Abby to be late. What if she made off with the shoes we loaded in her back seat, and she wants to sell them? I doubt Abby would go that far.

**20**

---

**JACK**

Ahand touches my arm, waking me. I open my eyes and wince as jabbing pain stabs at my skull. People talk nearby. A cart rolls down the hall. I try to sit up but can't. A moan escapes my dry mouth. I blink and say, "Where am I?"

A middle-aged nurse with short brown hair says, "You're in the hospital. They're about to take you to undergo a test. Do you need the urinal?"

I start to nod, but it hurts to move my head, and say, "Yeah."

She hands it to me. "I'll be right back." She draws a flimsy fabric curtain around the bed for privacy, and I position the urinal. A weak stream begins, and a man dressed in blue scrubs pulls back the curtains.

I say, "Not now."

The man goes away but leaves a gap in the curtain.

I'm doing my business when the nurse comes in, pushing aside the curtain the rest of the way. A man visiting the guy in the next bed looks over at me and glances away.

I groan. "Not yet."

She whips the curtain closed and walks away with brisk footsteps. As I finish emptying my bladder, I wonder what kind of sneakers she's wearing from the sound of her tread. I can't remember my own name, but for some reason, I'm drawn to sneakers. Maybe I'm a manufacturer's representative.

I press the call button and a few minutes later, the nurse comes in, taking the bottle from my hands. She eyes it, holds it up, and empties it into the toilet with a loud flush. I study my surroundings. I'm in a room with vinyl floors. A window lets in weak light, so it must be late afternoon or approaching evening. I have no idea what season we're in, and I can't see outside. I wonder what town I'm in.

I'm about to close my eyes when the visitor by the next bed turns and stares. He points at me and frowns, and my stomach clenches. Who is he and why do I feel afraid?

The nurse comes back. "The team will be here soon to take you to the test."

My body trembles. "What're they going to do?"

She says, "Take images. They'll explain it when you get there. You'll be back in your room in no time."

The man in the visitor chair furrows his thick dark

brows, and his black eyes bore into mine. With a shiver, I close my eyes and wish I was anywhere but in a hospital.

The nurse says, "Would you like a warm blanket?"

My teeth chatter, and I say, "Yes, please."

"I'll be right back with that."

She leaves the curtain open. Even with my eyes closed, I feel the penetrating gaze of the man by the other bed. What did I do to end up here? And why is that man staring at me?

A woman in the hall says, "A kayaker found him when they got out at the wharf. They called it in but left the scene. We have no clue who this guy is."

Hot tears of self-pity roll down my cheeks, and I turn toward the wall. If the woman in the hall is talking about me, I'm a lost cause. No one is looking for me, and I'm in a world of pain.

Alarms shriek, making me jerk, and lights flash on a monitor. The noise makes my head hurt even more. I try covering my ears, but tubes running from my arms restrict my movement. I croak, "Help. Someone help."

A nurse rushes in, glances at me, and checks the IV poles. Her cheeks are flushed.

"All I did was turn on my side," I say with a whimper.

She jabs at buttons on a monitor, and the beeping stops. She connects a cord to a device and says, "You disconnected your heart monitor. I'll get that warm blanket for you." She leaves and comes back carrying a folded blanket. "Here you are." She spreads the blanket over me, and warmth seeps into my body. My teeth stop chattering, my jaw relaxes and I sink into the mattress with a sigh.

She says, "Are you starting to remember anything?"

I shake my head, but the motion makes the room spin. "Nothing."

"Hopefully, it'll come back to you."

My eyes open wide, and I have no idea how to go about finding out who I am.

Two people in blue scrubs come in the room, and she says, "Here's your ride. They'll take you to have tests."

I try to sit up, but my skull throbs.

A man in his thirties with kind eyes says, "Stay where you are. We're taking the bed."

I shut my eyes, and the bed rolls out of the room. I hope the visitor by the other bed will be gone by the time I come back. In the hall, I open my eyes and ask the nurse, who is walking alongside, "Who is the man visiting in my room?"

She cocks her head. "There was no visitor."

"But I saw him. He was in a chair by the other bed."

"I'll make a note of it, but the other bed is empty, and we're expecting a new patient soon. Rest now and take it easy."

They roll me into an elevator, and the door shuts. The man in blue scrubs says to the woman, "How was your weekend? Mine was chill."

"Pretty good," she says.

They're talking about life for the living, but I'm in agony. I wonder if my head injury changed my personality. What if I can't go back to being the man I was? The question of my identity gnaws at me. Not only have I lost my memory, but I might be losing my mind. I swear I saw a dark-eyed man visiting the other patient in my room. Was I imagining things?

**21**

---

**ABBY**

I stop at my apartment to drop off the sneakers I took from Jack's place for a boost in the bank account. I take the two shoe boxes and trot from the parking lot, but my heart sinks when I see someone standing at my front door looking at their phone. My pulse picks up. It's Irena. What's she doing here?

I reverse course and slink back around the corner, shoving the sneakers under bushes. No one will see them there. Then I turn and saunter to my place, looking like I'm without a care in the world. La dee da, all is fine.

I stop and extend my hands. "Irena, what're you doing here? I was making a quick stop to use the bathroom before going to your place."

She folds her arms, scrutinizing me. Normally, her harsh stare would make me cough up the truth, but being this close to getting my hands on a chunk of cash keeps me calm.

She says, "It's not that far from Jack's to your place. Are you sure you're not up to something?"

A ripple of guilt passes through me, but I push it away. I say, "Of course not. Do I look like I'm up to anything?"

She frowns and taps a toe before letting her arms drop to her sides. "I must be getting paranoid. I'll see you in a few minutes at my place?"

"See you there," I say, and she strides away, as ever in a hurry. She's always in motion, the woman doesn't know how to sit still. That's not a life for me, always on the move. I'm more of a TV and popcorn person, but she rarely has time for that.

When I see Irena's retreating back, I hurry to retrieve the hidden shoes. I push green leaves aside, and my mouth drops open. The sneakers are gone. I glance around but don't see anyone.

I run to the parking lot as Irena gets to her car. She doesn't have anything in her arms, so she didn't take the shoes. I let out an exasperated breath and lean my forehead against a brick wall. What have I done and how can I make this right?

I comb through the bushes, getting twigs in my hair, scrambling on my knees in dense brush. Standing up, I burst into tears for all I've lost. Jack is gone and who knows if he'll return home. Irena is suspicious of me, and rightly so. If she shuts me out, I won't have any friends except Buzz, and all he cares about is spending time with Irena. I won't get to see Kelly, who I love. I'm out in the cold all by myself and it's my fault. I hate my kleptomania and wish I could stop.

I go in my apartment, use the toilet and weep. Brushing twigs from my hair, I tell myself, "Get it together. Stop taking things."

I take a last look outside for the sneakers, poking in the bushes. A glimpse of color catches my eye. A teenage girl is wearing a pair of the sneakers, and so is her brother. They live two apartments down and must have seen me stash the shoes outside their unit.

I run after them and say, "You're wearing my shoes, and I need them back."

They look at each other and laugh. The older brother looks down at me from his full height of five-foot-nine. "They're ours now. Finders' keepers."

The girl smiles. "Yeah, we found them. You shouldn't have left them there."

I say, "Give me back the shoes or I'll talk to your parents."

They grin. "Go ahead. It won't make any difference."

Their mother comes out and says, "Give her back the shoes. She asked nicely. I saw her leave them there."

The kids slump over and lumber to their apartment, where their mother is waiting. They pull off the shoes and throw them in the bushes. I wince because if they're dirty, I won't get the best price.

Their mom points at them. "Get those back and put them in the boxes. And next time, don't take what isn't yours."

They do as they're told and retrieve the shoes with glum faces, shoving them in shoes boxes with dirty fingers. I suppress a groan and take the shoes, saying to their mom, "Thanks for the help. See you around."

I hurry to my apartment and leave the shoes, declining in value due to being worn and smudged, under a blanket on the bed. Then I lock the door and race to Irena's house. Guilt trills in my ear, but not loud enough to make me want to give back the shoes.

## 22

# IRENA

I drive to my house and frown as a thought strikes me. When I waited at her apartment, I saw her approach and disappear around the corner before greeting me. But it's probably nothing, and she might have stopped to have a quick word with a neighbor.

I climb out of my car and my next-door neighbor says, "Do you have a minute?"

I'd rather deal with the shoes, but I go over to the fence and smile. "What's up?"

Kathy, a retired school teacher, pats her blond hair worn in a bob cut. "Didn't you break up with Bud Wiser and he moved out?"

I nod. "I did, and he's gone. But who knows, we might get back together someday. He's a nice guy, and he's good with Kelly."

She cocks her head. "He was a good kid in my class,

not like your friend Craig, who was always acting up and had to be the class clown."

"Craig is in jail. He's not that much of a friend anymore."

She nods. "I saw that in the paper. I called you over to say I saw Buzz go in your house while you were gone. He came out carrying something, but I didn't see what it was."

My stomach sinks. "Thanks for telling me. It slipped my mind to ask for my house key back with all that's going on. It looks like I should have changed the locks."

She picks at a rose bush that deer like to nibble. Roaming wild deer eat her flowers, and she wields a mean broom chasing them. She says, "When I had you and Buzz in fourth grade, I thought you'd both grow up to be something special. But when I saw him watching your house with binoculars, I almost changed my mind."

I clench my fists, wondering what he took. "I needed a break to straighten out my thoughts. Are you sure you didn't see what he took?"

Her eyes narrow. "Don't get tangled up in your thoughts or you'll miss the love of your life. We can all be pestered with doubts at one time or another. I should know because I passed up a lifetime with a wonderful man because my mother didn't like him. I look back and see what I missed, living every day with regrets."

I cringe, imagining my life filled with regrets because I

pushed Buzz away. "I'm sorry to hear that, and I'll think about what you said."

Kelly pops her head out the front door. "Mom? I think you'll want to see this. When you have time, that is. Hi, Kathy."

"Hi, Kelly." Kathy says to me, "I'm glad we had this little chat."

"Me too," I say. "Maybe Buzz forgot his shaving kit and came back for it." To Kelly, I call, "Be right there."

I wave goodbye to my neighbor and stride into my house. I was sure I gathered every last thing Buzz had at my place and dumped them out in the rain when I broke up with him. Kathy could be right, and I'll give Buzz the benefit of the doubt, or Buzz is a devious liar. If I catch him sniffing around my place again, I might have to call the cops. Is he a stalker and a creep, coming in my house when I'm not home? If so, bye, Buzz, so long. My mind swirls with conflicting tangled thoughts, and the truth changes depending on the lens I use to view events.

My eyes dart around the living room. Kelly looks up at me from the couch, and I wipe a look of concern from my face because I don't want her to worry. The sooner we get back to normal life, the better it'll be.

Kelly points to her tablet. "Look at how much this pair of sneakers is going for."

Plum nods and looks up at me.

I say, "Wowzah, right?"

They giggle at my phrase. But what are mothers for,

after all, if not to make fun of in front of friends? Looking at Kelly reminds me of Jack, and I want him to come back for her sake. She needs her father while growing up.

I say, "It'd be great if we can put one pair of sneakers up for sale in an auction tonight. Where should we post them for sale? And how do we pick a beginning bid? Do we start low to encourage bids or make it closer to the amount we'd accept?"

Kelly's fingers fly across the keypad. "I'm on it."

A car horn beeps twice out front in the considerate way we do it in our town. Residents don't lay on the horn hard because that wouldn't fit with our polite, laid-back lifestyle. Only tourists and city folks do that.

Plum jumps up and grabs her backpack. "That's my mom. Gotta go. See you at school." She runs out and closes the front door behind her.

I say, "Hon, we have to talk about something."

Kelly stares at the screen. "Uh huh."

I tap her shoulder. "Put that down, just for a minute."

She looks at me. "Okay. What's up?"

"Buzz came in the house when we weren't home. Kathy saw him leave with something. He was also watching our house with binoculars. I want you to be careful around him."

She wrinkles her nose. "Buzz is fine. He's a friend, and he's not a threat."

"Just keep your distance from him until I figure this out. He's acting strange, and it scares me. I don't want you getting hurt." I fake a calm face. No need for her to get as freaked out as I am.

She rolls her eyes. "Let's not have a stranger danger talk about Buzz. He's fine. We know him and can trust him. I mean, how many years have you known each other?"

I shove my hands in my pockets. "About thirty?"

She smiles. "Proving my point. You don't know someone for that long and find out they're a pervert or a stalker."

I say, "Maybe he's a different person deep down than how he comes off." A shiver runs up my spine at how I slept with him and didn't suspect any evil lurking inside. He puts on a good act; I'll give him that. Recent events have pushed me over the edge from suspicion into full blown paranoia.

Kelly picks up her tablet. "You're making a big deal out of it and being dramatic. Two people broke up. End of story. There's no Captain Evil suit under his shirt."

I get up from the sofa. "You may be right, but just be careful."

She nods, but I doubt she's paying attention to what I said. Just then, Abby bursts in, and we stare at her. Her nose, cheeks, and knees are smudged with dirt. When I left her, she wasn't like this.

I rush over and say, "I thought you'd be here by now. Are you okay? Where are the shoes?"

## 23

## ABBY

I slump on the sofa by Kelly and wipe my forehead with the back of my hand. I've got to make up a story to explain why I'm late and have dirt all over me. "You wouldn't believe what happened. I tripped and fell in the bushes as I was leaving my apartment."

My face heats with shame because I'm lying to those I love, but my penchant for taking things overrides a sense of right and wrong. I blow out a breath.

Irena says, "Let's go in the kitchen and clean you up before we get the shoes out of your car."

I follow her into the kitchen and swallow a guilty lump in my throat, taking a warm washcloth from her and scrubbing my face. I wring it out and hang it on the faucet. "Thanks, let's get the shoes from my back seat."

The three of us tromp outside, and I take a deep breath of crisp fall air. It's late September, and I want to hibernate and hide from my worst habits. Old patterns are tough to break.

I open my car and hand shoe boxes to Kelly and Irena, stacking them in their arms. I grab the last boxes and go inside. We set them on the floor, and I wonder if Jack misses me, wherever he is. If he was here, he'd tell a story and make us laugh.

I glance at Kelly and Irena, and my stomach clenches. I'll have a tough time replacing these two if I leave town. Friendships like these take a long time to form. Maybe I shouldn't rush off and ditch my life in Millersville. I'll mull that over when I have time.

We sit and strategize in the living room, sipping tea and mapping out a plan for Irena and Kelly to sell the sneakers. I listen carefully because I'll follow their blueprint when I sell the sneakers hidden in my apartment. As punishment for my bad deeds, I say, "After work tomorrow, I'll clean Jack's place. It's the least I can do."

Irena says, "Thanks. I appreciate that." But she gives me a long, careful look.

I say, "Why're you looking at me like that?"

She shrugs. "It's just that you're suddenly acting so helpful. Are you sure when you fell you didn't hurt your head and get a personality transplant?"

We laugh, but I wince inside because it would be the worst thing to have a brain injury. That would be frightening. I eye the sneakers on the floor and hope wherever Jack is, he's okay. I can't imagine life without him.

Kelly says, "I think the best site to sell the sneakers is BestSneaks. We'll sell one pair there in an online auction and see how it goes. Which shoes should we pick first?"

Irena's phone rings. She glances at the screen and says, "I've got to take this call."

She steps out of the room and comes back a few minutes later. "I'm sorry, but that was the Coast Guard. I've got to take a distress call."

Kelly moans. "Now? We're just getting started. And what about dinner?"

Irena pulls on her jacket and gives me a look. "Abby, can you help her? Call and get Thai food delivered and charge it to my credit card."

I nod. "Of course."

She opens the door. "Got to run. I'll be back when I can." She points at Kelly. "Whatever you do, don't get in the car with Buzz. I don't trust him. Not one inch."

My eyebrows shoot up. She is ticked off at my former husband, far more than I thought. She might think Buzz wanted the gold shoes. Or is she just stressed from clearing out Jack's place? Clean up on aisle ten is what he left her.

She goes out, slamming the door behind her. Framed photos of the three of us hanging on the wall rattle and tilt off-kilter.

I smile at Kelly. "Just us chickens left. Your mom sure has a lot of energy, doesn't she?"

Kelly sets down the tablet. "Sometimes too much."

"Do you want to eat first or set up the auction?"

"Auction, then eat."

I rub my hands together. "Let's do it. Come on money, roll in. Let's pay off Jack's debts, including the overdue child support."

Kelly's eyes flick open wide. "You're not supposed to know he owes her for child support. I think it's a secret."

I grin. "We don't have secrets between us. We've known each other far too long for that."

She gives me a long thoughtful gaze, and I chew the inside of my cheek, doing my best to look innocent. Whip smart, she's wise beyond her years. I don't stand a chance if she questions me about what I've been up to. I hold my breath and hope she won't suspect me of stealing sneakers.

Fortunately for me, she says, "Let's get this auction set up."

## 24

# IRENA

I get out of my car at the marina and hurry past the office, waving to my friend Mike at the front desk as I go by. Striding down the dock, I hop in my boat and check the engine oil. The dipstick shows I'm good to go. I start the engine, let it warm up, and pat the dash of my speedy racehorse of a boat. My stomach knots, because anything can happen while I'm on the water, and that's what I love about my job.

I shrug on my life vest, snap three clasps shut, and tug on them to be sure they're securely fastened. My mind drifts back to when I was swept into the sea with Jack. He disappeared in a dramatic fashion and, unbeknownst to me, he shared his plan beforehand with Buzz. I purse my lips, wishing my two friends had told me about the secret set up. Instead, I ran around in a panic searching for Jack, which was wasted effort when a body wasn't to be found.

Thanks a lot, Jack, for leaving chaos in your wake, making the rest of us stressed out, worried sick, and exhausted.

I step out to the boat deck and stow the fenders. The wind is picking up, and halyards on sailboats clang against masts in the ever-changing song of the wind. I release the lines holding the boat against the dock and head into the Salish Sea.

Steering toward the powerboat in trouble, I call the skipper at the number the Coast Guard gave me. I already called from the car to tell her I was on the way and to take her payment details. When she answers, I say, "This is Irena Fishbone with Nimbus Boat Rescue. What's your current position?"

She names the coordinates, and I nod. "I'll be there in five minutes."

She says, "Hurry, a wave hit our boat, and we're taking on water."

"Be there soon."

I push on the throttle to go faster and keep a close watch for floating logs that could damage my propeller and take my boat out of commission. Being the sole breadwinner means my boat is how I pay my bills. I found a calling that taps my need to help others and fix broken things. My mom worked two jobs, and as a child, I'd look out into the dark night from our dim apartment and send a silent message for someone to come rescue me. Now I rescue others and get paid to do it. I break into a smile as a thrill runs through me. I'm right where I want to be, racing across the water.

Steady wind opposing strong currents makes a hash of white caps. I approach the powerboat mid-channel off Cedar Island and come alongside. The other boat bucks in the waves. To the west, a tugboat towing a tanker is heading toward us.

My pulse quickens, and I say to the tall blond skipper who is biting her lower lip, "I'll tow you away from the shipping channel, then assess the damage."

"Thank goodness you're here," the skipper says. Her face is flushed, and her curly hair is wild. "We were heading for James Island when a huge wave came up all of a sudden and crashed onto our bow, breaking the windshield. My parents are with me, and they're worried."

I say, "Have everyone put on life jackets."

I lash the boats together at midships and tow the boat to a sheltered cove, hauling my tool kit across the gap between the two bound boats. Water splashes up, getting my feet wet, but it's part of the job.

On the damaged boat, two people in their seventies sit stone-faced on the settee. The skipper says, "These are my parents. They're pretty shook up, and water is flooding in."

"I'm on it," I say and hustle to the helm. Wind whistles and blows through where the windshield once was. Shattered glass covers the instrument panel, captain's chair and wet floor. I check to see if the hull is breached, and all is shipshape and sound. But then I check the instrument panel and see that a fuse is blown out, which would stop the boat.

I go to my boat, grab a set of fuses, and replace the shorted fuse. I step to the salon, where the parents are sitting staring ahead with blank faces.

I say, "It looks like your boat is structurally sound. When the water came in and broke your windshield, it shorted out one of your fuses. I replaced the fuse, so now you should be able to make headway to the marina."

She says, "Can you tow us to the marina?"

I nod. "I can, or you can drive it to the boat yard haul out."

She gives her parents a quick glance and shakes her head. "No, I'd rather you do it. I'm too rattled, and I want to sit with them while we're underway."

"I'll be glad to do that. Do they need medical assistance? I can call EMTs to meet us at the dock."

Her father says, "Yes, we'd like that."

Her mother says, "For both of us."

I say, "I'll call it in. Cover them with blankets to keep them warm and sit tight. I'll get you there in no time."

I grab my tool kit, lug it to my boat and get underway, towing the other boat, while calling 911. "Two people on a powerboat need medical assistance. They appear to be in shock after a wave crashed onto their boat and broke the windshield. I'm towing the boat and will be at the marina boat launch in fifteen minutes."

The dispatcher says, "Any signs of injury or bleeding?"

"Not that I saw."

Next, I call my friend Steph who runs the shipyard. "Can you take one more? A wave blew out the windshield on a thirty-six-foot Grand Banks powerboat."

"Bring her in, I'll make room."

I hang up, heart thudding, wanting to get to the dock to deliver the stunned parents. I grimace as I steer and consider what a shock it must have been when the windshield broke and water burst into the boat.

I turn into the marina and dock by the boat launch, quickly hopping off and tying lines to cleats. A red and white medical van waits, with two EMT's beside it. They come over with a stretcher, set it down and guide the skipper's parents off the damaged powerboat onto the dock. They examine the two and help them into the medical van.

The skipper hops off her boat and turns to me. "Will you take my boat to the boat yard? I want to go to the hospital with my parents."

I swallow the lump in my throat. This woman is so lucky to have two parents who love her, and she loves them. I say, "I'll take care of it. You go with them."

I drive away and deliver the wayward vessel to the boat yard. Waving to the dockhands, I head toward my boat slip but before docking I stop to sob. My mom died, my dad is in prison, Jack is gone, and I broke up with Buzz. I have my daughter and the sea sloshing against the hull as a comfort to me.

## 25

## KELLY

While my mom is out answering a distress call, Abby and I pick a pair of new orange sneakers to sell first. I'd love to have some like these in my size, but I get the feeling Mom wouldn't let them in the house. When she's upset with my dad, she scowls and mutters under her breath about the stinking orange sneakers that ended their marriage.

I search online for an idea of what we can get for them, and my jaw drops. "Dad was right. They're limited edition, with one hundred pair manufactured, and they were designed and signed by Ramsey Fast, the famous basketball player."

Abby says, "Your dad sure knows his sneakers."

I point at the screen. "They're worth a lot. Someone's selling a used pair for eight hundred bucks. Here's a new pair without the box for three thousand. What price should we set?"

"We've got the box, don't we?"

I nod. "Yeah."

"Let's list them for just under five thousand dollars. They're not making any more of them, and your father told me when Ramsey Fast passed away last year, so their value increased."

I say, "It's odd that ten-year old new shoes are more valuable than when they were first made."

She shrugs. "I guess collecting sneakers doesn't make sense to anyone but the people doing it. Investing is like that. When people want the same few items, it drives up the price. So, if a certain stock becomes popular, the price goes up."

I tilt my head. "You sound like you know a lot about investing."

A smile spreads across her face. "I do."

"I don't think your friends know that about you."

"No need to tell them. I tried a few times, but they didn't believe me. I'm more than my job at the ice cream factory, and I could manage my investments from anywhere in the world."

My eyes open wide. "You're not thinking of moving, are you?"

"Not now, but maybe someday. If I went away, I'd miss you so much."

She wraps her arms around me, giving me a hug, and I melt in her arms. She smells like vanilla, nutmeg and cream. I step back and say, "Your being here makes missing my dad a bit easier. Don't stop coming around, okay?"

Abby squeezes my shoulders and looks me in the eyes. "I won't."

I sniffle and wipe my eyes, missing my dad with an ache that won't stop.

She says, "Let's take photos of the shoes."

We set up in the kitchen, turning on lights. I cover the table with a blue tablecloth and set the shoe box and orange sneakers on it. The shoes almost give off a glow. I snap photos with my phone, and we pick the best ones to show online.

We sit on the couch while I upload pictures to the auction site. I type in a description and have Abby check the details before I push the button to make the auction go live. She leans back on the couch and says, "And now we wait."

With a sigh, I say, "I'd like new sneakers. I'm surrounded by shoes but can't wear them."

"Ask your mom, and she'll buy you a pair."

I roll my eyes. "All she cares about is her boat and rescuing boaters in distress."

Abby grins and pumps a fist in the air. "Irena to the rescue!"

We collapse on the sofa laughing. I say, "My mom was so angry, I thought she wouldn't let you come over anymore. I'm glad it worked out, and you're helping me."

She says, "You're like the daughter I never had." Tears fill her eyes and trickle down her cheeks. "If you ever want kids, don't wait too long like I did. Do it when you're young, like your parents, in your twenties or early thirties."

I cross my arms. "I might stay single like you and never have kids."

"You have your whole life ahead of you. I envy that."

My phone dings with an alert for the auction. "Incoming. Let's see."

We giggle and laugh, and I'm sorry my mom is missing this moment. I say, "Bids are coming in, and the price is going up."

Abby gets up and twirls around. "I love it. But your dad would've wanted us to keep the sneakers in case he comes back."

I nod. "He would've, but he owes too much money. We have to sell them."

"At least it looks like there are sneakerheads out there who want them."

My stomach growls. "Let's call and order dinner."

"Definitely. Green curry with chicken two stars?"

"And Pad Thai with three stars. White or jasmine rice?"

"Jasmine."

I order online and start to put in my mom's credit card, but Abby leans over watching me type in the numbers. I turn away so she can't see the last four digits and security code. No need to tempt her.

## 26

## JACK

Two people in blue scrubs wheel my bed down a hall and into a room where a machine with a long narrow tube open on both ends takes up most of the space. A tall technician with a wide chest pats a platform and says, "Are you able to get up here and lie down? This will move into the tube for the test."

I groan. I haven't gotten up and walked while in the hospital. My legs are weak. "I'm not sure. I get dizzy when I sit up."

He nods to the assistants in blue scrubs. "They'll help you. It's just a few steps."

A woman says, "Sit up and swing your legs over."

I frown because I'm afraid to sit up. Whoever I was, I've become a loser who feels sorry for himself.

A man says, "I'm going to raise the head of the bed now."

The head of the bed slowly rises. The room spins, and I moan, touching my head.

The technician, who appears to be in charge of my torture, says, "This won't take long."

Strong arms help me sit up and shift my legs so they hang over the edge of the bed. The bed is lowered, and soon, I feel the floor under the soles of my sock-covered feet. I glance down at the yellow socks and shuffle as the room whirls.

"Just a few footsteps," an orderly says, "and you'll be on the table for the test."

I sigh and get a whiff of my stale breath. I'm a disaster. I don't know when I last showered. I reek of body odor. Hands on my elbows and waist help me hobble to the platform. Letting out a whoosh of breath, I perch on the edge.

"I can't lie down," I say with my eyes shut. "My head hurts too much."

"We'll help you."

Firm hands guide me, lowering my torso to the table and lifting my legs. My head throbs, and I wince. It feels like a dozen ice axes are driving into my skull.

The technician says, "This will take about twenty or thirty minutes. We need to find out what's wrong, and hopefully this'll give us the information we need."

My lips are chapped, and my throat is dry. I manage to say, "Fine."

The technician says, "You'll have to put up with the noise in there."

"I don't like loud noises," I say.

"Stay still. If you move, we'll have to start all over again."

I say, "I wish I was in Costa Rica."

The technician says, "Don't we all. I'm right there with you. Dream of time on the beach while you're in the tube, and you'll be fine."

As my body moves into the tube, I snap my eyes closed, and the room spins in circles. Why did I say I wanted to be in Costa Rica? I shrug my shoulders because I have no idea.

"Remember, don't move," the technician says. "You've got to stay still."

I grit my teeth and clench my hands. The machine grows loud, rumbling like a train coming through a tunnel. It clangs and bangs. A tickle in my throat grows more and more intense. I swallow, but it gets worse. I can't think about anything else but needing to cough. I know I shouldn't move, but I can't stand it anymore. I bark out a few quick coughs and clear my throat. That's better.

The tech says in an exasperated tone of voice, "You moved, and now we have to start over. Don't cough and remember, take shallow breaths. Don't scratch your nose. Here we go again. Some people fall asleep in there. Maybe you can too."

I squeeze my eyes shut and try to block out the racket

going on around me. The machine buzzes and hums, sounding like a billion bolts sliding home all at once. Please, let me survive this. Please.

My nose itches, and the urge to scratch is unbearable. I keep my hands where they are and repeat to myself, "Just a few more minutes. I can do this. I will survive my medical ordeal. I'm on a beach in warm sand. I can do this."

A daunting thought slams into me, whipping up doubts. There's a chance my memory might not come back. Do I have the courage to start a new life? I'm not sure. Right now, I feel so fragile and full of fear.

## 27

## FRANKIE

Frankie turned her chair in the FBI white-collar crime unit in Seattle and looked up at her boss. Her gut churned. They'd been working non-stop, trying to find their missing man.

Alana frowned and wrinkled her forehead. "Still no sign of Jack Fishbone, our star witness?"

Frankie shook her head. "No. We've looked for him everywhere. He hasn't crossed the border, unless he crossed into Canada in the mountains by foot. Even then, the Mounties would catch him. And he didn't fly out of any airports or rent a car."

"We need to find him before the case goes to trial. The clock is ticking."

Frankie drummed her fingers on her knee. If she was going to rise in the ranks, she had to find Jack Fishbone. She wanted that promotion so badly she could smell it like the meatball sub with extra onions her partner, Mark Brick, was eating in the next cubicle.

She stood and jabbed at a map on the wall. "Using facial recognition, we haven't seen him in Millersville, the surrounding area, or Seattle."

Alana poked a finger at the map. "What happened between the time he fell off Craig's boat and he was supposed to swim to shore? Have you interviewed his friends?"

Frankie stiffened her shoulders. "We were just about to do that."

"Well, get on it. Someone like this doesn't just disappear. He has to be out there, and if anyone can find him, we can. Maybe he flew out of Vancouver, British Columbia. Did you check with the Canadians? He could've hopped on a private plane that flew out of Millersville. He could be hiding in the San Juan Islands, living off the grid on Lopez Island."

Frankie's mind spun with possibilities. "Got it, boss. I'm on it. I'll report back as soon as we have something."

Alana stared deep into her eyes. "You'd better have something for me within twenty-four hours. Your promotion rests on how you handle this. You'd better find Fishbone fast."

As her boss strode off, Frankie slumped in her chair. Fishbone could have high-tailed it out of town by boat over the border into Canada. But the Canadians monitored the border closely and were known to board boats that didn't check in with customs. Last month, drug runners hauling a boat load of cocaine were apprehended in a cross-border cooperative effort when a speed boat crossed from the Gulf Islands in British Columbia into the San Juan Islands in Washington State. Two smaller boats pulled up to the powerboat, and the perps were off-loading duffel bags filled with zip lock bags of white powder when the authorities swept in and made arrests. Frankie liked her job for doing what's right and being part of a team pursuing justice.

She tapped on her keyboard, gathering names of Fish-bone's known associates. She said under her breath, "I know you're out there, and I'll find you."

Brick stood in the next cubicle stood and looked over the flimsy wall barrier. He wiped his mouth on a white paper napkin. "Everything all right? Heard the boss reaming you out."

Frankie's face grew hot. To show weakness would make her vulnerable, and her colleagues would rib her mercilessly. "We'll get him."

Her boss strode past and barked an order. "You two, McNalley and Brick, work together and pick up the pace. Find him fast. I don't want to see your faces in this office until you bring in Jack Fishbone."

Frankie grabbed her laptop, tucked it in her bag with her wallet, and said, "Ready to roll?"

Mark grinned, showing a dimple in his left cheek. He pushed back a lock of curly brown hair. "You bet."

She nodded. "I'll drive. It'll take two hours to get there, if traffic isn't bad."

Her pulse picked up, and she plastered on a calm façade. She had to nab this guy Jack and hide him until the trial started. They had written documents proving the two friends ran a scam defrauding the elderly, but it was best to have an eyewitness take the stand to convince the judge and jury.

**28**

---

## BUZZ

I tell my staff at the bookstore I'm leaving and climb in my car. A strong urge pulls me to Irena's house, and I pull over at the curb, staring in her front window. It looks like Abby is visiting and hanging out with Kelly. I slide out of my seat and tiptoe to the window to listen.

Abby exclaims, "Look at that bid. Someone really wants the sneakers. Woohoo!"

Kelly says something, but I can't make out what she said.

I creep closer to the window to hear better, and a delivery van pulls up. The driver runs out carrying two large paper sacks. Before I can be spotted and thought a weirdo for stalking, I hop on the front steps and accept the order.

"Thank you," I say, taking the bags. My heart is racing, because I shouldn't be here. Irena told me not to come by.

The front door swings open, and Kelly's mouth drops open. She says, "Hey, Buzz, come on in. I sort of missed having you around."

I step inside, and Abby gives me a quick kiss on the cheek. She says, "What're you doing here, keeping tabs on us?"

I shove my hands in my pockets and shrug, doing my best to look as if I don't have a care in the world. But the truth is, I left my heart in this house the night Irena kicked me out. I run a hand through my hair and say, "I probably shouldn't be here. Irena wouldn't like it."

Abby glances at Kelly and says, "She can get over herself. Take a seat in the kitchen and eat with us."

My stomach sours at the thought of Irena walking in while I'm making myself at home where she forbade me to enter. "Another time, okay? I don't want to make her angry."

Kelly takes the food to the kitchen table and says, "She has a right to be angry. You lied to her about helping my dad get away."

I nod. "It wasn't my best move. I should've told her the truth about helping him get out of town, even though he made me promise not to tell."

Kelly says, "As far as I'm concerned, you're forgiven. Sit and eat, there's enough for all of us."

Abby pats the chair beside her. "Come on, you know you want to."

I release a breath and sink into a seat. My hands are clammy. Irena will blow up if she finds me in her home, and I want to be long gone before she walks in the door. But Kelly and Abby are like family, and I've missed being around them.

We dig into the food, and delicious flavors explode in my mouth. I say, "Thanks for inviting me in and sharing this. I miss what we had."

Abby says, "Our group of friends is blown to smithereens. I don't think we'll ever be the way we were, even if Jack comes back."

Kelly dabs her eyes.

Abby pats her hand. "Sorry, I didn't mean to blurt that out. I'm sure he'll come back for you. Of course, he will. He's got to. Right, Buzz?"

"Definitely," I say to back her up and make Kelly feel better. I'm not sure it's possible to deal with the loss of a dad. We're quiet as we slurp noodles and shovel green curry and jasmine rice into our mouths. Spoons and forks clang against porcelain bowls.

In the quiet, a sound makes my chest grow tight. The front door opens, and Irena calls, "Kelly, what's Buzz's car doing out front?"

She strides into the kitchen and drops her purse on the floor when she sees me. "This is the last thing I expected to see when I came home. You have nerve, coming back when I told you not to darken my door."

Abby and Kelly snicker. Abby says, "She's so dramatic when she's upset."

Kelly says, "I know, who says darken my door?"

They giggle, covering their mouths with their hands, and Irena puts her hands on her hips, glaring at me. Fire might as well be blazing from her eyes. She's an acetylene torch ready to incinerate me.

I jump to my feet and offer her my chair. "Sit down. I'll dish you up some food. It's really good. It's hot, how you like it."

Abby and Kelly smile and whisper, "Hot, how you like it."

I say to them, "Could you give us a few minutes please? I'd like to talk to Irena alone." They leave, and I give Irena my most open-hearted, vulnerable, puppy love eyes. "If that's okay with you, that is."

She grabs a beer from the fridge, pops it open, and chugs a swallow. I love her and miss her, but I can't appear desperate or needy. That would turn her off, and this is my moment to turn the situation around.

I let my arms fall to my sides. "Darling, I've missed you more than you'll ever know."

Her jaw clenches. She takes another sip from the beer bottle, and I watch her swallow, wondering if I'll ever get the chance to kiss that sweet neck again or take her to bed after a long day of rescuing people. She doesn't reply, so I take a step closer, staying a foot away so I won't scare her off.

My voice cracks when I say, "We've always been meant for each other. I'm sorry I've shaken our shared trust, and now is not the time to turn our backs on love. Please, we need to be together and support each other through this terrible time. We have to help Kelly get through this. She needs us."

She sets the beer bottle on the table with a thud. "I saw you laughing in the rain after you lied to me, so I'm not sure I can trust you. I've still got mixed emotions about us. But Kelly misses you, and you might take the blister off missing her father just a bit. I need more time to sort this out."

Her face softens, and she gives me a slight smile. "That was quite a speech you delivered just now."

I open my arms and say, "Thanks, I worked on it ahead of time, in case I had a chance to tell you how much I love you. I've missed you more than you'll ever know. Can I hug you?"

She sniffles before stepping away. "Not so fast, Mr. Slick. I followed you and saw you looking around Martin Wharf. Did you hurt Jack?"

My throat is dry, and I swallow. "I wouldn't do that. Kelly needs her dad. Why would you think that?"

She purses her lips. "I have a feeling something

happened when you parted ways." She points at me, and my heart skips a beat. "Don't tell me you're innocent. I saw you swallow just now, like you do when you're guilty."

I say, "You're making me out to be the bad guy, but you're frustrated that Jack left. Don't take it out on me. It's Jack you're angry with."

She glances at the hallway. "You could be right, but why did you come in my house and take something while we were out?"

My pulse pounds in my ears. My hands are sweaty, and I wipe them on my jeans. "I was just making sure my shaving kit wasn't left here. I couldn't find it. And I came in and took the dog bowl."

She crosses her arms and tilts her head. "I did forget to put the dog bowl with your things by the curb. But don't get any ideas about moving back in. Not so fast, buster."

Laughter erupts in the hallway.

Irena says, "Okay, you two, you can come back in the kitchen. It's not like you weren't listening to every word anyway."

Abby grins and says in a low voice, "I've missed you more than you'll ever know."

We all chuckle, and I catch Irena's eye. I say, "I'd better go." I turn to Kelly and Abby, "Thanks for inviting me in." To Irena, I say, "I hope you'll give me a chance. If we put our heads together, maybe we can figure out where Jack went."

She nods slowly. "Maybe. I'll think about it."

I ooze pure innocence when I gaze at her, but I know Jack will never come home, not after I left him at the cannery. I don't know where his body is or who moved it, but I don't care. Good riddance to my best friend who wanted to take Irena away from me.

I head to the door and say, "Later."

Kelly giggles. "Bye, Mr. Slick."

I flash Irena a smile and throw her an air kiss. Abby and Kelly erupt into a fresh round of laughter, holding their sides.

Abby bends over, gulping for breath. "Mr. Slick. I never thought of him as Mr. Slick."

I wave and gently close the door. Getting in my car, I start the engine and will the beating of my heart to slow its rapid pace. I smile and congratulate myself for presenting myself well under stress. I hope I carved out a chance of stepping back in as Irena's partner and Kelly's almost dad.

Irena's next-door neighbor and our former teacher scurries over like a beetle blown by the wind. She points and says, "Buzz, I saw you watching their house, and I saw you go inside when they weren't home. Be better, Bud Wiser. I expect more of you than that."

I say, "I will." I wave goodbye to her and pull away from the curb. Whatever else she says is lost in the wind as I head for home. At least I have a dog that loves me, unlike some of the humans in my life. If only Irena and I could share unconditional love like my dog shows.

I park in my driveway and hop out. My dog barks inside, and I smile, opening the front door and burying my face in his fur as he licks me, welcoming me home. I'll take him for a walk, give him his dinner and think about how to woo Irena back into my arms.

**29**

---

**JACK**

The torture machine holding my prone body stops making noise. I clench my teeth and stay still, because I don't want to be scolded by the technician a second time and have to start the test again. The experience of being in the hospital has made me more appreciative of what sick people go through.

The technician says, "You can move now. I think we have some good images."

With a whir, the platform slowly slides out of the tube. I scratch my nose and moan, because the movement, even though it is slow, sets off my vertigo. The room spins, and I feel queasy.

I put a hand to my belly and double over. "I'm going to be sick."

He says, "Here's a bag."

I take the plastic blue bag and put it over my mouth.

Lying on my side, the room whirls around, and I cough and hack, heaving up bitter bile. I feel weak. The surface of the platform I'm resting on is hard and unforgiving.

I bite my lip to stop myself from bursting into tears. I want off this emotional roller coaster. I open my eyes.

The aides in blue scrubs step forward. "We can help you get up. It's time for your next test."

I shuffle with their help to bed and wince at the feeling of knives driving into my skull. I say, "Can you see them?"

They settle me in bed and pull the covers up to my neck. The woman says, "See what?"

"My head, knives are being pounded into my brain. I can't take it anymore."

She pats my hand. "Give yourself time to heal."

I say, "I don't want to wait. What's wrong with me?"

They roll me out of the room on the bed, and he says, "We don't want to upset other patients. Please lower your voice."

Tears run down my face into my mouth, tasting of salt and devastation. I break down as we roll along a hall and sob. Whoever I was is lost, and I can't recover my past.

## 30

## ABBY

I say goodbye to Irena and Kelly and step outside, waving to their neighbor Kathy, who is gardening in dim light as dusk falls. A deer waits ten feet away for her to abandon her post near the rose bushes. It's a hopeless one-sided war, which the deer will win, because as soon as Kathy goes inside, deer will nibble her roses and dahlias. If I ever get a house, I'd like to try my hand at gardening.

As I drive home, a twinge of guilt flits past, making me frown. I shouldn't have taken the sneakers. Irena needs support, but I'm working against her. How low is that? I should give them back, but she'll ream me out with a scolding that will leave me mortified. I'm not sure I have the courage to admit what I've done to anyone.

My face heats with shame as I unlock my apartment door and go inside, turning on the lights. I like living alone, but I hate it at times because I wish Jack lived with me. I can't help it if my heart belongs to him, even though he still loves Irena.

A knock at the door makes me flinch. Looking out the peephole, I see the two kids who took the sneakers. I'm no better than them, in fact, I'm a horrible person. They took the shoes I left in the bushes, but I stole them from my friend's apartment. I open the door. "Yes?"

The boy scuffs his foot. "We're here to say we're sorry."

The girl smiles, showing a gap between her two front teeth. "Here's all of our savings. We shouldn't have taken your sneakers."

She drops pennies, dimes, and nickels into my cupped hands. I've sunk so low, I'm taking money from children. I say, "Your apology is enough. Please take your money back."

But they turn and walk away.

"Come back," I say. "Take your money back."

The girl says, "We wanted you to have it. It was our idea to make things right."

"Yeah," the boy says, "our mom didn't say we had to do it. But we wanted to."

My throat closes tight with tears, faced with two children who are better humans than I'll ever be. "Okay then. I have free ice cream from my job. Do you want some?"

Their faces brighten. He says, "Sure, but we have to tell our mom."

The girl grins. "We'll be right back."

"Invite your mom too," I say. "If she wants to come over."

I leave the door open, which I never do, and a breeze wafts in, bringing the scent of salt air. I dump the change, which amounts to three bucks if that, into a cleaned-out mayonnaise jar where I put a quarter for every bad habit I exhibit. Change clinks as coins tumble into the almost full jar. You'd think seeing visual proof of my sticky fingers habit, with one coin per episode, would make me stop, but so far, it's failed, like every other method I've tried. Meditation, visualizing, rubber bands snapped on my wrists, none of it has helped. Taking sneakers from under Irena's nose has to be my worst moment, betraying my best friend in the process. I've got to find a way to stop stealing.

"Knock, knock," the mom says. She hold a bouquet with bright flowers in pinks and purples out to me. "I brought you these as a thank you for going easy on my kids. They're learning, and it won't happen again."

I take the flowers and put them in another empty mayo jar waiting for more coins to remind me of my shame on a daily basis. I run water into the jar and arrange the flowers. "These are so pretty, thanks."

The kids hesitate at the threshold. "Come in," I say. "Make yourselves at home."

They flop into chairs and stare at my big screen television. "That's big," the boy says. "You're lucky," says the girl.

I pull cartons of ice cream from the freezer. We can eat as much ice cream at work as we like and take home two quarts of ice cream a week, which is more than I can consume on my own.

I say, "I saved up for the TV, so that's not due to luck. But I'm lucky I work at the ice cream factory and guess what?"

"What?"

"They give me free ice cream to take home. Anyone want to try some?"

The girl says, "What flavors do you have?"

"Mainly vanilla, because that's what I like best."

They glance at the floor, looking sad.

I hold up a carton of double chocolate chunk. "But we also make the best chocolate ice cream. Do you want to try that?"

"Yes, please," they both say.

I dish up ice cream and say, "I'm Abby. What're your names?"

The mom says, "I'm Becca, and this is Tyler and Tina."

Tina rolls her eyes. "I hate our matching names. They start with the same letter."

I shrug and scoop ice cream into bowls. "I guess you could change it when you get older and go by a different name."

Becca arches an eyebrow. "You're giving them wild ideas."

Tina glances at her brother. "My name is fine. I was just complaining."

I nod. "I love to complain. It's one of my hobbies, and I'm really good at it."

We all laugh. Soon we're perched on chairs letting ice cream melt in our mouths and exchanging stories about ourselves. Becca says, "We just moved from Arlington, and I'm looking for a job, if you hear of anything."

"The place I work is hiring, Lotus Creamery. You should apply there."

She smiles. "I will."

Spoons clink against the sides of ceramic bowls I bought at Goodwill. I'm big on saving money, and my friends have no clue as to the size of my savings account. It's a secret I intend to keep. Guilt nudges me, and I draw a deep breath. I should give the shoes back, if I want to live with myself and sleep at night. But they've been scuffed and worn. I wish I never took them.

Tina and Tyler get up and put their dishes in the sink. They're good kids, not at all like I imagined during the sneaker war disaster. They point at my mostly filled coin jar and two others filled to the brim on the counter.

Tyler says, "What're these for?"

Tina says, "Why do you have them?"

I grab a handful of change and put the coins in their hands. "So, I can give money to kids who stop by."

They say thanks. Tina tilts her head and says, "No, really, what're you doing with them? Why not spend the money?"

My stomach knots, and I decide to be honest. "They're

there to remind me of my bad habits. Each coin represents a time I could've been a better person."

Becca says, "That's a good idea. How long did it take for you to collect these?"

I shove my hands in my pockets and think back to the beginning of my collecting change in hopes of tempering my bad behaviors. Jack and I had been out at a bar, eating burgers with beers. I was tipsy and leaned into him in the alley. I threw my arms around his neck, inhaled his salty scent, and kissed him on the lips. His arms wrapped around my waist, and he drew me close. We hung there under the full moon in the sky, pausing in a rare moment when time stands still. My right foot lifted, and I let out a little moan.

But a car door slammed in the parking lot, bringing us back to reality, and Jack released me. I cleared my throat, and we glanced at each other with questioning eyes.

He said, "This can't happen again. I love Irena, and I don't want to be tempted. I'm waiting for her to come back to me."

My throat closed tight with tears as I hurried to my car, swearing on the bright full moon that I'd never push myself on him again. If only he loved me the way I loved him. If only we'd met before he fell for my best friend.

Letting out a sigh, I answer Becca. "About five years."

"Wow," the kids say. "That's a long time."

Becca says, "Good for you, for trying to change your habits. It's not easy."

"No, it's not, and I have a long way to go."

We say goodbye, and I close the door and flop on my bed, avoiding the shoe boxes. I've got to sneak these back into Jack's place. Better yet, I'll go in Irena's and add them to the collection of sneakers in her living room when they aren't home.

## 31

## FRANKIE

We're stuck in bumper-to-bumper traffic driving north on I-5 approaching Everett. They widened the road in this area a few years back, but it clumped up again and became clogged. I guess the American way is if you can drive instead of taking mass transit, by all means do it.

I glance at Special Agent Mark Brick. "How'd you get into this line of work?" A car stops ahead, and I slow, but his foot slams on an imaginary brake pedal.

"My dad was a police detective, so that's what I thought I'd do growing up. But I ended up here. How about you?"

I shrug. "I was recruited in college."

"Where'd you go?"

"University of Washington in computer sciences. I like

to code and solve problems, see patterns. That's why I like this job."

"Huh."

I haven't seen family photos on his desk, so I say, "You married and have kids?"

He looks out the side window. "Nope. Might not go that route, given the job. We'll see what happens though."

"I know what you mean."

I creep past Everett and continue north, hunched over the wheel, intent on tracking down my quarry. Where ever Jack Fishbone is, he'll regret messing up my plans for a promotion. Traffic glides ahead, and I say, "This guy we're looking for is seriously ticking me off. He looked at me with a straight face and told me point blank he'd be there no matter what in the meeting spot. I never saw him being a liar. What a fool I was."

Brick says, "First time fooled, never again."

I grit my teeth and form a plan to find the missing man. "Let's go over our approach. I'm thinking we'll interview his friends and family, check out the surrounding area, and head to the marina office. Maybe they'll know something."

"Right. And while we're here, let's stop by the jail and talk to the guy behind the scam."

I say, "Good idea, let's do that before we hit town."

Brick calls to make arrangements, and I take the freeway exit closest to the jail. We're let into a room, where the prisoner is cuffed and waiting. He scowls and glares at us.

We take seats facing him and identify ourselves. I say, "Craig, we're here because your friend, Jack Fishbone, is missing. Did you overhear anything that would've led you to believe he was planning an escape after your boat trip?"

He cocks his head. "Why should I tell you? You're not doing me any favors. From what I heard through the grapevine, you offered Jack a special deal to turn on me and give evidence. No way you'll get me to say anything." He turns and stares at the gray cinder block wall.

I say, "I understand why you wouldn't want to help us. But there's a chance we could make your life easier if you tell us what you know."

He spits on the floor. "I'm not helping the Feds build a better case against me. I'm innocent. I wasn't involved in that scam. Jack did it all by himself. I told him to stop, but he wouldn't. He took advantage of old people who didn't have friends or family. You've got it the wrong way around."

Brick says, "We know it's a difficult time while you're awaiting trial. Maybe we could get the judge to reduce your bail and release you."

Craig chuckles. "Fat chance of that. I don't have the money to post bail, and my rich parents refuse to help. They want me to rot in jail and learn a lesson. So, you can take what you're offering, which I doubt is real, and get out of here."

Brick gives me a look and tilts his head, so I know he's turning it over to me. I say, "Before we go, tell us one thing. Who is the most important person in Jack's life?"

Craig snickers. "That's easy. Jack loves his ex-wife almost as much as his sneaker collection. That's all you'll get from me. I want my lawyer."

We rise from our seats, and I say, "Thank you for your time. We'll be in touch."

"Go through my lawyer next time," Craig says as we leave. "I'm through talking to you."

In the car, I drive to Millersville and say, "That didn't go well, but at least we know there's a chance that Fishbone is at his ex-wife's house."

Brick says, "Or at his apartment gloating over his sneakers before leaving town."

The marina appears up ahead, and I say, "Let's talk to the marina manager, get the lay of the land, before we see his friends and family."

"Sounds good. I'll update the boss while you drive."

He calls and relays what we're up to, getting stern orders in response. I listen to his conversation, and the pit of my stomach churns with worry. Can I prove myself in this job? Maybe I'm cut out for computer coding more than dealing with people and finding lost souls.

In the marina office, I ask for the manager. An older man with gray hair comes out of the back. He's wearing a flannel checked shirt and jeans. His gray beard is trimmed short. We introduce ourselves, and he says, "My name's Mike. What can I do for you?"

Brick says, "We're looking for a man named Jack Fishbone. Do you know him and where he might be?"

Mike nods. "He's a friend of mine. I've known him for years. He fell overboard and disappeared. I heard he wanted to start a new life somewhere else so he could wear shorts and flip flops all year round."

I give Brick a side look. That's good intel. The fugitive likes warm weather. Maybe he's driving south. I say, "Did he mention wanting to go somewhere? A favorite place he'd like to live?"

Mike pats the counter and smiles. "Costa Rica was where he wanted to live. He dreamed about moving there, but Irena, his ex-wife, wouldn't go with him. They share a daughter, you know, and she's torn up about her dad disappearing."

Brick says, "Are they close, Fishbone and his ex-wife? Do you think he might be hiding at her place?"

Mike laughs, resting a hand on his belly. "Not in this lifetime. He'd give anything to be back with her, but she can't stand how much he spends on sneakers. And he never wears them. The shoes sit in his apartment on specially lit shelves. He won't let anyone touch them."

I say, "Thanks very much, that's helpful. Anything else you can add?"

He blinks and looks down. "No, but I hope he's alive. He's a great guy."

## 32

# JACK

As my bed is wheeled into my hospital room, going past a patient in the bed by the door. His lined face is pale and worn, but I don't want to look in the mirror and see the horror show I've become. An orderly pushes a rolling IV pole hung with clear liquid in bags dripping into my arms through tubes. I'm a pin cushion radiating fear and body odor, on the verge of full-out panic.

The aides lock the wheels of the bed and pull up the rails. After the MRI, they took me to get an X-ray. A heavy lead vest was placed on my chest, and I was told to stay still, which I managed to do. The best I can do is wait to get better.

A nurse comes in. "How're you feeling?"

"My head's killing me. It really hurts."

She says, "The doctor will be in. Did you remember your name?"

I shake my head, and a spike of pain hits me between the eyes. "No, nothing yet."

I close my eyes and wake when a woman in a white lab coat pats my wrist. She says, "I'm Dr. Wang, and I'm here to ask you some questions."

I squint at her. Bright lights give me a splitting headache. Her black hair is pulled back, and she's wearing blue disposable gloves.

I say, in a hoarse voice, "My head really hurts."

"We'll see what we can do about that. Do you know where you live?"

I say, "In a house built of bungie cords and rubber bands."

Her brown eyes flicker. "Do you know where you are?"

"In a hospital."

"Do you know your name?"

I sigh and wish I could give a different answer. "I have no idea."

"What town are you in?"

"I don't know."

She pats the metal bed rail. "You have a head injury that may have left you with memory loss. Do you remember anything about when you hurt your head?"

I lick my dry lips and try to summon up the past. "Waves, water, that's all I recall. It's dark and murky."

She makes notes on a device. "Is the memory dark and murky or were you in a dark place physically?"

"I wouldn't call it a memory. More of a feeling."

She nods. "Anything else?"

I blink back tears. "I think someone close to me betrayed me. It's a feeling is all."

She waits, but I have nothing else to say. The effort of trying to recall exhausts me. My heavy limbs sink into the mattress, and I stare at the ceiling, letting sadness and self-pity wash over me.

"We'll review your test results and be back later," she says. Her sneakered feet squeak as she leaves. If I had to bet, I'd say she was wearing Skoopla sneakers with black waffle soles. I wonder why I know so much about sneakers. Maybe I was a famous athlete. The idea rings true and feels right, and I hold on to a glimmer of hope that I was a professional basketball player. I close my eyes and smile, imagining my athletic prowess. I bet I was a king on the court and a star slam-dunker.

Heavy footsteps on the linoleum floor approach my neighbor's bed. Apprehension sweeps over me, and I open one eye. The visitor is back, and he's tinkering with the other guy's tubes. Wait, is that a syringe in his hand?

He holds it up, pushes out a squirt of liquid and shoves it into the arm of the sleeping man. The patient gasps, and his eyes fling open wide. The visitor turns and strides from the room.

Alarms go off, and bells chime. Monitors beep, and I

cringe in the chaos. My chest grows tight. What if the stranger comes for me and kills me? I reach over and hit the red call button to help the other patient before it's too late. No one appears. Why aren't they rushing to help him?

A nurse hurries in and says to me, "Do you need something?"

I point to the next bed. "The man over there needs help. Someone came in and stuck a needle in his arm. I think he might be dead. Go check on him."

She glances at the bed and says to me slowly, "While you were undergoing tests, we did have a man in that bed for a brief time before he was taken into surgery. I'm afraid he didn't make it. It's such a shame. We want all of our patients to have positive outcomes."

I gulp and say, "He's dead?"

"Yes." She's talking about life and death, but she's calm. Maybe that comes from working in a hospital, where not everyone makes it out alive.

I say, "Why am I seeing people who aren't there? Am I going to be all right?"

She hesitates before answering and says, "I suppose it depends on your definition of all right. Take it one day at a time with small steps on the road to recovery. There may be permanent damage you'll have to learn to live with, and there will be emotional ups and downs."

I wince. "Was I hurt in my groin? I want to have kids. Did something happen to me, and I won't be able to?"

"That appears to be in working order. The doctor will come in and talk to you."

I say, "Can I still play basketball? I think I played sports professionally."

She tilts her head. "Rest now. The doctor will be in later."

"I'm hungry. Can I have something to eat?"

"Not yet. You may need to go into surgery."

My pulse races. "I don't want surgery. I could die on the operating table."

"Just rest."

She leaves the room, and I stare at the sink, clenching my jaw and wondering what happened to my head. I have a feeling someone hurt me, but that's all. I might as well try to make sneakers out of cotton candy. My situation is hopeless.

## 33

## KELLY

Abby leaves, and I sit with my mom while she wolfs down food. I put the dinner dishes in the dishwasher while she takes a shower, which she does after a day of handling distress calls. She used to sing in the shower, but after Dad went missing and Buzz moved out, she lost her joy.

I sigh and wonder where my father is. It hurts that he was willing to leave without taking me along. I would've gone with him, and the same might be true of my mom. I know she still loves him, but as she says, she can't live with him because of his habit of hoarding sneakers and spending more than he earns bartending part time.

But I miss Buzz almost as much as my dad. I liked having him around, and he's a better cook than my mom. Now that our neighbor tattled on him to my mother, I doubt she'll relent and ask Buzz to live with us again. The first few weeks after he moved in with us, she was carefree and happy. I need to remind her of that.

My mom's phone rings while she's in the shower. I glance at the number and answer it. Abby says in a tearful voice, "I haven't been the best friend to your family. I want you and your mom to know I'm going to do better. I really am, and I love you guys and appreciate your support during this difficult time. Goodbye."

She hangs up, and I set the phone down and whistle. That was strange.

My mom comes in the kitchen rubbing a towel over her hair. "Who was that?"

"Abby. She called to apologize. She said she loves us, she's glad we're friends, and she's going to do better."

My mom walks over to the sink and fills a glass with tap water, drinking it down. She wipes her mouth and says, "Everyone is acting weird and dramatic since your dad went missing. When we find him, I hope everyone will calm down."

She strides out of the room, leaving me gazing out the window wondering if my dad will come back. Maybe he's had enough of us and doesn't want to be found. Tears run down my cheeks, and I wipe them away. Feeling sorry for myself isn't going to solve anything, as my mom would say. She's been preoccupied with cleaning out his apartment and selling his shoes, so I'll try tracking him down.

I check the online auction we're running for the first

pair of sneakers and squeal. My mom comes running in the kitchen. "What is it? A mouse?"

"Dad's orange shoes. Look at the last bid for them. We'll close it tomorrow."

My mom's eyes grow wide, and she hugs me. "We'll get rid of his debts."

"We need to insure them when we ship them, in case they get lost or stolen."

"Good idea. Let me know anything else you find out. We'll put another pair up for sale tomorrow."

I say, "And we have to clean out the apartment."

She smacks her forehead. "I'll get on that tomorrow. It's too late tonight."

She pulls out her laptop and goes in the living room. My science project is due tomorrow, but I ignore it. My heart isn't in school work. All I care about is my dad and helping my mom. She's all I have left.

I sit on the couch beside her and research what price the next pair of shoes should go for. Dad's leaving all this behind strikes me as a selfish move. I hope he's happy wherever he is, and it was worth the price of hurting us.

I say, "How are you going to track Dad down?"

She glances up from entering numbers in a spreadsheet. "What do you mean?"

"What specifically were you going to do to find him?"

She shrugs. "I plan to tackle that when the apartment is empty, the shoes are sold and his debts are paid off. The

FBI wouldn't release any information about him or his whereabouts."

"Wait, you called them and didn't tell me?"

"Sure."

"Next time, tell me. Maybe I can help, since you're busy with your regular job and taking care of Dad's stuff."

She goes back to her bookkeeping. "Sure, go ahead. I think it'll be pretty tough to find him though."

## 34

# IRENA

I sit beside Kelly on the sofa and update my sales spreadsheet. I'm behind on my record keeping, and my bookkeeper is bugging me for the numbers. I save the file and lean back with a sigh. "Want a cup of tea?"

Kelly hunches over her laptop and says without looking up, "Peppermint, please."

I get up, heat the water in the electric tea kettle we gave my mom for Christmas before she passed away, and bring back two mugs with tea bags, putting them on the coffee table. She sets her laptop aside, and we sit quietly sipping.

I say, "A lot has happened lately. How're you feeling about it?"

Her brows knit together. "I'm angry Dad left. Who would do that to a daughter?"

I pat her knee. "I'm sure he didn't mean to hurt you, but he did, didn't he? With all this commotion, you've been lost in the shuffle, and I've been too focused on clearing his things out to sit and talk with you."

She shudders and drinks tea, holding the mug with both hands. I'm not a shrink, but if I had to guess, I'd say she's protecting her heart from harm. I say in a soft voice, "I wish we could have a do-over. Maybe if I'd stayed married to your dad, this wouldn't have happened."

"Don't doubt yourself," she says. "You always tell me that. You guys fought all the time about money. I'd hate growing up hearing that in our house."

I let out a sigh and wait for her to say more.

She says, "It hurts that he didn't even say goodbye or ask me to come with him. And it's not fair. Why does Plum get to have her dad at home, and I don't?"

I bite my lower lip and say, "You're right, it's not fair, not one bit. Not one iota or scintilla or however you want to say it, it isn't fair. And it was selfish how he up and left without a goodbye. I'm sorry, sweet girl. You deserve better than that. You deserve everything going right for you forever and always." I reach over and rub her back. "But if you had left with him, I'd miss you more than you'd know. I hope you know how much I love you. You are my wind and sea, keeping me afloat."

She nods. "I worry about that. What'll you do when I finish high school and move away? You'll be here all alone. You should ask Buzz to move back in, because when he lived with us, you were laughing all the time and in a good mood. I liked that version of you."

I cringe at how I've been coming off. "But he lied to my face when I was running around looking for your dad and didn't mention he left your dad by the old cannery. I can't be in love with someone who puts me in second place."

Kelly sets down her mug and squeezes my hand. "But you're forgetting Buzz was protecting Dad from the thugs who wanted to hurt him, like the fake pizza guy with a gun. You should cut Buzz some slack. He was helping Dad."

I rub my temples. "I'll think about it. I wonder where the fake pizza guy is now? I hope he left town when he didn't find your dad."

# MR. ABERNATHY

Mr. Abernathy put down his book about World War I, Volume 7, and got out of his reading chair. Someone pounded on Jack's apartment door. A man yelled, "Open the door, Jack Fishbone. I know you're in there. You owe Mother Mercy money, and I'm here for payback."

Wood splintered, sounding like someone was kicking in Jack's door. Mr. Abernathy trembled and reached for his phone, dialing the police with shaking hands. He reported someone breaking in across the hall. While he waited on hold, a man screamed and what sounded like a baseball bat smashing furniture made Mr. Abernathy wince.

The dispatcher said, "Yours is the second call we've received about this. We'll send an officer right over."

He hung up, looked out the window, and paced the room while calling Irena. When she answered, he said,

"Someone's in Jack's apartment breaking things, and it might be the guy with the gun. I called the police. Don't come over because it's too dangerous."

Irena said, "Stay in your apartment. I don't want you getting hurt. I'll be there in five minutes."

She hung up as he said, "Let the police handle it."

Across the hall, a woman screamed, "Get your hands off me. I reported you to the police. They're on their way."

It sounded like Abby's voice, but he couldn't be sure. He hoped whoever it was wouldn't get hurt. He crossed his arms and waited for the cops to arrive in a squad car.

A man roared, "Get out of my way or I'll shoot you."

Mr. Abernathy said to himself, "Man up and do the right thing. I can't let him hurt her."

He jerked open the hall closet, grabbed his crossbow and marched across the hall to confront the thug and save Abby. Outside, sirens wailed, coming closer. He stepped into Jack's apartment and crouched, pulling back the crossbow and aiming the arrow at the man's broad back. The creep had Abby in a choke hold, and she was gasping for air, flailing with her hands, kicking at his knees.

Mr. Abernathy debated whether to plant an arrow in the target without warning, but he said, "Let her go or I'll shoot."

35

## ABBY

Sweat drips down my arms as I clean Jack's apartment, vacuuming and wiping dust from cupboards, running around scrubbing. I'm doing this partly as a penalty for lying and stealing from my friend. Besides, Irena is busy, and I want to do her a favor.

Dirt, crumbs, and pine needles clink up into the black vacuum hose as I clean the kitchen floor. I do a quick round of dusting with damp paper towels in the living room and bump into a hammer on top of a file cabinet, leaving it where it is. This is a big job, and I'll have to come back tomorrow after work to clean up the grime.

I fill a bucket with hot soapy water and grab a mop, scrubbing the floor. Someone pounds on the door, and a man yells, looking for Jack. I jerk and drop the mop.

I yell through the closed door, "Go away, he's not here. He left town."

"Liar," a man says. "I know you're hiding him. Let me in."

A foot pounds on the door, wood splinters, and walls shake. My heart races, and I pull out my phone, dialing 911. My palms are sweaty. My knees are weak. My voice trembles when I give the address to the dispatcher and say, "A man is breaking in. Send someone fast."

Just as I pocket the phone, the door flies open, and a man bursts in. He's big and tall, wearing a plaid flannel shirt. His dark eyes dart around the room. "Where is he?"

I grab the mop, wielding it as a weapon in front of me, and sidle over to the hammer that is just out of reach. "He's not here. You better go because I called the cops."

He grabs the mop from me, tossing it aside. I pick up the bucket of soapy water and fling it at him, but he just blinks and holds up a gun. "I'll shoot you if I have to. Tell me where Jack Fishbone is."

"I don't know." I lunge for the hammer, but he advances before I can reach it and puts me in a choke-hold. I gasp for breath, but his arm tightens around my neck. I claw at his eyes and kick at his groin. I scrabble around with my hands, searching for something to use as a weapon.

A man that sounds like Mr. Abernathy says, "Let her go or I'll shoot you."

The brute turns to look at Mr. Abernathy, and the grip on my neck loosens. He says, "Give up the act, old man. You can't hurt me with that."

My hand grasps a smooth wooden handle. I whip around and wallop the beast on his head with a hammer, but he dodges the blow, and the hammer smacks his shoulder. He lunges for me, and his eyes suddenly grow wide. He howls in pain, sliding to the floor with his hands on his leg, where an arrow protrudes from the back of his thigh. He screams, "I'm going to kill you."

Two police officers rush in and scan the room. A frowning female officer with short black hair says, "He's alive but wounded. Call the EMTs."

A male officer in his early twenties calls it in. The woman turns to us and says, "Tell us what happened."

I say, "This man broke in, looking for Jack Fishbone, and he tried to kill me when I couldn't tell him where Jack was. Mr. Abernathy warned him and shot him with an arrow."

Just then, Irena barges in with Kelly in her wake.

## 36

# IRENA

Kelly and I run past a police car and into Jack's apartment. The door is open. Inside, two police officers are standing over a big man on the floor with an arrow sticking out of the back of his thigh. Blood oozes out. An acrid smell of body odor wafts through the room, coming from the man. I stop and stare at the jerk who came here before pretending to deliver pizza. He brandished a gun and slugged Jack's neighbor, Mr. Abernathy, in the stomach.

Beads of sweat break out on the big man's brow. He frowns and says, "I don't do cops. I'm getting out of here." He tries to get up but flops back on the floor, groaning, grimacing, and clutching his leg.

Two officers bend over the prone man, cuffing his hands behind his back, and asking his name. "I'm not saying," he says. They repeat the question in stern tones, and the female officer pulls out his wallet and reads from his driver's license. "His name is Elgin Johnson."

I hurry over to Mr. Abernathy, who is gripping a crossbow and glaring at the man. He says, "He was choking Abby and wouldn't stop, so I had to shoot him."

I pat his shoulder. "You did the right thing because he could've killed her. I'm so glad you were here."

He nods and swallows hard.

I go over to Abby, who is touching her raw, red throat, and give her a hug. "How awful. You must be terrified. I know I would be. How are you holding up?"

She coughs and says, "My throat hurts, but I'll live. I was cleaning, because I wanted to help you, but he broke in and came after me. I used a mop to defend myself and then I got hold of a hammer."

I say, "You did this for me?"

She nods and her eyes fill with tears. "You're busy, so I came over to clean. I was mopping the floor when this jerk broke in."

I say, "Love you," and she says the words back. Maybe little by little, we'll recover from the shipwreck of Jack's disappearance. I wipe tears from my eyes and scan the room. The dining table that wobbled is smashed to smithereens, as are the chairs. The wood frame of the couch is broken into pieces. A coffee table is destroyed, parts splintered. A baseball bat lies on the floor.

I say to Abby, "You're lucky to be alive."

She holds up a hammer. "I got a good swing at him before he went down."

Two medics arrive carrying a stretcher. They check the man's vitals and examine the arrow lodged in the back of his thigh. "We'll take him to the hospital."

Medics lift him onto a stretcher, and the police cuff him to it. He says, "Get your hands off me." His eyes narrow, and he points at Mr. Abernathy. "It's his fault this happened. You should arrest him. Don't let him get away with almost murdering me."

They haul him out, arrow protruding from his thigh, and I say, "Good riddance. I hope they lock you up forever."

The police interview us and take notes. The female officer stands tall, with a grim expression on her face. The young male police officer looks fresh out of high school.

Abby touches her throat and says in a hoarse voice, "He choked me and was going to kill me. But I whacked him with the hammer."

Mr. Abernathy says, "He was strangling Abby and threatened me. I had to shoot him, so he'd let her go."

The female officer says, "Don't leave town in case we have questions for you. You acted in self-defense, so we won't arrest you."

Abby and Mr. Abernathy stand side by side, their hands trembling. When the police leave, I throw my arms around Mr. Abernathy and say, "You saved her life. You're my hero."

He blushes and rubs his cheek. "I did what anyone would do in my position."

Abby puts a hand on her hip. "What about me? Doesn't self-defense with a hammer count?"

I grin. "You're both heroes in my book and welcome on my boat and in my house anytime."

Kelly says, "That's right."

Mr. Abernathy says, "I'd like a boat ride. I miss being on the water."

I nod. "We'll take a boat ride with you two when all this is sorted out." I smile and open my arms. "It'll be the survivors tour for courageous heroes."

We laugh but Kelly rolls her eyes.

Abby says, "Can we go under Jackson Bridge and see where Jack was picked up by Buzz and taken to the wharf?"

"Sure, we'll make it a beyond the bridge tour," I say, but I glance at Kelly, who is biting her lower lip, reminded of being abandoned by her dad.

I survey the wrecked living room and switch to a safer subject. "There's not much left to move or give away, so I'll get junk haulers to clear this out. And Abby, thank you for coming over to clean. I was harsh with you before, but you showed up to help anyway. I appreciate it."

Kelly says, "Yeah, thanks, Abs."

The young male police officer knocks on the open door. His face is flushed, and he's wearing white disposable gloves. The female officer stands behind him. He says, "I forgot to take the weapons from you for chain of custody. Would you hand them over?"

Abby holds out a bloodied hammer, which he places in a bag. Mr. Abernathy hands him the crossbow.

"Nice bow," the young officer says.

Mr. Abernathy says, "Never thought I'd use it on a human."

As the police leave for the second time, Mr. Abernathy goes over to the door and fiddles with it. "Looks like you can close and lock it. I'm going back to my apartment to have a drink."

I say, "Thanks for everything."

"Yeah, thanks," Abby says. "I'd be dead on the floor and this'd be a crime scene if you hadn't shown up. I owe you one."

He smiles. "It's nothing special," he says with a chuckle. "Just another day of saving a life."

Kelly giggles. She's known Mr. Abernathy her whole life, and he always puts her in a good mood. We wave goodbye, and I turn to Kelly. "Let's take a look and see what you want to take home."

She frowns. "I'm not sure I want to take anything. It doesn't feel like Dad's place anymore. It even smells different."

Abby wrinkles her nose. "The jerk who choked me reeked of sweat."

I say, "If I ever see that Elgin Johnson sniffing around here again, I'll call the police as fast as you can hit a log near Upright Head."

Kelly groans. "Too many boating metaphors." She goes in the kitchen, and Abby and I follow her. She puts a small drinking glass decorated with pink tulips in her pocket. In the living room, a box where she kept her extra clothes is empty, the contents thrown around the room. She pokes a toe at a pair of ripped gray sweatpants on the floor. "Nothing here now but bad memories and nightmares."

I squeeze her shoulder and say, "We'll get through this."

She goes in the bathroom and shakes her head. "Nope, nothing I want here."

I hold up a toothbrush. "Is this your father's?"

She eyes the worn bristles and nods. I take the toothbrush and go in the kitchen, slipping it in a plastic bag and zipping it closed. If Jack is dead deep in the woods somewhere, I may need this for DNA identification.

Kelly goes in the bedroom and lets out a sigh. Jack's mattress is slit and pushed on the floor. The bedframe is broken. The contents of dresser drawers are scattered around the room.

She walks over to a framed drawing she made in

kindergarten and takes it off the wall. The glass is cracked, but her artwork is intact. "I made this for him."

She feels the back. "Something is under the paper," She rips brown paper off the back, and a key falls out on the floor. She picks it up and shoots me a smile. "Do you know where it goes?"

I say, "I don't, but it looks like a key to a bank safe deposit box. The question is, which one?"

**37**

---

## JACK

An orderly with wire-rimmed glasses and a short woman wearing blue scrubs wheel a hospital bed into the empty space next to me. She pulls up the side rails, and they click into place. I stare at her purple sneakers because they remind of something, but I can't think of what it is. I grit my teeth. Not remembering is driving me crazy. In the next bed, a big guy is on his side, facing away from me with heavy bandages on a leg and one hand handcuffed to the bedframe.

The orderly closes the curtain between us. The mauve and yellow plaid fabric doesn't match where the curtains come together and the colors bother me. I blink my eyes and consider the man with the bandaged leg. This situation must be a set up to test my sanity.

I chuckle and say in a hoarse voice, "You can't fool me. I know he's not a patient, and this is a test. You're trying to see if I'm sane. But you didn't have to add handcuffs. That's over the top and what clued me into your scheme."

The effort of making a short speech exhausts me. I slump back and say, "For all I know, this room might not be real, and you are figments of my imagination. Whatever you do, you can't lock me up. I won't let you, no matter how hard you try." A cackle escapes my lips and dies.

The two blue-scrubbed workers stand staring at the foot of my bed before turning toward the door. The woman says in a low voice, "So sad."

He says quietly, "Head injuries are the worst."

The door closes with a click. Except for the humming of machines hooked up to me, all is quiet. A noise from the next bed makes me twitch.

A man clears his throat and says, "I'm real, you know, not a fig bar of your imagination. What's wrong with you anyways? Sounds like you lost your mind."

I stare at the plaid curtain. My armpits smell. I need a shower and deodorant. I'm a smelly mess of a man who is losing my mind.

I say, "I saw people in and by that bed, before, but it turned out they weren't real. I lost my memory from a head injury. I have no idea who I am."

"That's rough, but that's life, one bummer after another. Do you know your line of work? Maybe that'll help you figure it out."

I stare at the curtain. Something about his large size

and raspy voice is familiar, but I swat the ridiculous thought away. I don't know this stranger. Besides, I'm not sure I'm talking to a real person. My brain could be tricking me again in life's latest joke.

"I'm not sure. All I know is I have a feeling I was headed somewhere important, and I loved someone. But I ended up here instead."

He says in a gravelly voice, "I get it. One day we're bound for glory and a goner in love, but out of the blue we're stuck in nowhere land with a roommate to boot."

I sigh and consider all I've lost. It's a blur, so I don't miss anything specific, just vague twinges of leaving someone behind and deep regrets. I say, "But I seem to know a lot about sneakers. So, maybe I was a shoe designer or a sales rep. That's my best guess."

He snickers. "A designer of sneakers? I have to congratulate you for your original thought. That's way out there, my friend."

My face heats. "Or I was a famous basketball star. I have a feeling I was."

He cackles, and his bed rattles. "You're crazy, pal. If you were famous at all, people would be looking for you. But I didn't see anyone with you when they wheeled me in. Where are your fans? And your PR person?"

I swallow bitter tears. No friend or family member sits by my bedside to comfort me and translate what doctors say. Is anyone wondering where I am? I bite my lip and hope I wasn't a horrible person who was disliked, making others glad to see me gone. I say, "You're probably right. I'm all alone."

The guy in the next bed says, "But I'll give you this, you made me forget how bad this arrow hurts, so thanks for that. Listen, buddy, I'm no shrink, but I think you may have what they call delusions of grandeur. Has anyone ever called you a narcissist?"

I frown. "No, not that I remember."

"Check the dictionary for the definition of a narcissist. Bet your mug shot will be next to it."

I squint at the ceiling. What a jerk. "I don't want to talk to you anymore. Let's just end this conversation."

"Fine, the feeling's mutual."

An alarm goes off on my IV monitor, beeping and making my head ache even more. I cringe and hit the red call button. How can anyone rest with this noise?

He says, "Where's the nurse? I can't find my call button."

I clamp my eyes closed, trying to block out the beeping alarm. "I called her."

A blue-scrubbed nurse with her hair up in a pony tail comes in the room. A white plastic badge shows her name is Alyssa. She says, "Do you need help?"

I point to the next bed. "He wants to see you, and my machine's beeping."

She resets my monitor, and I eye her orange and salmon-colored trainers that have a thick tread. Sturdy sneakers, good arch support, excellent for jogging, running, and hiking. How do I know so much about sneakers?

The man in the next bed says, "I need something for pain. You wouldn't believe how much it hurts. It's driving me crazy."

She says, "The doctor will be in."

He groans. "I can't take this anymore."

She says, "They're busy with other patients."

He says, "I don't like doctors or hospitals. I don't want to be here, chained up like an animal."

I nod, feeling the same way. Let me go home, wherever that is.

She says, "We need to keep a close eye on your wound. The police are here, and they want to talk to you."

A feeling of dread fills me, and I hope I don't have a criminal record. My heart beats fast. What if the police are here to arrest me? I start to scoot my butt to the edge of the bed, ready to run, but the room spins. I'm woozy and in no shape to evade the authorities.

I say, "I don't want to talk to them. Don't let them near me."

She comes over. "They're not here to see you. They want to interview your neighbor." She tugs the curtains blocking my bed all the way around and walks away.

The man in the next bed says, "Hey, pal, your voice sounds familiar. Wonder if I know you."

I roll my eyes. Whoever I was, I'd never associate with someone like that. "I doubt it."

## 38

## FRANKIE

Driving from the county jail, I say to Mark, "Let's work with the local cops on this one. Maybe they've learned something about Fishbone's location. And let's check his bank accounts a second time." I clench my jaw. "We can't let him disappear. It makes us look bad."

He types on his laptop, riding shotgun. "The local police are interviewing a guy right now who broke into Fishbone's apartment. His name is Elgin Johnson, like the FBI case in the 1950's where an agent was murdered. Someone shot an arrow in his leg when he broke in and choked a cleaning woman. He's at Riverside Hospital in Mt. Vernon. Let's go talk to this guy. He must know something about Fishbone. At the very least, we'll find out what he was doing at our witness's apartment."

I stab at the GPS to get directions to the hospital. "The

creep with an arrow in his leg sounds like a national treasure."

He nods. "He sounds like another winner."

We stride into the hospital and take an elevator to the third floor, going in Room 366, which has two beds. One bed has a curtain drawn around it, so I can't catch a glimpse of the other patient. I shift my attention to the two police officers in blue standing at the culprit's bedside talking to him.

The suspect in bed is a big man with black eyes close together. Elgin Johnson is on his side, moaning. There's a huge bandage around his right thigh. He scowls at us and grimaces.

The police officers turn to us, and we flash our badges, introducing ourselves. I say to them, "What do you have so far?"

A middle-aged male officer with a beer-drinker's belly says, "He says he made an innocent mistake and went in the wrong apartment, thought it was his girlfriend's place."

I smirk at the far-fetched story and say to Johnson, "Why'd you choke the cleaning lady?"

He says, "What'd you mean? She attacked me, and I had to protect myself. I acted in self-defense."

The female officer says, "Her weapon was a mop."

I resist the urge to roll my eyes. "What about your leg? How'd that happen?"

He says, "A guy came in the place and shot me with a

crossbow. I wasn't doing anything. I happened to be in the wrong apartment is all."

Mark gives me a side glance, and I nod for him to take over. He says, "You've been at that apartment before and threatened Mr. Fishbone's family and neighbors. Why were you there? Are you working for somebody?"

A choking sound comes from behind an ugly plaid fabric curtain separating the two beds. I say, "Everything okay over there? Do you need a nurse?"

A man in the other bed coughs. "No, I'm good."

Mark stares at Johnson, who fiddles with a pillow under his arm, and says, "What drew you to Jack Fishbone's apartment? Why'd you go there twice?"

Coughing in the next bed draws my attention, but I turn back to Johnson and glare at him. "Answer him."

The police nod.

Johnson looks at his bandaged thigh and whimpers. "I was following orders. I was told to trash the place to send a message to deadbeats who don't pay what they owe and to hurt anyone who gets in my way. My boss doesn't like to be stiffed. She won't let people take advantage of her."

I say, "What's the name of the woman you work for?"

He shakes his head. "I can't tell you. She'd hurt me."

My hands clench, and I reach over and squeeze the bandage. "Tell us."

He gasps. A monitor beeps, and a warning blinks about high blood pressure. I say, "With all the charges against you at this point, you're probably going to prison for quite some time. If you talk to us now, we can probably help you and put you in a place where nobody can get at you."

He is quiet for a beat and finally says, "She goes by Mother Mercy. But please, please, don't let her know I gave you her name."

A nurse rushes in, sneakered feet squeaking on the floor. She pushes a button to silence the alarm and says to Johnson, "Are these people upsetting you?"

He groans. "Yes, they are."

I hold up my hands. "We were just talking."

The nurse frowns. "You need to leave. You're upsetting him, and he needs to rest."

"Fine," I say, "we were about to go anyway."

Mark says to Johnson, "We may need to talk to you again."

"Forget it," he says. "I'm not saying another word."

We move into the hallway. Staff in blue scrubs hurry by. The sound of monitors beeping in rooms gives me a headache. Nurses line one side of the hall standing at mobile computer monitors, entering data.

I say to the police officers, "Can you stake out Jack Fishbone's place in case someone else shows up?"

They shake their heads. "We lack the man power. Budget and staffing issues and all that."

I nod. "Understood."

Mark says, "How long can you hold him?"

They look at each other and shrug. She says, "We'll do

the best we can, but at this point it's his word against theirs."

Mark says, "Are you familiar with Mother Mercy? Or do you think he made that up to get us off his back?"

The middle-aged officer tugs on his ear. "There've been whispers but nothing substantiated as far as I know."

His partner says, "Yep."

We thank them for their help and head to the car.

Mark says, "We'll look into this Mother Mercy when we're back in the office."

"Could be a wild goose chase," I say, "but you never know."

# 39

## JACK

The police enter the room, and I turn to face the wall. I can tell from their voices they aren't the ones I spoke with earlier. They ask the man in the next bed a bunch of questions, and he says, "It's not my fault. I'm innocent."

I stare at the mint green wall. The paint color feels like it was around thirty years ago, and I narrow my eyes, wondering why I thought that. Maybe I worked in a hospital? I clamp my jaw shut, frustrated that I can dredge up unimportant facts but can't retrieve my name or where I live. Tears roll down my cheeks. It isn't fair. I did nothing to deserve this. Or did I?

Two more people come in the room introducing themselves. The new woman and man are from the FBI. My eyebrows rise. The guy in the next bed is in deep trouble if the Feds are coming after him.

The FBI pair grill my roommate. He offers lame excuses about why he broke into an apartment. He choked a cleaning woman, and that's cold. But it sounds like he enjoys doing that sort of thing, so I guess it takes all kinds.

I roll on my back and cover my face with my hands in case they look behind the curtain. I wish they'd leave. I want to take a nap, but their voices are keeping me awake. They're really interested in this Fishbone fellow's apartment.

The back of my head pulses with pain. I close my eyes, wondering what Fishbone did to attract attention from both the police and the FBI. A chill sweeps up my spine, and I pull the blankets up to my chin. I'm glad the guy in the next bed is being questioned and not me. Something about the police and the FBI being here makes me tremble with fear.

The man in the next bed yelps, and my eyes fly open. A monitor erupts with an ear-piercing beeping. I grit my teeth and hope someone will make it stop.

A nurse rushes in and sends the cops away. I'd better be careful and not tick him off, because it sounds like he has a quick temper. I don't want to end up dead in a hospital room after a scuffle, and I'm in no shape to defend myself. I stare at the curtain, afraid to go to sleep with a menacing man in the next bed.

A ponytailed nurse comes in and starts to open the

curtain, but I say, "Please, leave it. I like the privacy." She nods. "Sure, I understand that."

She checks my IV drip, and I say, "What are you giving me?"

"Saline, to keep you hydrated."

"Can I have something to eat?"

"Not yet. The doctor will be in soon. I saw her down the hall earlier."

I say, "I can't remember my name, but I know I don't like doctors."

She smiles, showing a dimple in her left cheek. "You're not alone in feeling that. But you need help. We've got to get your head fixed."

I squint. "The lights are too bright. Can you turn them off? And I need something for the pain."

"The doctor needs to see you first." She flicks off the overhead lights, pulls on white disposable gloves and examines my eyes. She smells of fresh air, exercise, and a cheese sandwich. My stomach rumbles. She opens my eyes wide and shines a pen light.

I say, "What do you see?"

"Enlarged pupils. Are you seeing double, by chance? Or is everything blurry?"

"No, but the light hurts. I want to go home, wherever that is."

"We're working on finding out who you are. Just rest." She leaves, and I close my eyes.

The man in the next bed says, "It sucks in here. I've had an arrow stuck in my leg, and it took them forever to get it out. It shouldn't be a big deal, just yank it out. I'd have done it myself, but I couldn't reach back there and get a good grip."

I clamp my lips closed and stay still. I don't want to engage with this guy or attract his attention. He says, "Can't get you talking, eh? Going quiet on me. Suit yourself. You're probably a high and mighty stuck-up guy anyways. I hate those types."

I swallow hard. For all I know I was a stuck-up jerk in my former life before landing here. I have no grounds to defend myself. I grimace and hope I didn't hurt anyone in the past. Maybe I'm no better than the guy in the next bed.

His bed creaks, like he's getting up. I slowly turn on my side to face the wall. My head throbs.

He stands breathing hard near my bed and yanks back the curtain. "Let me get a good look at you, hiding behind the ugliest curtain I ever saw. The plaids don't even match at the seams. Did you notice that?"

Anger radiates off him in a foul garlic smell mixed with potent body odor. "The colors make me sick. Who picks mauve to go with yellow, anyway? I hate the color yellow. Can't stand it."

I wrinkle my nose and lie still, squeezing my eyes shut, and hoping he'll go away. My pulse pounds in my ears. How did I end up in this bed? I try to recall, but nothing comes to me.

He shakes my bed and says in a gruff voice, "I've got to get out of here. This noise drives me crazy."

My eyes open wide, and I stare at the wall, wanting the nurse to come in and rescue me. The blood pressure cuff on my arm tightens, and a machine beeps repeatedly with a warning. I push the call button for the nurse, and she strides in.

She says to my menacing roommate, "Get back in bed and leave this poor man alone. Patients deserve privacy."

He grumbles and shuffles away. He says to the nurse, "He's giving me the silent treatment, and I hate it when someone ignores me. Makes me want to hit them."

"This hospital is a violence-free zone. He's here to heal. Don't talk to him or we'll have to move you to the hall."

She swishes the curtain closed, and I let out a sigh. "Thank you," I whisper.

"Of course. Now rest until the doctor comes in."

My roommate says, "Are they coming to see me?"

"Not yet. You'll have to wait."

She walks out, and my roommate says, "Thanks for throwing me under the bus and making me look bad. Thanks a lot, man. When I get out of here, maybe I'll look you up and make your life miserable."

Before I can stop myself, I blurt out, "You already are."

He chuckles. "Glad to hear that. I make people miserable and get paid to do it. I'm the best there is at my job. I didn't get your name. What is it? You can tell me. I can keep a secret. You're probably scamming the system, pretending you hit your head and lost your memory. Is that right?"

I take a breath and will myself to remember who I am, so I can pick up where I left off. But nothing comes to me. It's a blank. A feeling of helplessness washes over me, and it takes all my strength to not break down and sob. My skull aches. My shoulders shake as I cry, mucus running from my nose. If I don't like who I was, what will I do then?

"Everything all right over there?" my roommate says in a snide tone of voice. "Sounds like you're crying, Blubber Baby. That's what I'll call you."

My chest heaves, and I fight the urge to weep out loud. But when I gasp for breath, a sob escapes my lips, and I whimper.

My neighbor says, "Don't go feeling sorry for yourself. You're not the only one with problems, you know."

The nurse comes in and parts the curtain at the foot of the bed, where my obnoxious neighbor can't see in. She says, "The doctor is on her way. Here are some tissues."

I take them and blow my nose, making a honking sound, and she pulls the curtain closed. "Thanks," I say in a quiet voice.

My roommate says to the nurse, "Sad sack there is feeling pretty sorry for himself."

"You should try being a bit kinder. Everyone has their

own issues and problems. We're not all as fortunate as you to have only had an arrow in a leg."

He laughs. "I like your attitude, honey. You've got some spunk. Maybe we should go out sometime. We could have pizza and watch a movie at my place."

"I don't date patients."

"There must be exceptions. Rules are made to be broken, after all. Maybe you'd like to go out with Mr. Sorry for himself over there when all this is over?"

Her sneakers squeak as she turns and walks out the door, leaving it open. A cart rolls down the hall, and people are talking outside the room. I sigh. When will this ordeal end? I wish I had a roll of duct tape to cover my roommate's mouth and shut him up. I'm hurt and searching for answers, but that menacing creep is making it very hard.

## 40

## IRENA

I check the auction results online for the first pair of Jack's shoes we put up for sale. Bids for the orange sneakers are flying in fast as the deadline looms. The dollar amount rises as each minute ticks by. I say to Kelly, who is sitting by me at the kitchen table, "Looks like a lot of people want these shoes."

She bites her lip. "I wish we could've kept them for Dad, though. If he comes back, he'll be disappointed that we didn't keep them."

I pat her shoulder. "You can blame it on me if that happens. That's what mothers are for. But you know, we're doing this for his sake to pay off his bills. Your father was irresponsible and didn't pay his debts."

Out of the blue, a storm cloud of sorrow wallops me, and all I want to do is cry. A sharp pain pulses at the back of my head. The image of my ex-husband Jack appears in my mind, as clear as if he were standing here in front of us.

I grip the table edge, and tears run down my cheeks. Where is Jack? Has he gone somewhere to lead the good life? Or is he hurt and needs help? I drum my fingers on the table. I have no idea where he is, so I have no way of riding to his rescue.

Goosebumps prick my flesh. I'm certain Jack needs help. I wince as icepicks of pain stab at my skull. When I touch the back of my head, I almost hear Jack moaning.

Kelly touches my arm. "Are you okay? What just happened?"

A shiver passes through me, and I massage my temples. "I'm not sure. A wave of emotions swept over me, and all I could think of was your dad. I have a feeling he needs us."

"How can we find him?"

"I don't know, but I need to think of how to do that." Jack could be flat on his back in the woods. An image of blood oozing from his head flashes before me, and I grimace.

Her voice trembles when she says, "I miss him and think about him all the time."

I rest a hand on her back and say, "I hit a brick wall with the FBI. It was like shouting into the wind. I'll think of something."

"Do it soon," she says, tears welling in her eyes. "Before it's too late."

I rub my forehead and vow to track down the truth, which may take longer than I'd like, with cleaning out Jack's apartment and selling his shoes and rescuing boats and tending to Kelly. Just rattling off that list makes my bones weary. I can't wait for the confusion to clear and for us to learn where Jack is.

I say, "I hope after your dad's debts are paid and Craig's trial is over that he'll come back to us. He should be out of danger by then."

My laptop dings with an auction alert. I say, "If the orange sneakers are this popular, just think what we'll get for the gold leather shoes. Those will bring in boat loads of money."

Kelly rolls her eyes. "Your boat jokes are corny."

I smile and give her a side hug. "And I'm your corny mom."

She says, "Aren't you supposed to be practicing your violin?"

I make a face. "I haven't had time. I've been preoccupied since your dad left."

Her brows furrow. "What did dad's note mean about the violin maker knows everything? Did you ask him?"

"I asked, but he wouldn't tell me yet." I get up and say, "Tell you what, I'll go practice for a half hour. But you might want to use ear plugs."

A loud knock at the front door startles us. We look at each other with wide eyes, and I say, "Are you expecting anyone?"

She shakes her head.

A stern voice at the front door says, "Irena Fishbone, this is the FBI. Please open the door. We want to talk to you."

Kelly says, "Mom, is everything all right?"

I shudder and hurry to the door. "I hope so. Let's see what they want."

I wipe my moist palms on my jeans and open the door to a woman and man in dark blue jackets with FBI written in yellow letters. The woman has short brown hair, and she's in her early-thirties. She gazes at me, sizing me up. A muscled man with a cleft chin about her age clenches his jaw. They're dead serious.

My breath grows shallow. I hope they aren't here to tell us Jack is dead. I don't think Kelly and I could recover from that news.

The woman says, "I'm Agent Frankie McNalley, and this is Agent Mark Brick. Do you mind if we come in and sit down?"

I gesture to the couch. My throat is dry. "Would you like some water?"

"No, thanks," she says. They perch on armchairs. He says, "Please, take a seat."

Kelly and I glance at each other and sit on the couch.

Agent McNalley clears her throat. "I'm sorry to tell you this, but your ex-husband is missing. He was supposed to show up at a rendezvous spot, where we'd take him to a place and protect him until your friend Craig's trial was over. But he never showed, and we need to track him down."

Agent Brick says, "When was the last time you saw him?"

I clear my throat. "Right before we were both swept overboard off Craig's boat."

"Same here," Kelly says.

McNalley leans forward and stares at me. "We understand you argued with your ex-husband before you two were swept overboard?"

Kelly looks at me. "Mom?"

"He wouldn't put on a life jacket. The skipper sent me to tell him to put one on, but Jack refused and said it'd be uncomfortable. He always does what he wants anyway." I cringe, picturing Jack bleeding in the bushes. There are many isolated places near our town where a person could die and not be found for days.

Brick says, "Did you have any disagreements with Jack in the past?"

I shrug. "Sure, doesn't everyone? Especially when they're divorced?"

They glance at each other, giving a quick shake of their heads. McNalley says, "We understand he owed you money for child support. That could be cause to harm him."

My fists clench. "I loved him. I wouldn't hurt him."

Brick says, "He named you as his beneficiary on his accounts. That gives you motive."

My heart races. "I didn't know that. And you shouldn't be questioning me. You should be talking to Bud Wiser, who goes by the nickname Buzz. He was the last one to see Jack. He picked him up after he fell overboard and took him to the old cannery."

McNalley abruptly stands. "We'll be in touch."

Brick rises and pockets his notepad. "Don't leave town. We may need to talk with you again."

I take a shaky breath and stand, ushering them out. I turn to Kelly and wrap my arms around her trembling body.

She says, "Do you think Dad is dead?"

"I don't think so, but it sounds like no one knows what happened to him."

"I don't understand what's going on."

"I don't either, hon. I thought he went into witness protection or something like that. But we've got to hang in there and get through this. One day, we'll be on the other side looking back."

Tears stream down her cheeks and she says, "The FBI basically accused you of doing something to Dad, maybe even killing him."

I blow out a breath. "I'm sure they're treating everyone as a suspect." But many questions tumble through my mind. Will they accuse me and arrest me for killing my ex-husband and hiding his body? But they have no evidence. What will Kelly do if I end up in jail? Buzz is the one they should arrest. He saw Jack last, and he was staring at what might have been blood on the ground by the wharf. And where is Jack anyway?

I take Kelly's hand and squeeze it. "We've got to be strong to get through this."

She hesitates before nodding. "I wonder how Dad's doing."

I sigh. "I'm wondering the same thing. It's so frustrating not to know anything."

I plod into the kitchen with slow weary steps. I have no idea what the future holds, but I will do my best to fix this. My daughter deserves answers and to not live in limbo about her father's fate. I want to find the man I love but can't live with. Something is seriously wrong if he didn't show up to meet the FBI.

I pick up a mug and take it to the sink. Piercing pain strikes the back of my skull, and the cup falls from my hands, shattering on the floor. I moan and rub the back of my head. An image of Jack lying on his back flashes before me.

Kelly says, "What's wrong? Are you okay?"

I lean on the cold porcelain sink and rest a hand on my forehead. "I just had a feeling something's wrong with your father."

"But we don't know where he is, or if he's even alive."

I look out the window as darkness settles. "You're right, and we have no idea where to look. But we've got to try to figure it out."

She folds her arms. "The FBI is trying to find him. Maybe we should just let them do their thing?"

I shake my head. "They don't know your dad like I do."

I sweep up broken ceramic mug pieces and dump them in the trash. Porcelain bits clink and clunk, falling into the bin. First of all, I need to interrogate Buzz, get the truth out of him and find out what happened to Jack.

My cell phone rings, and Mercury Thunder, the violin teacher, is calling. "Hello?"

He says, "I hope it's not too late to call. I wanted to hear how your practicing is coming along. Do you have any questions for me?"

"Other than what was Jack involved in and how you two know each other?"

He says, "As I mentioned before, that's off the table for now. But later on, I might tell you more after we get to know each other better. It takes time to build trust."

My brow furrows, and Kelly whispers, "Who is it?"

I whisper, "Mercury Thunder, the violin maker."

She puts a hand over her mouth and giggles. "What kind of name is that?"

He clears his throat. "The name was given to me at birth, and it took time for me to grow into it. You know about teasing on the playground. Children can be beasts."

"I agree," I say, recalling what Buzz and I went through growing up because of our names. A shiver of longing passes through me, and I wish he was here. The man knows how to cook, I'll give him that. He's the best listener, and I miss his hugs and how he made Kelly laugh.

Mercury Thunder says, "How much have you practiced? Are you making progress?"

I sigh. "To tell you the truth, not much, maybe a half hour? But I'm juggling a lot at the moment and tying up loose ends at Jack's place. And I have the boat business to run and a daughter to take care of, which is the most important job."

Kelly flashes me a smile, and I nod, sending her an air kiss.

"I'm sure it is," he says. "I appreciate your honesty, although I'd hoped to hear you were practicing an hour or more a day. Jack said you were eager to learn. Perhaps you'll move it up on your priority list. You won't learn to properly play if you don't apply yourself."

I say, "When Jack's apartment is empty and his shoes are sold, I'll practice more."

"There's always an excuse to be found," he says. "But the bright spot in our conversation is that you told me the truth and we laid the groundwork for building trust. I can work with that. Come in for another lesson when you've practiced an hour a day for two weeks. Then I'll tell you something about Jack."

"But this is urgent," I say. "We're trying to find him. I need your help."

"From what I hear, the authorities are after him. Leave it to them."

I hang up and shake my head. "That was a weird conversation."

Kelly says, "Go practice. Get out the violin and play. Dad would want that."

I say, "I wouldn't call it playing, but here I go."

Moving into my bedroom, I close the door and open the blue practice book. I pull out the violin, nestle it under my chin and pick up the bow, focusing on fingering and forgetting my worries. I'm eleven years old and taking music lessons, like I wanted. The violin makes me a time-traveler back to my wished for past.

41

## BUZZ

I sit at my desk in my bookstore office combing the internet for sneakers like the limited-edition gold leather shoes I have in my possession. Irena will thank me one day for doing this, and after we're married ten years, I might tell her what I did. My pulse thrums. My employees are doing inventory, which is a bear of a task while the bookstore is open with customers underfoot, and I should be out there helping them.

I wipe my brow and don't find any shoes for sale like the ones I have. Typing fast, I set up an auction to sell the gold leather sneakers and press a button to go live. I sit back in my creaking wooden chair, but something catches my eye. A pair of orange sneakers are being sold in an auction that Irena must have set up. Bids are coming in, and a wall clock ticks, marking the passing of each second. A loud knock on my office door makes me start. I told my staff I wasn't to be interrupted. "Who is it?"

"This is the FBI. We have questions for you."

## 42

### ABBY

I hurry down a dark path to my apartment and let myself in, locking the door behind me. I lean against the door, hands shaking, knees trembling, and rub my aching throat where the man choked me at Jack's apartment.

I pull an ice pack from the freezer and sit on the loveseat, applying cold to my aching neck. I bet I'll have a bad bruise after what that creep did. I kick off my shoes and put my feet up on the arm rest. Cold seeps into my skin and I shudder, recalling being choked and gasping for air. I'm glad Mr. Abernathy shot the thug in the leg. He deserved it. I hope they charge him with intent to murder or whatever they call it. He wanted to hurt Jack and busted up his stuff to prove a point, but I had no idea Jack was involved with dangerous people like that. What was the guy's name? Elgin Johnson is what he told the cops. I'll look him up online and see if I can find anything about him, but I suspect underworld thugs like him keep a low profile with no social media presence.

I eye the lump under the bedspread. I could give the stolen shoes back to Irena and face her wrath, or I could brush off the dirt and sell them using a business name my friends don't know about.

My phone rings, startling me, and the icepack drops on the floor. Irena is calling. It's as if she could read my mind and know I was thinking about her. I answer and say, "That was crazy at Jack's place, wasn't it? I hope the guy who choked me rots in jail."

She says, "It was, and I hope so too. Listen, the FBI was just here. They said Jack didn't show up where he was supposed to meet them, and they're looking for him. I think they're going to talk to Buzz next, but they might want to talk to you."

My hands turn sweaty. I put her on speaker, set down the phone, and wipe my hands on my jeans.

She says, "Are you still there? Did we get cut off?"

I whoosh out a breath. "Yeah, I'm here. Thanks for letting me know."

"They might come by tonight."

I screw up my face. "What did they look like?"

Irena says, "They're in their early thirties. The female agent is tough. The guy might be a bit more approachable. They're super intense, like nothing escapes them."

I swallow and glance around the studio apartment. I say, "I'd better go. Thanks for calling."

I shove the ice pack in the freezer and rush around, putting the stolen sneakers on a shelf in the closet. Then I hide my checking account registers under the silverware tray in a drawer in the kitchenette. My hands tremble, and I glance around. I'm as ready as I'll ever be for a visit by the Feds.

**43**

---

## JACK

Someone knocks and enters my hospital room. I wipe my eyes, take a shaky breath and tell myself to step off the roller coaster of emotions I'm riding. At least I'm alive, even though I don't know who I am.

Curtains open at the end of my bed, and a woman in her thirties with black hair pulled back in a clip says, "Hello, I'm Dr. Wang. We met earlier." She touches a stethoscope draped around her neck and gazes at me. I wipe my nose with the back of my hand.

My mouth is dry, and I clear my throat. I wonder what she's about to tell me. "What's wrong with me?"

"We evaluated your test results. You've a severe traumatic brain injury from a violent blow to the head." She pauses, perhaps to let me process it. "Do you recall how you hit your head?"

I clench my fists. "I have no idea what happened. I must have friends and family. Where are they?"

"We're not sure. It could be that you're not from the area. You might've gone hiking, gotten lost and wandered to where someone found you."

I squint and stare at the sink. "I don't feel like I liked to hike."

She tugs on the lapels of her white coat. "Let's discuss your case. We take severe traumatic brain injury very seriously. You have an acute epidural hematoma from a blood vessel bursting and leaking, forming a mass pressing on brain tissue. Trauma can cause an epidural hematoma, and it can be deadly. We need to go in and operate."

My heart hammers in my chest, and I say, "I don't want an operation."

She pats the bedside rail. "I can understand that, but you must realize it's a matter of life and death. Surgery should help prevent permanent brain damage. I'd like to bring in a group of residents and interns who are training. Would that be okay with you?"

I break out in a sweat. "I don't want people watching me. It makes me feel sick."

The doctor says, "I understand. By participating, future patients will benefit. Your case will help them provide better medical care to others."

I let out a sigh. "Fine, go ahead, but don't take long."

"We won't."

She goes out and returns with a group of people who

look like they're in high school or early college. They file in and stand around my bed staring. I'm in a zoo, and inquisitive tourists expect me to entertain them.

I say, "Please don't stare. I don't like that."

They study the floor.

The doctor says, "Let's get started. We have a man in his forties, we estimate."

I interrupt. "I'm twenty-five, at most."

Their eyes flit back and forth. She says, "We believe he has both retrograde and anterograde post-traumatic amnesia. Do you have any questions?"

A guy clears his throat. His chin is begging for the first whisker to come in. I'll play along for the sake of medical research, but the group clustered around me is closing in on me. He raises his hand. "Do you recall anything about what happened to you?"

I say, "I have no clue. All I know is I ended up here. But I believe I was either a basketball star or a sneaker designer."

The residents and interns give each other side glances. A young man covers his mouth, and I detect a slight smile underneath.

I say, "What's so funny?"

A young woman wearing black framed glasses says, "What makes you think you played basketball for a living?"

I shrug. "It's just a feeling because I know all about sneakers."

From the next bed comes a mimicking voice. "It's just a feeling. I'm famous, but no one recognizes me."

I snap my eyes shut, wanting to leap out of bed and strangle the man in the next bed.

The doctor tugs on her stethoscope. "What about alcohol consumption? How many drinks a day do you have?"

I clench my jaw. "I don't know."

She nods. "And what about aspirin? Do you take that or other blood-thinning medications?"

"I have no idea." I take a deep breath and shout, "I'm a helpless idiot who doesn't know who I am or if I like beer or vodka or if I stick to water."

My roommate says, "Cry me a river, will ya, sob sport?"

The doctor turns to the group. "Patients with traumatic brain injuries may exhibit sudden mood changes, severe emotional reactions, and outbursts. They might suffer from irritability, anxiety, and depression."

I say, "I'm irritable because I can't stand sharing a room with a toad."

The guy in the next bed says, "Right back at you buddy."

My throat is dry, and I say, "Can I have a glass of water?"

The doctor turns to a tall young woman with pink framed glasses. "Julie, how would you respond to that?"

Julie points to the whiteboard on the wall. "You're

NPO, so it's not allowed. We can give you ice chips, or a moist swab for your lips."

I groan. "I'll take ice chips. Here's why I suspect I'm a basketball player. I know a lot about sneakers, and I can guess the brand from the sound the soles make. I figure only a pro would know that, and I'm coordinated and strong."

The doctor says, "Any comments?"

Someone whispers, "Delusions of grandeur."

A young man with curly hair raises his hand. "A TBI can trigger narcissism."

I frown. "I'm not a narcissist. I'm just trying to solve the puzzle of who I am."

An aide hands me a white paper cup, which is a third-full of ice chips, and a plastic spoon. I suck on ice chips and swallow. The doctor says, "We're going to perform a craniotomy and hematoma evacuation. We'll take out a piece of your skull, remove the blood clot, and stop bleeding sites. We'll put the skull bone back in place when the swelling has gone down and secure it with screws."

My mouth drops open. "I can't go through with that. No way I'll let you saw out part of my skull."

The doctor looks me in the eyes. "If we don't operate, you could die or have permanent brain damage. We need to operate to save your life."

I bite my lip and say, "I don't want to die without knowing who I am."

The doctor says, "We'll be with you every step of the way. And after you come out of surgery, you'll have a private room."

My stomach clenches. The group stares at me, and I moan. "I feel sick."

A nurse in blue scrubs hands me a blue cylindrical barf bag. I grip it with a slick, sweaty hand and stare at the white blanket to block out the pairs of eyes boring into me.

The doctor says to the group, "What do we know about brain injuries and memory?"

I open my eyes a tiny bit and see Julie's hand shoot up right away, but the doctor calls on a short guy standing by the sink. "Derek?"

"Personalities can change, and patients can have false memories after a head injury. Triggers like loud noises or smells or crowds may remind them of when they were hurt and cause a negative reaction."

I clear my throat. "Is there a cure for what I have?"

The doctor says, "We'll reduce the swelling in your brain and some of your symptoms, like seeing people who aren't there, may ease."

I fling the cup with ice chips at the wall, and Derek ducks. "I saw a man murder a patient who was there."

The doctor says, "You need to be calm until we take you into surgery."

I press my lips together and stay silent.

She says, "A psychiatrist will be in to evaluate you. We'll let you rest."

"I have every reason to be upset. My memory is gone, and my head will be sliced open."

The doctor says, "We'll help you. That's what we do."

They file out of the room, and Julie looks back before leaving me to my forsaken plight. I whimper, "I don't want to be here. Help me. Come back."

The guy in the next bed says, "Get a grip and close your trap. Some of us are trying to rest."

Tears stream down my face, and sorrow washes over me. Even if I survive an operation on my skull, my future is blighted because I don't know who I am. Fatigue overcomes me, and my eyelids grow heavy. I escape into dreams of being held by a beautiful woman with a heart-shaped face.

## 44

## FRANKIE

Brick and I approach Bud Wiser's house, where the carport is empty. We ease our way through the front gate, and I knock at the door. A dog barks inside, but no one answers. The dog peers through a side window, panting.

"Good boy," Brick says.

I say, "I'd like to get a golden retriever, but I'm not home enough. This guy owns a bookstore. Let's see if he's there."

Dusk is falling when we park outside the bookstore. We climb out of the car and I say, "Growing up with a name like Bud Wiser would put a chip on your shoulder."

Brick says, "It'd make you tough, that's for sure. Let's see what he has to say and if Irena Fishbone was right about him being the last person to see Jack."

The smell of old books, coffee, and baked goods greets

us when we walk in the door. People sit at tables nursing cups of coffee hunched over laptops. In a kids' section, children sit looking at books. I don't have time for a relationship or to consider having a family, but I might change my mind one day. Kids are unpredictable, like criminals, and they frighten me with sudden emotional changes.

Brick stops at the counter and asks for Bud Wiser, the owner. A woman in her mid-twenties furrows her brow. "You mean Buzz, but he's not available. And you are?"

I step forward, ignoring a squalling child, and say, "FBI. Where's his office?"

She points to a closed door labelled Private Office. "He said not to disturb him."

I march over to the door, with Brick following, and knock. "FBI, we're here to ask you questions. Open up."

A chair scrapes inside, and I open the door as an image of a pair of sneakers fades on a computer screen. Why would a bookstore owner be looking at sneakers online? I shrug. Maybe owning a small business is high pressure, and this is a hobby of his.

I say, "Are you Bud Wiser?"

He's about forty, and his biceps look like he works out. "Yes, I am. What's this about?"

"I'm Special Agent McNalley, and this is Special Agent Brick. We have some questions about Jack Fishbone. You were the last person to see him, according to a witness."

His eyes open wide. "A witness? What did they see?"

I glance at Brick and nod to give him the go ahead. He says, "Why don't you tell us? Let's start from the beginning. What happened after Jack went overboard?"

Buzz swallows, his prominent Adam's apple bobbing up and down. "A group of us went out on Craig's boat to celebrate his promotion. Irena was on the bow with Jack, and a wave reared up out of nowhere and swept them both overboard. One minute they were there, the next they weren't."

My partner says, "And then what happened?"

Buzz leans against this desk, blocking my view of his computer monitor, and crosses his arms. "We saved Irena. Her daughter and the rest of us were frantic. But we couldn't find Jack."

I say, "Did you help him set up a scheme to escape? And make it look like an accident where he died but his body wasn't found?"

He nods. "That's the way it was supposed to work. But Jack had a flair for drama and liked being the center of attention, so he left clues for Irena to follow after he fell in, like a shirt nailed to a log with writing on the collar. I told him not to do it because it made it obvious he wanted to disappear. It would've been best if he left town and there was no sign of him after he fell in. We would've assumed he was dead and the body wasn't recovered."

Brick says, "What's your interest in all this? Why did you help him?"

Buzz cocks his head. "He's my best friend, that's why. I'd do anything for him."

I squint at him and say, "Do you believe he's dead?"

He shakes his head a little too fast for my liking, like people do when they're guilty. We'll keep this guy on our radar as a suspect in Jack Fishbone's disappearance. He says, "No, and I hope he's happy wherever he is."

Brick says, "Where did you last see him?"

Buzz says, "I picked him up under Jackson Bridge and took him to Martin Wharf by the old cannery. I dropped him off, waved goodbye, and wished him well. That was it." He rubs his right hand, locks eyes with me and covers his hand. "I didn't do anything. Honest."

Brick says, "Show us your hand."

"What?"

I say, "Hold out your hands. Let us see them."

He slowly puts his hands in front, palms up. His hands are as big as small plates. My stomach growls, but I ignore it and say, "Turn your hands over."

His hands tremble, and he turns them over, holding them out. Knuckles on his right hand are red and raw, and the skin is swollen. His face turns beet red.

Brick brings out his phone and snaps a picture. "Did you have a scuffle before you two said goodbye?"

The room is stuffy and warm. Sweat pricks my armpits. I say, "Yeah, how final was your goodbye? Did you take him to the wharf, knock him out, and push him in the water, leaving him to drown? Maybe that's why he didn't show up at our meeting place."

A bead of sweat breaks out on his upper lip, and he says, "I swear, I dropped him at the wharf and left him there. If something happened to him, I didn't have anything to do with it."

I say, "How'd you hurt your hand? It looks like you hit something hard."

He glances at his hand. "I was unloading boxes of books. Must've grazed my knuckles." He shakes it out.

I resist the urge to roll my eyes at his theatrical performance.

Brick says, "Looks more like you hit a brick wall or someone's head."

Buzz nods. "I did hit a brick wall. I was so frustrated my best friend wanted to leave town, that I punched a brick wall. Stupid, right?"

Brick and I exchange a quick look.

Buzz wipes his brow. We'll need to gather more evidence before bringing him in for questioning. All we have is hearsay from his former girlfriend, who may or may not have a reason for pointing a finger at Buzz.

Someone knocks on the door, cracking it open. "Sorry to interrupt, but we have questions about inventory."

Buzz says, "I'll be right there." He says to us, "Look into Abby Love as a suspect and question her. She's had a crush on Jack for years and might've whisked him away before he met you. Maybe he decided to run off and start a new life."

Brick says, "She's on our list."

I say, "We'll be in touch."

We walk out and climb in the car. I say, "You hungry? I am."

Brick nods. "Sure, let's get something to eat before we see this Abby Love."

## 45

# FRANKIE

Brick says, "I saw a place to eat on the way into town." He directs me to an older two-story house where lights are on inside. A tall tree looms over the building, with a sign out front for Gigi's Café. Laughter drifts out as I open the door. Bells jingles, marking our entrance, and people's heads turn. Silence greets us.

A woman in her twenties with a pierced nose and pink hair smiles and says, "Sit anywhere you like. I'll be right with you."

We slide into seats, and the hum of chatter in the room resumes. The place is packed, leaning toward a gray-haired crowd. The young woman comes over carrying a coffee pot. "I'm Karina, the owner. I'm experimenting with offering dinner service, but we're closing in an hour. Would you like coffee?"

"Yes, please." We push two white mugs on the table toward her. I could use a caffeine injection after running around. Jiggling my leg under the table with restless energy, I have the sense we're about to uncover a solid lead.

Brick opens a menu, looking it over. "Quiche and scones? That's all you offer?"

She smiles and a diamond in her nose sparkles. "That's right, for now anyway. Gigi refused to add to the menu." She blinks away tears and says, "She was my grandmother and she raised me, but she passed away recently and left me this place."

An older man gestures to her from another table, and she says, "Do you know what you'd like? Or do you need a few minutes?"

I nod to Brick who orders a slice of quiche and a scone with jam.

I slap the menu closed. "Same for me, thanks."

"Coming right up. Oh, and if you're interested in buying my artwork, those are my paintings on the wall, and my pottery is on the table over there."

She leaves to help another customer, and I pick up my cup, savoring the rich aroma of fresh brewed coffee. I swallow and set it down. "We're getting closer."

Brick nods. "We'll find him."

I scan the café for potential troublemakers out of habit, but no one sticks out. An older man at the cash register is wearing a white short-sleeved shirt and black framed glasses. He brings over two plates and sets them down before us. My mouth waters, smelling warm quiche with bacon and a scone.

Hunkered over our food, I gaze at other diners. A woman in a pink sweatshirt and sweatpants at the next table talks about books to a woman with curly hair. A gray-haired man with a trimmed beard sips coffee with three older men talking about boats and bottom paint. When the bearded man changes the topic and mentions Irena, I listen closely.

I tap on the table with a fingertip to get Brick's attention and tilt my head toward the table of four men. He nods, and we listen as the man says, "Irena's going through it."

The others nod. One says, "You can say that again."

The bearded boater says, "Makes you wonder what happened to Jack Fishbone. Where did he go? You don't just vanish into thin air."

A man taps the table with a gnarled knuckle. "Heard the FBI has him."

"He's in witness protection," says a man. "That's why we haven't seen him."

A fourth man runs a hand through his gray hair. "He was a great guy. Used to buy rounds of beer at the bar sometimes. Life of the party."

The woman in the pink sweat suit points at us and says, "Are you with the FBI? It's on your jackets. I bet you know what happened to Jack Fishbone."

The woman with her says, "Tell us what happened. Is that why you're in town?"

An older man says, "We've been wondering."

The bearded boater says, "Tell us what you know. We want to help."

I shovel food in my mouth and set down my fork. Brick pushes away his clean plate and swallows the last of his coffee. We stand up and to maintain a good reputation in the local community, I say, "We're not at liberty to discuss details about Jack Fishbone, but we are looking into his disappearance. Anyone with information about where he was last seen at the wharf out of town, please contact me. I'll leave a card at the cash register."

The woman in pink rises. "Can I have your autograph?" She shoves a menu at me, along with a pen, and I politely decline. I turn to Brick, 'Let's pay and get out of here."

We split the bill, and I leave my business card at the register with the older man in the short-sleeved shirt. He holds it with two hands, as if it's a treasure, and says, "I'm glad you're looking into it. Jack's disappearance has rocked our community. Any answers will be welcome."

I say, "We're Agents McNalley and Brick. And you are?"

"Frackus," he says, fiddling with his black framed glasses. "Bernard Frackus."

"Nice to meet you," Brick says. "You know where to

find us if you remember anything about Jack Fishbone's last movements."

Bernard taps his chin. "There was something I overheard. But it's just hearsay."

I say, "Go ahead."

He says, "I heard someone was in the marsh when Jack fell overboard and thought they saw him climb out of the water and pick up a backpack near Jackson Bridge."

We nod. "Could you tell us who this someone was?"

He leans across the counter. "I'm not sure. Right now, it's just a rumor, but I'll keep my ears open and call if I hear anything else."

Karina, the owner, bursts out of the kitchen waving her hands. "The dishwasher is leaking."

Mr. Frackus looks at us and says, "I hope you find him." He hurries into the back.

We step outside, and a gust of cool air blasts us. I pull my coat closed and climb in the car. Brick buckles his seat belt and chuckles. "Pretty funny back there."

I drive and say, "What do you mean?"

"Autographs? Seriously? You've got a fan club."

We laugh and pull up outside Abby Love's apartment.

I say, "I hope this Love person can tell us something we can use."

Brick nods. "Hope so too, or we're running around wasting time. So far, the tip line pulled in a lot of crank calls."

We trod along a dimly lit path to the apartment and knock on the door.

## 46

## ABBY

I'm watching an episode of Jeopardy when a knock on the door startles me. I pick up the remote, put the show on pause, and look out the door's peephole. "Who is it?"

A man says, "FBI. We'd like to talk to you."

"Show me your badges before I let you inside."

A woman whips out a badge, and he flashes his.

"Just a minute while I make myself presentable."

I stay where I am but stick my ear to the door to hear what they might say. He says, "Nice place, eh?"

She says, "What're you, Canadian, with the ehs?"

They chuckle, and I decide they must not be too bad. Opening the door, I gesture to the loveseat and two chairs. "Take a seat."

She says, "I'm Agent McNalley, and this is Agent Brick."

They sit in chairs, and I perch on the loveseat, knees trembling. I clear my throat. "What can I help you with?"

She says, "When did you last see Jack Fishbone?"

My throat closes tight with tears, and I draw a shaky breath. "It's been a while. I was out of town for work when he disappeared."

Agent Brick says, "Where did you go?"

I shrug. "I went to Tukwila for an ice cream convention."

He says, "And where do you work?"

"At an ice cream factory just out of town."

He says, "Sounds like a fun job."

I tilt my head. "It sometimes is, but the factory is noisy with machines going all the time. I fill in as a taste tester, that's the part I like best."

She says, "How would you characterize your relationship with Jack?"

My palms are moist. "What do you mean?"

Her eyes bore into mine. "Were you friends? Lovers? Both?"

My heart thuds. I'm stripped bare by the question reminding me of how Jack turned me down one night. They stare at me, so I open up and say, "We're friends, although I wouldn't have minded more. He wasn't into it, though. He made that clear." I cover my eyes, recalling my utter humiliation when Jack turned me down after drinks and burgers one night. My face heats.

He says, "We apologize if our questions make you

uncomfortable, but your answers will help with our investigation."

My eyes open wide. "What investigation? Didn't Jack go off with the FBI? That's what my friends told me."

McNalley shakes her head. "I'm sorry to tell you this, but Jack Fishbone is missing. He didn't show up at our designated spot."

I clap a hand to my mouth. "Where do you think he could be?"

She gives her partner a side glance. "We're not sure, and that's why we're checking leads. He might've run off to Costa Rica. What do you think of that?"

I tap a finger to my lips. "He talked about moving there. He wanted to live where he could wear shorts year-round. Of course, some people do that anyways around here. Like the woman who owned the garden store. But I don't think he'd up and leave."

She says, "Why not?"

"He loves his ex-wife, Irena, and his daughter Kelly. They're everything to him."

The agents exchange a look. He says, "If you were trying to find Jack, where would you look? You seem to know him pretty well, so maybe you can help us out."

I purse my lips and stare at the ceiling. "I'd ask questions about his supposed secret girlfriend. Someone must know something. Maybe he left with her."

McNalley says, "A secret girlfriend? Where did you hear this?"

"Kelly told me that Jack said she'd get to meet his new girlfriend, but he disappeared before that happened."

The female agent frowns. "He might've planted a lie to distract from the truth."

I shrug. "It feels like the missing piece to me. Find the girlfriend, and you might find him."

She says, "Are you sure you don't know who this girlfriend is? Do you have any ideas at all?"

I stand up. "I have no idea who she is. They were quite secretive, it seems."

They rise and hand me a card, telling me to contact them if I hear anything. When they leave, I close and lock the door. Alone at last, I flop down on my belly on the bed and cry my heart out, missing Jack.

A half hour later, I sniffle, wipe my eyes, and hurry to my laptop. I go online and check prices of collectible sneakers. A burning sensation in my throat reminds me that I shouldn't sell the stolen sneakers but give them to Irena. My mouth falls open when my search turns up a pair of limited-edition gold leather sneakers with red stars on the sides for sale in an online auction. Someone is selling the gold shoes I tried to steal from Irena's. Bids are coming in, and the offer price is climbing.

I grab my phone and call Irena. When she picks up, I say, "Are you selling the gold leather sneakers online? Because if you aren't, someone else is."

She yelps, and I move the phone away from my ear, putting her on speaker. She says, "We haven't listed them yet. We planned to sell them last, after clearing out the rest."

I say, "I think someone took the sneakers, but it wasn't me, I swear."

"We have them, but I'll double check. Hold on."

While I wait, I go to the foot of the bed and pull out the stolen sneakers, staring at them and wondering what I should do. Irena comes back on the line. "The shoes are here, but they don't have the number stamp under the tongue, which is weird."

I say, "Someone could've switched the real ones with a knock off pair. I didn't touch them after I left your place."

She says in a stern voice, "But did you take any of Jack's sneakers?"

My stomach sours. I say, "Diarrhea is coming on. I've got to go."

"Don't hang up on me," she says. "Answer the question, tell me the truth."

I hang up and race to the bathroom, retching. Only the scum of the earth would betray her best friend like that. I need to be a better person. I lean against the wall, panting, resting a hand on my churning gut.

47
———

# IRENA

I hang up the phone and stare at the pair of gold leather sneakers in white tissue paper in a box. My chest is tight. Without the limited-edition shoes, I'm not sure I'll be able to pay off Jack's debts, including the child support he owes me.

I check under the tongue for a second time but don't see a number. The limited-edition pair delivered to my home from Jack showed the number one under the tongue, and this pair is missing the mark. The leather is a different shade of gold than the real pair.

Resting my head in my hands, I break down weeping. The real gold shoes were a key part of my plan to quell the disaster Jack left behind. I want to walk away from the hassle of selling his shoes, but I can't. If I get Jack out of debt, I hope he'll come home to see Kelly after testifying in Craig's trial. I groan, wishing Jack never got caught up in the scam Craig ran on the elderly.

Kelly comes in the room. "What's wrong?"

I point at the shoe box. "Someone stole the gold sneakers. These are knock-offs."

She sits by me and examines the shoes. "Who did this?"

"I doubt it was Abby. She let me know they're being auctioned, and she swears she didn't do it. She means well, deep down."

"She does."

I say, "No one's perfect, as we know. Who has a key to the house? Kathy next door does, but she wouldn't come in and take them."

We're quiet for a beat and turn to each other, saying at the same time, "Buzz."

I put a hand to my chest. "But I doubt he'd steal something from us. Buzz knows I need to sell the shoes to pay off your dad's debts, so he can come back."

Kelly bites her lower lip. "What're we going to do?"

"I'll go to the bookstore and ask him about it. I'll know if he's hiding something."

Kelly says, "And let's see who's selling the shoes online, like Abby said."

Hunched over my laptop, we find the auction. Bids are coming in, and the price is going up. I say, "I can't see who is selling the shoes, can you?"

She takes the laptop, clicking on links. "No, it doesn't say."

I blow out a breath. "This is so frustrating. I wish your dad was here, and he wasn't in debt. I just want to sell the shoes and clean up his mess, so we can move on with our lives."

She wipes tears from her eyes. "I should've gotten a part-time job to help Dad with his money problems, instead of taking dancing lessons. Then he wouldn't have had to leave us."

I give her a hug. "Hon, this is not your fault. You didn't do anything wrong. Drop that idea like an anchor in the Salish Sea."

She rolls her eyes. "Here we go with the maritime references again."

I reach out to take the laptop, but she says, "Wait, when does the auction end?" She scrolls down on the screen. "We have twenty-four hours."

I stretch my arms. "I'd better go interrogate Buzz about the gold shoes."

Kelly says, "Don't approach it like fixing a boat and barge in, but like a dance, finessing your way in. Be subtle."

I stand and grin. "I'm not sure that's possible, but I'll do my best." I pull on my jacket and grab my purse. "I'm not sure when I'll be back."

With a gleam in her eyes, she gets up. "I'm going with you."

I shake my head. "I'll be in and out in no time."

"I'm not changing my mind. I've already lost one parent. I'll go to make sure nothing happens to you."

I nod, realizing she could help ferret out information. "Fine, let's go."

The car is chilly as I drive, and I turn on the heat. "I'm nervous about confronting Buzz, but this can't wait."

Kelly says, "Don't blow up at him, like you did with Dad. Keep it cool."

I park across the street from the bookstore, which is a beacon of light in the growing darkness. "I wasn't that bad with your dad, was I?"

Her eyebrows arch. "Let's just say you wouldn't be proud of yourself if you saw a replay."

I cringe and vow to set a better example in the future. Opening the door to the bookstore, I gesture for Kelly to go first. Customers prowl the aisles. Like the full shelves in his store, Buzz's house is packed with books. Out of our friends, Buzz hoards books, Jack collects sneakers, Abby loves clothes, Craig craves wealth, and I live for the adrenaline rush of saving boats from sinking. Craig often said, "The more money the better. One day, I'll be a billionaire. You can count on it." And look where that got him. He ended up in jail.

Buzz stands at the counter, and I stride over to him, tapping on the counter to get his attention. He looks up and sets down his pencil. He says in a soft voice, "What're you doing here?"

Kelly stands next to me, and I uncross my arms, letting them hang by my sides. Taking a deep breath, I say, "We'd like to talk to you in private and ask you a few questions."

His jaw tenses. "This isn't a good time. I wished you called ahead. We're doing inventory while the store is open, and you know that's a nightmare."

I nod. "I get it. But this'll just a take a minute or two."

He gazes at Kelly and says, "I'll do this for Kelly's sake, but let's be quick."

We move toward his office, and he says to me, "I've missed you."

I say, "I miss you too. But I didn't like how you lied to me."

He opens the door, and we file into his cozy office, where a half-empty cup of coffee sits. I've become a glass half empty kind of person and overwhelmed by what I must do now that Jack is gone. A computer sits on a desk with a screen saver on. I'd love to see if Buzz is selling the gold sneakers, but there's no chance of that while he's in the room, and I don't know his passwords.

He leans on the desk and faces us, arms folded. "You have five minutes, then I need to get back to work. What's up?"

Kelly says, "Someone took my dad's gold sneakers with the red stars, and they're selling them online. Our neighbor saw you go in our place and come out carrying something. Tell us the truth. Did you take my dad's shoes?"

We stand side by side staring at him. A bead of sweat forms on his brow. His cheeks turn red. We wait. Silence grows in the still, small room.

He coughs and covers his mouth. I clamp my mouth shut and keep quiet, not wanting to jinx the moment. Kelly says, "Do you have the gold sneakers with the number one under the tongue?"

He whooshes out a breath and holds up his hands. "Fine, fine. I'll tell you because I'm not a good liar, and you'd see right through me. I didn't take the shoes, but I have an idea of who did."

I lean in. "Who was it?"

He stares at the worn wooden floor boards. "I shouldn't say."

"Come on," I say, "tell us."

"I bet Abby did. She could've climbed through a window. She knew about the sneakers, and she has a habit of stealing things."

Kelly says, "But she takes small things, like jewelry and hair brushes, not something this big or valuable."

Buzz says, "I'd look into her, if I were you. It's a small step from a hair clip to a pair of limited-edition sneakers." He glances at a wall clock, reminding me time is ticking, and every minute matters until the auction for the gold sneakers ends. We have less than a day to find the stolen shoes. He says, "I've got to get back out there and help."

I rub the back of my neck and frown. "One quick question first. Did you wait for someone to pick Jack up when you dropped him off at the wharf?"

He shakes his head. "He told me to leave."

"Did he hit his head before you left?"

His jaw drops open. "Why are you asking that?"

Kelly says, "It's one of her hunches. She thinks he fell and cracked his skull."

He frowns. "If you'll excuse me, I have to get back to work, which is something I don't think Jack ever said in his life. I've got a bookstore to run."

As we walk out, I stare at his broad back, not sure if he hurt Jack and took the shoes. He could be my best friend, or deceiving me, and I have no clue what is true.

He says in a gruff voice before stepping to the sales counter, "I miss you both."

I take him in, the boy I've known since grade school, and feel a tug in my chest. I glance at my daughter, whose lower lip trembles, and say, "We miss you too."

I step out into cool evening air and glance back inside. Illuminated by overhead lights, Buzz is holding an animated conversation with a smiling female customer in her thirties. A pang of jealousy stabs me, and I wipe a tear from my eyes.

I clear my throat and say to Kelly, "Let's see if Abby has the sneakers."

## 48

## KELLY

My mom hunches over the wheel with her jaw clenched while she drives to Abby's apartment. I pull out my phone and say, "I'll let Abby know we're coming over."

She frowns. "Please don't. She might hide the shoes, and we'll never find them."

She parks near Abby's place, and we climb out of the car. She slams the car door and says, "It's best if we surprise her."

We walk along a sidewalk and turn on a paved path. I say, "You don't sound like you're talking about a friend. You're suspicious of everyone since Dad disappeared."

She shrugs. "Our group changed when your dad went missing. I suspect Buzz is hiding secrets. Abby is stealing more often because she's stressed. I'm freaking out and dealing with it by charging around getting things done.

The only one I trust is you." She touches my arm, and we stop at Abby's gate. "You're the same perfect person you've always been."

I wince and look down. She doesn't realize the depth of my sadness. I put up a fake front and act calm, but inside I'm a cold dark cave. My sunlight left with my dad. He's the fun parent, but my mom would hate it if she knew I thought that.

She says, "We'll wait until someone comes through the gate, and let's be quiet, so she won't hear us coming. I've got to get the gold shoes back."

My eyes narrow. Who cares about the shoes? I don't. I just want my dad back. But because my mom wants the shoes, I'll help her.

A woman with two kids comes up to the gate and opens it. My mom says, "We're here to see Abby Love. Would you let us in?"

The woman looks at us, and her kids go ahead. "What's your name?"

"Irena Fishbone and this is my daughter Kelly. We're long-time friends with Abby. I've known her since high school."

"Okay," the woman says, holding the gate open for us. "I hope I don't get in trouble for this."

I say, "Thanks, we want to surprise her."

"Too bad about Abby's new sneakers," the woman says, walking behind us on a dimly lit path.

My mom turns and stares. "What did you say?"

The woman shrugs. "She had two pairs of new sneakers and left them under some bushes. My kids put them on, but we had a lesson about not taking other people's stuff."

My mom says, "We'll make sure to see her new shoes."

The woman says, "The odd thing is they weren't her size." She says goodbye and goes in her apartment. We stop at Abby's door. My mom says in a low voice, "Let me do the talking."

I nod and wish everything would go back to the way it was before we went out on Craig's boat. I was happy, before disaster struck. Now I know how it feels to walk around with a hole in my heart.

I take a deep breath. Because my mom needs me, I say, "I'll be your back up."

**49**

---

**IRENA**

I rap on Abby's door. I'm a hot wind blowing from the south, ready to rain down on my friend. It could end our friendship if she stole some of Jack's shoes.

Abby opens the door a crack. "It's not a good time. Let's get together tomorrow."

I crane my neck to see if someone's inside, and if that someone is my ex-husband. For all I know, she could be hiding him. She's always had a thing for Jack, although I suspect it wasn't reciprocated. But what do I know? My friends have secrets and private lives I never suspected.

Someone sits on the loveseat with their back to the door, so she does have company. I spot two shoe boxes at the end of the bed partly hidden by a blanket, and I stride into her apartment.

Kelly says, "Sorry, Abs. She's in a bad mood."

Abby says, "Aren't we all? Nothing's right without your dad around."

I whip the blanket off the shoe boxes and turn to Abby with my hands on my hips. "You stole these from Jack's. How could you do that?"

The person on the loveseat stands and steps between us. A middle-aged woman wearing a dog collar sticks her hand out to shake. "Hello, I'm Gladys Knight, and I don't like how you're speaking to her."

I shake her warm hand and try to extricate myself from an embarrassing situation by saying, "Like Gladys Knight and the Pips?"

The minister chuckles. "I get that all the time."

Abby's lower lip trembles, and a tear trickles down her cheek.

The minister says, "Abby knows she has a problem, and we were just discussing it. You shaming her won't help her recovery, and in fact, it might make it worse. Most of us thrive on praise instead of the stick, don't you think?"

I gulp and nod. "Yes, and this is my daughter, Kelly."

The minister smiles. "Nice to meet you. I'm with Family Counselling Services, if you'd like to call and set up an appointment. From what I hear, it's been a stressful time for all of you, including dear Abby."

Abby catches my eye, because we always laugh when someone calls her dear Abby. It's a childish joke we've shared since our teens. I glance at my daughter. When I was her age, I was itching to get into trouble. I wonder if

Kelly needs to see a counsellor like this one. I would have refused to when I was her age.

Gladys Knight pats my elbow. "You might want to see me sometime. Abby mentioned you moved to Millersville when your father went to prison?"

I break into a coughing fit, feeling exposed, but it's no secret. My father had a mean streak, and we were glad to move to the other side of the mountains.

She hands Kelly her card and gives one to me. "I must be off, but remember to be kind to each other during this difficult time. Goodbye." She turns to Abby and says, "Remember, count to ten when the urge strikes you and do something else. Walk away from temptation." She sweeps out the door, gently closing it behind her.

Abby turns to me. "How could you accuse me with someone here? A good friend doesn't barge in like you did. What's the matter with you?"

"A good friend doesn't steal from her friends." But Gladys Knight's words echo in my mind. I say, "I'm sorry. You're right, I was rude. But your neighbor told us you had two pairs of new sneakers. Did you take them from Jack's place?"

She stares at the tan carpet. "I did, and I was so ashamed that I called my counsellor. She came right over."

I tilt my head. "Where are the gold sneakers? I don't see them."

Her eyes grow wide. "The last time I saw them was at your house."

I rub my lips, mulling it over. She looks like she's telling the truth. Maybe Buzz took them and lied to put me off the scent. But if it wasn't Buzz, who has them?

Abby opens her arms, gesturing to the studio apartment. "Go ahead, take a look and search my car while you're at it. I don't have the gold sneakers."

## 50

## JACK

I shift on the thin hospital mattress, trying to get comfortable. My backside is sore from sitting. Someone knocks on the door and parts the curtain at the end of my bed. A tall Black man in his forties is wearing tortoise shell framed glasses, a white lab coat, and blue scrubs. "I'm Dr. Rhodes, a neurosurgeon. How are you feeling?"

I wince. "My head really hurts."

"You'll have surgery tomorrow morning. Do you feel faint?"

I say, "I'm dizzy and a bit woozy."

"Are you experiencing any confusion?"

"I don't know my name or how I got hurt. Nothing's coming back."

"Not even a vague recollection?"

A tear slides down my cheek. A jab of cold fear stabs

me, and I swallow. I've got to toughen up and get through this. "I have a feeling someone was there, but that's all."

"Any numbness or tingling in the arms or legs?"

"No."

"Can you move them?"

I wiggle my hands and fingers and lift my legs.

"I'll check your eyes." He pulls out a penlight, shines it in my eyes, and slides it into his pocket. "Can you walk? Take a few steps?"

"I don't know."

He raises the head of the bed, and when I swing my legs over the edge of the bed, a dizzy spell slams into me. The room whirls around. I whimper and say, "The room's spinning. I feel sick." He hands me a barf bag, and I hold it, taking slow breaths.

He says, "You'll feel better after surgery, when the swelling goes down."

I close my eyes. "I don't want to have surgery."

"We need to stop the bleeding and relieve the pressure on your brain."

"What if I do nothing?"

"Your risk of mortality is between five and fifty percent if you don't have surgery."

The room falls quiet, except for the beeping of monitors. Warm air blows from a heating vent on the wall beside me. A toilet flushes in the next room.

My roommate says, "Don't be a coward. Get the operation."

The doctor says, "Your scans indicate surgical intervention is required."

I break out in a sweat. "I don't want people staring at me while I'm knocked out on the operating table."

The doctor says, "We'll be focused on the back of your head, not your face. We'll cut out a portion of your skull to relieve pressure and drain blood from the brain."

My pulse races, and a monitor beeps with a high-pitched warning. The doctor pushes a button, and the beeping stops. He says, "Surgery will give you the best chance of living a normal life."

"What are the risks of having the operation?"

"You could have a stroke, bleeding, and brain injury. The chances of those happening to you are very small. I've performed thousands of these procedures, and the benefits of surgery outweigh the risks."

I sink into the pillow, and my skull throbs. I say, "Will the operation make my memory come back?"

The doctor adjusts his glasses and says, "It's possible, but severe head injuries, such as you had, may cause permanent amnesia. I'll send someone in with forms for you to sign giving permission to perform surgery. If your condition worsens, we may need to take you into surgery earlier."

When he leaves, I close my eyes and frown. They're about to cut into my skull, and I may die. A vague memory tickles at the back of my mind, and I have a feeling my heart was broken by a woman I loved. I can't put a finger on more than that, but it feels like a fresh wound. Tears run down my cheeks.

A man says, "Housekeeping."

The curtains are open at the foot of my bed, leaving a two-foot gap. A man mops the floor and nods to me. He has tattoos on his shaved head and arms. He gives me a quick smile and moves on his way. His sneakers are bright orange, and I wonder what they'd look like if they were covered with diamonds.

## 51

## KELLY

My mother says to me, "Help me search her place for the gold sneakers." I blow out a breath and gaze at my mom's best friend. Pawing through Abby's stuff seems wrong and will show we don't trust her. But I don't want my mom to be mad at me. She's more uptight than I've ever seen her. I say, "Fine," and open a closet, checking the shelves and looking on the floor. I say, "I'm sorry we're invading your space, Abs."

Abby crosses her arms and taps a toe. Her eyes fill with tears. I glance under the bed, inhale dust, and sneeze three times, just like my dad does. I give up and flop on the love seat, fiddling with a key in my pocket. I want to find out where the safe deposit box key goes that I found in my dad's bedroom. I heave out a sigh at how my dad deserted me and wipe tears from my eyes. Abby sits by me and wraps an arm around my shoulders, pulling me close.

She says, "I know it hurts a lot, but someday it'll hurt a little less. And in the meantime, I'm here for you."

I sniffle and say, "Thanks."

She hands me a tissue, and I blow my nose, leaning into her. I'm safe and warm with Abby, my second mother. Life is better when she's around. I let my eyes close for a moment, but my mom says, "Let's talk about these."

Abby and I hop up and hurry over to my mom, who is standing at the foot of the bed. I hope she didn't find the gold sneakers, because I want Abby in my life. My dad left, and if Mom cuts Abby out as a friend, I'll have two less people who love me in my life.

My mom points to the shoe boxes holding two pair of my dad's special sneakers. They're not the gold ones, but still, it's wrong. I cringe at what's coming and cross my arms.

My mom says, "These were Jack's, weren't they?"

Abby nods and swallows.

"What did you plan to do with them?"

Abby's hands flutter, like birds flying. "I wasn't sure. I was thinking about giving them back, but I felt so guilty about swiping them."

"I hope so."

Abby's face flushes. "When the kids next door wore them, I felt even worse."

I lean against the wall.

My mom says, "I love you, Abs, but this is a big problem. Is it getting worse?"

Abby nods. "Yeah, that's why I called Gladys Knight. I'm trying to change, but it's a deep-seated habit. Jack's going missing hit me hard and reminded me of my dad's death. I'm sorry. I know what I did was wrong. You're my best friend, and I hope you'll understand and have some compassion."

My heart thumps. My mom takes a deep breath, pointing a finger at Abby, but I jump in before she can utter words she'll regret. Stepping away from the wall, I say, "My mom always says it takes a big person to forgive someone if they hurt you. What I think she was about to say is, we love you and we support you getting help. Right, Mom?"

My mom raises her eyebrows and says, "That's right."

I say, "We'll take the shoes with us and sell them."

My mom says, "Did you need money? Is that why you took them?"

Abby bursts into tears. "I thought Jack moved to Costa Rica, like he talked about. I was going to track him down and follow him. I really miss him. I love him."

My mom shoots me a glance. I didn't know Abby loved my father. I sit beside her and pat her back. "We all love him."

She moans. "No, I mean, I really love him, not just as a friend. But he only had eyes for your mother." She weeps some more, and I hand her a bunch of tissues pulled from a box by the bedside.

Mom says, "Maybe you could've lived with him better than I did and put up with his sneaker obsession."

Abby blows her nose and says, "I could've, I really could've. But he didn't give me a chance. I waited all those years, but he wasn't interested."

My mom says, "I might as well tell you now. After the trial is over, I plan to ask Jack to move in with us. It'll be good for Kelly to have her dad around."

I stare at my mother. She can't stand it when he gets fired from jobs, or when he buys expensive sneakers. They'd argue about money all the time. I see a glint in her eyes. She's competing with Abby over Dad. But they'll have the same problems. Dad spends too much. It's who he is. He doesn't mind owing people money, but my mom won't let a bill go unpaid.

I say, "But what about Buzz? Aren't you going to have him move back in with us?"

Mom says, "Probably not. I'm upset he lied to me."

"But he was protecting Dad by keeping a promise not to say where Dad was."

Mom shoves her hands in her back pockets. "I hear you, but deep down something feels off, and I'm not sure what it is. The trip on Craig's boat sure changed our lives."

Abby says, "It did, and I wasn't even here. How are we going to find Jack if the FBI doesn't know where he is?"

I say, "I was going to post on socials asking where and

when he was last seen. But then I realized the people he owes money to would see it, and they could find him and hurt him."

Abby and Mom say at the same time, "And we don't want that to happen."

Abby says, "Jinx."

Mom smiles and picks up two sneaker boxes, handing me one. She says to Abby, "You won't get a trip to Costa Rica out of these, but they're going to a good cause. Jack can start a new life without being in debt. He'll break his bad habits."

I roll my eyes. "I don't think it works if you expect someone to change, especially at his age. He's old."

My mom turns to Abby and puts the shoe box on a chair. "Did you hear that? We're old."

Abby says, "I don't feel like it."

They dance around, hooting and hollering. Mom shakes her hips and says, "Is this what old looks like?"

Abby says, "No way. Watch this move."

I release a sigh, relieved the leak in the boat of our lives, as my mom would say, is fixed, at least for now. Then I set the shoes down and join in, dancing.

## ABBY

I say goodbye to Irena and Kelly, hugging them as they leave, and lock my door. Looking around my cozy apartment, my eyes fall on my laptop. I want to be the first to find Jack and look into his eyes, so I didn't tell Irena and Kelly that I posted a photo of Jack on social media a few hours ago and wrote, "Have you seen this man? If so, please DM me the date, time and location. Thanks in advance."

I log onto Meadow Book and see someone sent me a message. Squirming in my seat, my heart races as I read: "Go to the hospital in Mt. Vernon. You'll be surprised what you'll find." I message the person back, typing fast with flying fingers. "What do you mean check the hospital? Which room?"

I wait and pace the floor, making a cup of tea to fill the time. It gives off a pleasant aroma of peppermint, but I can't drink it. My hands are trembling, and I'm too nervous to hold a mug of hot tea without spilling it.

After ten minutes, I can't wait any longer. I shrug on my white fake fur coat with a hood, slip my phone into my pocket, grab my car keys and purse and slip out the door. But a warning of caution niggles at the back of my brain, and I go back inside, checking the cook top.

A burner glows red. I turn it off and blow out a breath. I've been secretly saving money for the last fifteen years and paying to repair fire damage isn't how I want to spend it. And I don't want my neighbors to be hurt.

Pulling up my hood, I hurry through the rain to my car and drive to the hospital. Tires swish on wet pavement, and traffic is light. By this time of day, commuters are home watching TV or hunched over tablets. Rain drops pepper the windshield. Wiper blades squeal. Gripping the steering wheel tight, my mind fills with fears about what I might find. Jack might have been in a horrible car accident. Please, no, anything but that.

My jaw clenches tight. The best scenario will be if I find Jack and welcome him into my home. We'll chat about our day over warm lasagna from Costco, smiling with love in our eyes. We'll move into a bigger place, and Kelly will be welcome anytime, with a room of her own. She'll be treated like a princess at our home.

I locate the hospital parking lot and park, shaking my head at my starry-eyed dream. The fact is, it'll never happen. Get real, I tell myself. Give up hope. Jack's ship sailed long ago for Irena, and you never left the dock.

My phone dings with a message, and I pull it out with shaking hands. The mysterious person messaged me back. "Check Room 366. I can't say more, or I'll lose my job."

I take a deep breath and climb out of my car. If Jack isn't there, I'll leave. He needs me, I'm sure of it, but the hard truth is he might not want to see me. I swallow a lump in my throat and stride ahead.

Inside, I find the elevators and stab at button with an arrow pointing up. I'll say I'm the wife of a patient if a nurse stops me. With a loud ding, the elevator doors open, and I step inside, pressing the button for the third floor. My pulse whooshes in my ears, and I cross my fingers on the ride up, hoping but fearing what I might find.

## 53

## JACK

The urge to urinate grows stronger, but I don't see a urinal, so I push the call button. I'm a trained monkey, doing what they tell me while trapped in bed. I signed permission forms as John Doe acknowledging I was aware of the risks of having a stroke on the operating table. Monitors beep and bleep at different rates, aggravating my headache. After my operation, I'll run from this noisy room.

A nurse comes in. "Yes?"

"My bladder's bursting. Can you bring me the thing, whatever you call it?"

She looks around and hands me a plastic jug with a handle. "Here's the urinal. I'll give you privacy and be back in a few minutes."

"Thanks."

I take care of business, and the nurse comes back,

parting the curtain at the end of my bed. She walks in and takes the urinal, which is a third full. "That's a good color. Excellent."

I say, "What'd you mean?" While I'm in the hospital, I might as well learn something and keep my mind from worrying about what comes next.

She says, "If it was tinged with red, that'd indicate a problem with the kidneys, bladder, or both. But you're doing fine in that department."

"When will they let me leave? Right after the operation?"

"They'll keep you under observation here until they're sure you're okay."

I groan. "I want to go home, wherever that is."

My roommate says, "I hear you, buddy. Me too."

She nods to me and leaves. Someone knocks on the door and steps inside with light footsteps. The staff's steps don't sound like this. I'd like to see who it is, but the curtain is closed around my bed except for a two-foot gap at the end of my bed that lets me see the sink.

My roommate says in a gruff voice, "What're you doing here? You hit me with a hammer, and that guy shot me in the leg. That wouldn't have happened except for you. Go on, get out of here and stop gloating. It's your fault I'm stuck in this bed."

My eyebrows shoot up. Who is he talking to? Has he lost it, and he's talking to himself?

A woman says, "You're the biggest jerk I've ever met,

choking innocent people. I'm lucky I lived. I hope they lock you up forever."

I furrow my brow. Her sweet voice rings a bell, but I'm not sure why. My hands clench. Not remembering things makes me want to bash a hole in the wall, except I'm too dizzy to stand on my own.

She steps to the sink and turns on the faucet, washing her hands with her back to me. She says, "If I see you in Millersville again, I'll call the police."

He says, "Oh, that scares me. I shaking."

She glances my way, and my heart skips a beat. There before me is the woman with the heart-shaped face. She's the one I love. I remember that much.

My blood pressure alarm blares with a loud beeping. I cover my ears, and a nurse rushes in, saying to the visitor, "You're upsetting him. You have to leave."

The most beautiful woman in the world ignores her and says to me, "Is that you?"

I don't reply, because I don't know who I am. She has asked a huge question.

The nurse says, "Leave, or I'll call security."

Her mouth hangs open. She locks eyes with me and says, "Where've you been? What happened to your hair?"

I open my mouth to answer, but the nurse ushers her out. I hear raised voices in the hall, and they fade. I whisper, "I love you. You found me. I think you're my wife."

My roommate chuckles. "Too bad she had to go. I was going to throw choice words at her for ruining my life."

I say, "What's her name?"

"I have no idea, but she's trouble on wheels. I was doing my job, and she clubbed me with a hammer. You couldn't handle a woman that hot. She's a tiger, and you're a soft teddy bear."

I smack a fist into my hand, and monitors erupt with shrieking frenzied beeping.

The nurse comes in and eyes the monitors before pushing buttons to quiet the room. She says, "Your pulse is elevated, and your blood pressure is high. I'll speak to the doctor, but they may have to take you into surgery early." She steps away.

With a knock on the door, a woman says, "Dinner time."

The wheels of a cart roll, and the smell of hot food makes my mouth water. My stomach growls.

My roommate says, "What is it?"

"Meat loaf, a corn muffin and green beans, with apple compote."

"Thanks," he says.

Dr. Rhodes, the neurosurgeon, appears at my bedside. He's frowning and wearing a white lab coat over blue scrubs. "We're taking you into surgery. We can't wait until tomorrow."

"My wife was here, but a nurse made her leave. I want her here when I wake up."

He nods. "I'll look into that."

He walks away, and my head throbs with pain. I don't

bother to check and see what kind of shoes he's wearing because that isn't important in this moment. What matters is I may die on the operating table. A sense of dread fills me, and my stomach churns with acid. If only the angel who I just saw was by my side.

The guy in the next bed says, "No way that's your wife. She's gorgeous and feisty."

I close my eyes, drifting away. My wife was here. She'll tell me who I am.

In the hall, a nurse says in a loud voice, "She didn't leave her contact information. She's gone."

I flick my eyes open and say to my roommate, "What was her name?"

"No idea. She fought me with a mop in her hand. She's one tough cookie."

Two people in blue scrubs appear at the foot of my bed. A young woman with long dark hair pulled back in a ponytail says, "We're taking you to surgery."

Freckles dot the face of a short middle-aged man with her. He smiles and says, "You're going for a ride."

She says, "We'll wheel you in bed." She touches the curtain, and I bury my face in a pillow, turning away from my roommate. I don't want to be watched by him or anyone. The bed moves, and a wave of dizziness slams into me.

I say, "I'm dizzy. I don't feel good."

The man says, "This won't take long, so hang in there."

He places a cylindrical barf bag in my hands. "In case you need it."

The bed rolls down the hall and the wheels of fate turn, carrying me to my future. My hands are clammy. They're going to cut into my skull. Will I survive the operation? I want the woman with the heart-shaped face to come back and hold my hand, telling me who I am. I swallow tears of self-pity and squeeze my eyes shut.

The bed stops moving. I peek out from my cocoon of terror, and two doors swing open. They wheel me into a stark, cold room, and I'm trembling with fear. People dressed in surgical gowns move around the room, focused on tasks. Bright overhead lights cast a ghoulish glow.

I let out a sigh and surrender to what will happen. I may never know the truth about my past. But I have a choice going forward to be the best person I can be. I won't be a jerk. I'll be a kind person who helps others, like the people working at this hospital.

A woman in a surgical gown and mask examines the IV in my right arm. "I'm going to give you something to relax you. Count backwards from one hundred for me."

I say, "A hundred, ninety-nine, ninety-eight, ninety-seven." I yawn. "Ninety-five."

## 54

## ABBY

I glide down the hall pretending I'm a family member visiting someone in the hospital. The staff are helping patients in rooms or typing at computers on tall wheeled carts lining the wall. I swallow hard when I come to Room 366 and glance around to be sure no one is watching me. All eyes are focused elsewhere.

I knock on the open door and slip inside. A plaid curtain is around the bed against the far wall. But my jaw drops when I see the creep who choked me in the bed nearest the door. I touch my aching neck and glare. His heavily bandaged leg marks the spot where Mr. Abernathy shot him. He deserves to feel pain after breaking in and hurting me. If Mr. Abernathy hadn't come in, I might have died.

The man jabs a finger at me. "What're you doing here?"

I cross my arms and stare. "I hope they lock you up to rot in a cold, dark cell."

He says, "You come in acting tough, but try being me for a day. Someone's got to do the dirty work."

I glare at him and put my hands on my hips. A splitting headache throbs behind my eyes. "You broke into Jack's apartment, wrecked his things, and choked me. You're the lowest of the low. It makes me want to hit your leg, so you'll feel the pain you give to others."

He leers. "I'm a hired man, and I've got bills to pay. This is all I know how to do. If you hurt me, you'll be as bad as I am. There's not much difference between imagining the deed and actually acting it out."

My hands are slick with sweat. My pulse races. I want to see if Jack is in the next bed, but I don't have much time before a nurse comes in and kicks me out. I march over to the sink and wash my hands. "There's a huge difference between thinking and acting. You strangled me. I was lucky I didn't die."

I turn off the water and dry my hands on a paper towel, tossing it in the trash. I spin around and peer in a gap between the curtains around the other bed. A man about my age, in his early forties, is in bed. His brown hair is super short with ragged edges. He has a black eye with purple bruises. His brow is furrowed, and it looks like he's in pain.

I study the face, and it dawns on me that this man might be Jack. My throat tightens with tears, and I say, "Is that you? Where have you been?"

A nurse strides in. The man mumbles about the shape of my face and mentions his wife. I blink back tears. If this man is Jack, he must think he's still married to Irena.

The nurse points to the door. "Our patients need rest, and we can't have people bothering them. You must leave immediately or I'll call security."

She guides me to the door, and I say, "I think that might be my friend. What's wrong with him?"

She points to the exit sign. "That's private information. The exit is that way. I'll watch to make sure you leave and don't come back."

I take the elevator to the emergency room and sink into a chair. Bending over, I cover my face with my hands and silently weep for the love I never had. You can't force someone to love you, no matter what you do. Tears stream down my cheeks, and mucus runs from my nose. I take a deep breath and fumble around in my jeans pocket for a tissue. If only, if only, if only I didn't care for him, if only we'd met before he fell for Irena in high school.

I blot my eyes, blow my nose, and rise, throwing the tissue in the trash. Goodbye, past. I'm not sure, but I may have found Jack Fishbone. If I visited again, my heart would be broken for the thousandth time, and I couldn't take that.

I stride to my car and hop in. Turning the wheel, I'm

not sure where to go. Darkness is closing in, and nothing is going right. My stomach rumbles, and I pull over at a Mexican restaurant and go in carrying my laptop. I'll soothe my soul on this night with a chicken enchilada smothered in green sauce and by making a plan for my next steps.

I say to the hostess by the front door, "One for dinner please."

She gestures to a packed bar. "Would you like to sit in the bar or the restaurant?"

Laughter erupts from the bar. Families gather around tables in the restaurant. I hadn't planned for my solo excursion to be surrounded by loud, happy people. But that's the life I ended up with, so I might as well face it. "A table in the restaurant, please. In a quiet spot, if possible. I need to do some work."

She nods. "Right this way. Follow me." Her black braids sway against her yellow blouse. She gestures to a small table by the kitchen door, and I slide into a seat. Jack might be the washed-out helpless patient in a hospital bed. If it is, what happened to him? Maybe the trauma of falling overboard and fighting for his life changed him drastically.

I order tequila on the rocks and a chicken enchilada with rice and beans. While I wait to be served, I open my laptop and search for clues online, typing in symptoms I saw exhibited by the man in the bed. The many results give me a headache, and I snap the laptop shut, storing it in my bag. I'm better off thinking through this on my own.

The waitress sets down my drink and a glass of water. I sip bitter, smoky tequila and swallow, the liquid burning on the way down my throat. I nod to myself and come up with a plan. I must go back to the hospital, see if I can identify Jack, and talk with him. If it is Jack in that worn-out shell of a body, everyone, including Irena, will want a piece of him. When I'm sure it's Jack in that bed and we've had a few moments alone, I'll tell Irena and Kelly. They'll be relieved to hear that he's alive.

The waitress sets a steaming plate of food before me and says, "Don't touch the plate. It's very hot."

I thank her and drink ice water. What my brain heard was *touch the plate*, but I put my hands in my lap. Like the plate, the situation with the mysterious man in the bed is heated. I'll keep a lid on what I saw at the hospital until I can confirm my suspicions. If Jack is in Room 366, then I have found my missing man, and I want him all to myself before the hordes descend.

## 55

## IRENA

Kelly and I leave Abby's place with the two shoe boxes and put them in the car. Driving home, I say, "Abby seems to be working on changing and stopping her bad habits, and I can admire that. I think we all could use some self-improvement, like less running around and a little more laid-back couch potato lifestyle. What do you think?"

Kelly smiles. "You should focus on more lazing around. That's your goal."

We chuckle, and I say, "But first, I want to sell your dad's shoes, clean out his place, and pay off his debts. Then I'll relax and bake cookies all day."

She groans. "You say that, but something always comes up, and you go rescue someone."

I nod. "Guilty as charged." I don't add that this is how I pay the bills. If I didn't race to help boats in distress, we'd be out of money. But despite my reasons, Kelly is right, and I want to spend more time hanging out with her. In what will feel like the blink of an eye, she'll be out of the house living her own life, and I'll miss her with an ache in my heart.

Kelly says, "What're you thinking about?"

I glance at her with a smile. "You'll love this. I was thinking how after high school, if you move to Seattle, I'll be a becalmed sail boat. A kayaker without her paddle."

She groans. "Stop with the boating references. And you won't be lonely, you'll have your friends."

"I did, before all this happened. I'm adrift now, and my anchor line has been cut."

She laughs. "Stop, please."

"All right, I will."

She says, "I want to do something different for work, so I'm not always responding to calls. Maybe I'll work at the ice cream factory with Abby."

I drive down our block. I had hopes that Kelly would work for me and take over the company eventually. I press my lips together, staying silent, because pushing will only make her resist more.

Kelly says, "I want to call the hospitals and see if they have Dad."

"I think the FBI and the police already did that."

She opens her hands. "But it's worth a try."

I pull up and park in our driveway. "Let's do it

tomorrow after we sell his sneakers and clean out his apartment."

She says in a soft voice, "Okay."

We climb out of the car, grabbing the sneakers Abby stole. Her eyes are downcast, and her shoulders are slumped. I say, "Fine, if it means that much to you, we'll call first thing."

She meets my eyes and says, "Good."

We make our way to the front door, and I say, "I should call Violet. Maybe her security firm can find out who is selling your dad's gold sneakers. Whoever it was took them from under our noses."

The porch light is burned out, and I'm about to go up the front steps when a tall man comes out of the shadows. I yelp and thrust an arm in front of Kelly to protect her.

He clears his throat and bends on one knee, extending his hand and opening a small jewelry box. Light from a street lamp makes a ring sparkle and illuminates Buzz's face. Seeing him, my stomach does a flip.

Buzz says, "I didn't mean to scare you, but I must ask this question. Will you take me back and marry me, Irena Fishbone? I'll be the father Kelly needs, and we'll be a family."

# BUZZ

Kelly comes over and hugs me. Irena's eyes grow wide, but she doesn't say yes, which makes my stomach knot. I stand and hold the ring out to her. "You love me, I know you do. You told me you've loved me ever since grade school. Try it on. We'll get it sized to fit, or you can pick out a different one. Whatever you want. Let's just spend our lives together. The three of us will be a trilogy. We'll be related with different stories."

Irena covers her mouth, and my chest tightens. She says, "It's such a surprise, you being here. I'm not ready to commit. Jack's going missing changed us, and not for the better."

I swallow, setting the ring in the velvet box I bought using a home equity line of credit and pocket it. I made the local jeweler's day when I stopped in.

I let out a sigh and open my arms, hoping for the best

despite being spurned. I say, "Let's hug it out, the three of us."

Kelly moves into my arms and motions to Irena. "Come on, Mom, one hug won't hurt you. He's just a boy who loves you. That's what you said before he moved in."

Irena hesitates, so I say, "We've been hurt by Jack leaving. Let's stick together."

Irena steps in, and she smells of the salty sea, diesel oil, and floral scented shampoo. I wrap my arm around Irena's waist and say, "I want to make you two happy, that's what I care about, along with taking care of Happy."

Kelly sniffles. "I miss your dog."

I say, "I'd like to be the one to cook dinner for you two. We'll be a family, like we talked about."

Irena blinks back tears. "You're offering us a perfect world, and I'm sorry, but I'm not ready. I'm confused after all that's happened. There's a lot of things I need to think about it."

I say, "Trust me, I'm as solid as Elwha Rock off Orcas Island. I'm here for you, babe."

Irena gives me a quick smile and says, "Comparing yourself to a rock that took out a ferry isn't your best move."

She moves close and whispers in my ear, sending shivers up my spine, "I loved you, but if you hurt my baby girl's heart like Jack did leaving her, I'll kill you."

## 56

## KELLY

Mom invites Buzz to come inside, but he can't spend the night because she needs time to ponder his proposal. I've known him since I was born, and I'm fine if she marries him. Mom and I go in the kitchen to make tea, and Buzz sets up a fire in the living room fireplace.

As we wait for water to boil in the tea kettle, she drums her fingers on the counter. I lean in and say, "Are you going to marry him?"

She says, "A part of me wants to say yes, but I don't believe I can trust him. What do you think?"

I shrug. "I'm fine with him being around. Besides, Buzz may have saved Dad's life by keeping him from people who want to hurt him."

The tea kettle whistles, and Mom pours hot water into

mugs. She says, "I get that Buzz may have saved your dad's life. But I have a feeling there's more to the story."

Buzz comes in the kitchen and shoves his hands in his pockets. "I did save his life. He had to get out of town or the thugs were going to kill him."

Mom massages her temples. "I know you're both right, but I need a partner who tells me the truth, no matter what. Can you do that?" She points at Buzz, and a look flickers past his eyes for a moment and fades.

He nods. "Of course I can, and I will. What's a partnership if one person is holding back keeping secrets? I'm in all the way, babe, or I wouldn't have proposed to you a second time. I'm standing here as vulnerable as I can be, exposing my soul, asking you to trust me."

I stare out the kitchen window, waiting for the lovers to finish whatever word dance they're doing.

Mom says, "Well, that's good to know. About Jack's place, tomorrow, I want to sell his sneakers and call the junk collectors to clean out his apartment. We'll run an auction every day until they're gone, even the scuffed-up ones Abby stole. Let's go in the living room."

I glance at my mother and give a slight shake of my head to tell her she is reverting to bad habits by being defensive and guarded, using items on her to-do list to protect her heart. It doesn't work, but she doesn't realize that right now.

Buzz takes a cup and says, "Abby took a pair of Jack's sneakers?"

I carry a warm mug and sit on the sofa. "She took two pair, but they're not the most expensive ones."

A flash of concern flits across Buzz's face, and he settles in a chair by the fire.

Mom sits next to me and says, "We can still sell them though."

I say, "She's trying to stop stealing."

Buzz runs a hand through his hair. "It's pretty tough to change ingrained habits, so the best of luck to her."

Sitting in the living room sipping tea feels like old times. The fire spits and splutters. A spark flies up, hits the fireplace screen, and falls to the tiled hearth. Watching it, I make a wish and hope my dad is alive, where ever he is.

Buzz leans back and puts his feet on the coffee table. But he sits up when my mom says, "I texted Violet to see if she can find out who is selling the gold sneakers. I want those shoes back before they change hands."

Buzz stiffens and swallows. My mom gives him a close look and says, "Why are you looking like that, with your Adam's apple bobbing up and down? Did you have something to do with the shoes going missing from our place?"

His face turns red, and his hands grip the arms of the chair. "No, I didn't, and I'm insulted you think I had anything to do with it. I'm nervous because my heart is hanging out there. I proposed a second time and the waiting is killing me."

My mom says, "I'm sorry if you feel insulted. There's just a lot of things that don't make sense, with Jack being gone and shoes disappearing. After I pay off his debts and clean out his place, I'll decide about us."

Buzz stands. "Guess that's my cue to go. It's always about Jack. No matter what I do for you, it's Jack this and Jack that. Will it ever be different? Do I have a chance at all, or were you playing me and stringing me along?"

I cringe at being a witness to their quarrel and stand to escape to my bedroom and hide under the covers with a pillow over my head.

Buzz puts his hand on the door knob. "Did you see Abby's post about Jack on Meadow Book? She posted his photo and asked anyone who saw him to message her. Did she mention that to you?"

Mom and I shake our heads. She says, "I guess we missed it, being so busy. I wonder if anyone responded to her?"

He says, "I was wondering that too. I'll ask her."

I brush away a tear. "I hope her post won't make it easier for the guy with a gun to find him. Dad has to be alive. Don't you think?"

Buzz nods. "I hope so. Maybe he's in Costa Rica on a permanent vacation like he always wanted."

My mom wraps an arm around my shoulders. "I bet he's on a white sandy beach in board shorts with bare feet, looking over beautiful blue water."

I say in a choked voice, "But he's missing us and making plans to come home."

Buzz says goodbye and leaves, closing the door softly.

Mom strides over and locks it. "We can't take chances, with a sneaker-stealer coming in our house."

I shudder and cross my arms. "It creeps me out that someone was in our house."

She hugs me. "I'll protect you. Don't worry."

I bite my lip and wonder who is protecting my father. I say, "We need to call the hospitals and see if Dad's there."

She sighs. "It's a long shot, and it's late. Let's do it first thing tomorrow morning." Her phone rings, and she grabs it, saying, "I've got to take this. It's the Coast Guard."

## 57

**ABBY**

While I'm eating dinner at the restaurant, I mull over what I saw at the hospital. The jerk who choked me is in the hospital, and his roommate might be Jack. His voice was familiar, but the Jack I knew radiated sunshine and laughter. The man in bed was listless, pale, and weak.

I push away the plate with a half-eaten chicken enchilada. The guy's hair was chopped off, like someone took kitchen shears to it in a hurry. But his face, although gaunt, looked like Jack's. His brown eyes bored into my soul for an instant, like Jack used to look at me.

I tap a fingernail on the table. If something happened to Jack, and he's in the hospital, he could need my help. The longer I sit there, the more convinced I am that I saw Jack. I must go back to the hospital.

I shake my head and hope I won't get kicked out of his

room. Was he in a motorcycle accident? A bar fight? I grimace, because Irena's father hit a guy in the head in a bar fight and killed him, sending her dad to prison.

I put out my credit card for the waitress and glance at my purse and laptop, figuring if I sit by Jack's side, I'll have time on my hands while he sleeps. While I'm there, I'll message the person who told me to go to the hospital room and thank them. A quick thought flashes through my mind, and I open my laptop, checking my brokerage account. The amount in my investment account is climbing steadily. My friends know I work at a factory, but on the side, I've trained myself how to trade stocks and manage my money. I check the Japanese stock market, which is open while Millersville sleeps, and buy some yen. If I'm right, I'll make a mint, and I don't mean mint ice cream.

I frown, thinking back to when Jack hatched a misguided scheme of buying shares of a sneaker company on a margin call. I tried to dissuade him, but he brushed me off. We were eating breakfast at Gigi's Café, and I was footing the bill as usual like a fool.

I said, "I seriously caution you not to do that. You don't know what you're doing. You could get in over your head and owe a ton of money by betting on a margin call."

He said, "Abs, I love you." My heart soared, and I smiled and sighed. Then he said, "But you don't know about investments. You work at an ice cream factory. I looked into the stock market, and I know what I'm doing."

I groaned. He was an innocent who thought he knew better, lured by get rich quick dreams. I leaned forward, gripping the table with both hands, and said in a steely voice, "I know what I'm doing. I've studied the market and have been investing for fifteen years. And by the way, I'm doing very well."

He turned to Karina, the owner of Gigi's Café who approached with a coffee pot. "We'd like more coffee, please."

Karina poured steaming hot coffee and chatted with Jack while I swallowed bitter bile. Fine, I thought to myself, bringing the mug to my mouth. Brush it off and don't believe me, but I'll show you and all our friends. I'll build my investment portfolio behind your backs, and you'll never suspect that I'm the millionaire next door.

I come back to the present and close my laptop, grabbing my purse. I pay and hurry to my car. If Jack is the one in the hospital bed, I could help him until he gets on his feet. I have the means to support him, as long as he doesn't do something crazy, like buying high-end sneakers. Irena thought she could change him, but I'll keep him busy, so he won't have time to shop for shoes. I know people say that you can't change anyone, but Jack could be the exception to the rule.

I drive through rain crossing over a bridge, and thick mist rises from the river. I bite the inside of my cheek. I should tell Irena about my possible sighting of Jack in the hospital, and that I'm on the way there. Although they were no longer married, she's monopolized his time and attention, and I've wanted him for myself. If it's really him, I'll hang out and help him before letting her know what's going on. I whisper to myself, "I hope, I hope, I really hope I'll find Jack in that bed. Please, let it be him."

I park in the hospital lot and get out, popping up an umbrella. Rain patters down as I lock the car and march toward the hospital, not sure if I'll find Jack in a bed or a brown-eyed stranger. I pop a piece of peppermint gum in my mouth and bite down. I'm walking into a situation with unknowns, and although I have a good feeling about this, it could go sideways.

I take the elevator up to the third floor and tap my toe on the ride up. Stepping into Room 366, my mouth falls open. The space where the second bed by the far wall was is empty, and the man who might have been Jack is gone.

The brute who choked me says in a gravelly voice, "They carted that guy away. Sit with me instead."

"Not on your life." I turn and march into the hall to ask a nurse what happened to the missing patient. I hope he didn't die.

I catch the attention of a curly haired male nurse in blue scrubs. "Do you know what happened to the man in the far bed in Room 366?"

He tilts his head, brown eyes gazing into mine. "Are you family? We can't discuss it with visitors, due to patient privacy rules."

I open my mouth to answer, ready to fib on the spot.

I'll say the man is my long-lost brother, and I've been looking for him all over. But the nurse who shooed me out earlier comes over and says, "Are you John Doe's wife?"

My eyes open wide, and I nod. My hands tighten on my computer bag and purse. I'll play along and see where it leads.

She says, "We've been looking for you. Right this way."

I follow her down the hall, monitors beeping in rooms. We pass the creep in Room 366, and I shake my head and say, "The man in Room 366 attacked me when I was cleaning a friend's apartment."

The nurse says, "Did you report it to the police?"

"Yes, and I hope he spends a lot of time in jail."

# 58

## IRENA

I shrug on my boat gear, grab my phone, give Kelly a hug, saying, "I'll be back as soon as I can. Keep the doors locked and the curtains closed. Don't let anyone inside. Until I get this straightened out, we can't trust anyone."

Kelly's eyes open wide. "Thanks for scaring me to death and leaving me all alone."

I say, "Well then, come with me. Or I can drop you at Abby's."

She sighs. "Fine, I'll go with you."

We get in the car, and my phone dings with a text. I say, "Violet wants me to call her. I asked her to see who was selling the gold sneakers." I dial Violet, who runs Outrigger Services, and put the phone on speaker. I say, "Hi, what's up? I don't have long to talk."

She says, "We learned who's selling the limited-edition

gold leather sneakers. It's Buzzard LLC and the company's registered agent is none other than."

I frown and can't help jumping in and interrupting. "Bud Wiser."

Kelly gives me a side glance.

Another call comes in, beeping and overriding whatever Violet says. I say, "Another call's coming in, and I've got to take it. Call you later."

I swipe to answer the other call. A woman says in a panicked voice, "When will you get here? His hand is stuck in the anchor rode."

I glance at Kelly and cringe. "We're on our way. We should be there in fifteen minutes."

She says, "Please hurry."

"See you soon."

I park at the marina, and Kelly and I run for the boat through rain. We hop in my boat and I start the engine. We rub a towel over our wet hair and shrug on life vests. Minutes later, we pull away from the dock, on our way to rescue another stranded soul who met with a boating mishap on the Salish Sea.

Kelly pulls in the fenders and joins me inside, snapping into her seat harness. "What's wrong with their boat?"

"It was bobbing up and down in waves, and they wanted to move to a quieter spot. But the skipper's hand got caught between the anchor chain and the windlass. A helicopter is on the way, but we've got to free his hand before they can medivac him."

She says, "We should be able to get that done quickly, shouldn't we?"

I plow through two-foot seas and flip on the search lights. "That's right."

Kelly says, "Who do you think has the gold sneakers and is selling them?"

"We'll find out as soon as we wrap up this call."

A thirty-four-foot power boat bucks up and down off the southern tip of Cypress Island. I bring my boat alongside the other boat, lashing the boats together at midships. Kelly and I step over the gap. Water splashes up between the boats, soaking us.

I greet the gray-haired woman onboard, who is wearing a life jacket.

She says, "Please help my husband. I wasn't sure how to work the windlass to get his hand free."

My pulse picks up. "I will."

A helicopter hovers overhead, whipping up waves with prop wash. I get on the marine radio and tell them to go away and give me a few minutes to free the man's hand before coming back.

I turn to Kelly and say, "Get on the windlass and at my command, back off to release tension."

She taps the head set she's wearing. "Got it."

The woman's face is flushed from wind exposure and worry. She says, "Is she old enough to help you?"

I say, "She's fine. She knows her way around boats. Kelly's my assistant."

I hurry outside and hunch over, fighting the wind, walking with careful footsteps to the bow, where a man grimaces in pain. The anchor chain is wrapped around his wrist. I'm no medical expert, but it doesn't look broken.

I say, "We'll get you out of here, and the chopper will take you to the hospital."

He grits his teeth. Wind blows his gray hair in his face. "Do what you have to. I can't take much more of this."

I say into my headset, "Kelly, you there?"

"Copy that."

I put my hand on the man's wrist and say into the mic, "When I say go, back off on the windlass."

"Roger that."

"Go."

Tension lets up on the windlass, enough so I can pull the man's wrist out of the vice-like grip of the heavy anchor chain. I say, "Let's go inside until the helicopter comes back. I'll help you."

He moans, stumbling as he walks, and I support him. He steps inside into the woman's arms, and she wraps her arms around him. "Oh, sweetie, how awful."

Using the marine radio, I hail the Coast Guard helicopter. Moments later, the chopper hovers over the water near the boat. The power boat vibrates and shudders from the helicopter propeller wash. A diver in a wet suit drops out of the helicopter, splashing down in the dark sea and swimming over to us. I hurry to the swim step to help, and a basket is lowered from the helicopter.

The diver hops up on the swim step, graceful as a seal, and grins. She says, "J.J. Longmont at your service. Where's the injured person?"

I smile at the woman with round, rosy cheeks. "Right this way."

In the cabin, J.J. says to the wounded man, "We'll airlift you, and that involves getting you into that basket."

The woman says, "Can I go with him?"

J.J. says, "I'm afraid not."

I say, "I'll tow your boat into the marina, and you can stay onboard."

She says to me, "Thanks for doing this."

I smile. "All in a day's work."

Soon, the injured man is loaded into the basket and brought up to the helicopter. A rope ladder is tossed out of the chopper, and J.J. Longmont waves goodbye and climbs into the hovering helicopter. She waves and slams the door shut, and the chopper takes off.

I say to Kelly, "I've got to pull up the anchor to get us out of here. Work the windlass, will you? I'll tell you when to turn it on."

She says, "Will do."

We're about to go about our tasks when the woman says, "Aren't you two quite the team? What a positive relationship you have."

I say, "Thanks. My daughter's the best." I smile to Kelly and say, "Come on, let's pull up this anchor and get out of here."

An hour later, we're back in our marina slip. My boat is set for the night, with extra lines protecting against a storm that's blowing in. Going down the dock, I squeeze my daughter's shoulder. "You're a wonder. You know that, don't you? I love you."

She smiles. "Thanks. Love you too."

## 59

## JACK

A woman's voice says, "Wake up, and open your eyes." My eyelids flutter open. She is backlit by overhead florescent lights giving off a glare. "They'll take you to the recovery room."

People move around an operating room, and metal instruments clatter.

I say, "Is it over?"

"Yes, it is."

Aides roll the bed I'm on into a hall, and I say in a groggy voice, "She found me. She knows who I am." I close my eyes and dream.

A hand pats my arm. "You're in the recovery room," a woman says. "I'm Bettina, your nurse." Patients in beds face me along the opposite wall. Their mouths are slack, and they're sleeping. She says, "You're in the recovery room, and you just had surgery."

I blink, trying to recall why I'm here. "Why did I have surgery?"

She says in a soothing voice, "To relieve pressure on your brain."

I furrow my brow. "Where's my wife? I saw her before I was taken to surgery."

"Family isn't allowed in this area."

"I need to see her."

"Rest, and I'll bring you some pills and a glass of water."

My eyelids close, and I nod off. She taps my arm and says, "Take these two pills with small sips of water." I place the pills in my mouth and swallow a mouthful of water. She says, "Would you like juice? I have orange, grape, and apple juice."

"Grape," I manage to say. My limbs are heavy, and my eyelids droop.

She moves away, and I surrender to sleep. When I wake, the space across the room where the beds were is empty, so those people moved on. A tray next to me holds a cup with a straw, so I reach out and bring it to my mouth, sipping a cold, sweet liquid.

Bettina comes over with two aides. "They'll take you to the eighth floor."

I say, "Did they cut into my skull and take out a piece?"

"The doctor stopped to see you. Do you remember him coming by?"

I shake my head but stop because it hurts. "No."

"He'll see you later, when you're more alert."

Aides roll me to the elevator, and a thought flits through my mind. Maybe I'll leave the past behind and begin again. I'll start a new life.

A man in a white coat walks by and nods to me. I smile, because from now on, I can be whoever I want. Nothing's going to hold me back.

## ABBY

The nurse who scolded me earlier says, "I didn't realize you were family. He's leaving the recovery room, and they're moving him to Room 801. Take the elevator and join him there."

"Thank you," I say and hurry to the elevator at a pace Irena would appreciate. The doors open and I step in, stabbing a button for the eighth floor. I touch my sore neck and swallow. My hands shake. I'm just a nobody working in a factory, and Irena's the one guys like. If she knew I was here, she'd come in and take over, but I'm grabbing my chance to see Jack, if it is him, alone.

The elevator doors slide open with a ding. I stride down the hall to Room 801, determined to drop my wallflower act and take charge. I walk down the hall with questions buzzing in my mind, wondering if it will be Jack in the room and if it is, what is wrong with him. The only way to find answers is to face it full on.

**60**

---

**JACK**

My head is elevated, and I look around when the hospital bed is wheeled into a room with a wide window. A woman sitting in a chair stands as two aides in scrubs place the head of the bed against a wall. I say, "Everyone's so nice. Thank you for taking care of me."

They set the brakes on the bed and leave as a nurse comes in. She has yellow framed glasses, and brown hair pulled up in a pony tail, revealing a small tattoo of a butterfly behind her ear.

"I'm Grace, and I'll be your nurse tonight. Can I get you anything? A warm blanket? Ice water? I might be able to round up cheese and crackers if you like."

"Ice water sounds great. And a warm blanket. And cheese and crackers."

The woman with a heart-faced face comes over and

holds my hand. Tears wet her cheeks. "I can't believe I found you. I was so worried about you, my missing man."

Goosebumps prick my flesh. Her breath is sweet, and her hand is warm. I blink to be sure I'm not dreaming. My eyes fill with tears.

Grace the nurse says, "We had him listed as a John Doe. What is his name?"

She holds my gaze. "The one and only Jack Fishbone."

I frown. "I'm not sure I like that name."

She says, "You'll get used to it."

Grace says, "I'll let the administrators know. And if you'd like to spend the night, the recliner pulls out into a bed. Would you like a warm blanket too?"

She smiles. "Sure, I'll take a blanket, thanks."

Grace says, "I'll be back," and leaves the room.

I clear my throat and say, "I don't remember your name. What is it?"

Her eyes grow wide. "I'm Abby Love. Don't you remember?"

"I lost my memory when I hit my head."

She chews on her lower lip. "That's awful."

"Are we married? Because I hope we are."

"We're friends. Very good friends. And we love each other."

I say, "I thought so."

"But not in that kind of way. More like hanging out, drinking beer buddies."

"If that's all it was, I must've been an idiot. How did you put up with me?"

Her brown eyes sparkle. "It was easy."

"Are you sure we weren't married? Because I feel like we are. A beautiful woman like you probably has a hundred guys lining up to be with you."

She slowly shakes her head. "Nobody's lining up. I mostly keep to myself, except for some close friends. I don't like to be the center of attention."

"I know what you mean. Before the operation, people came in and stared at me. I couldn't stand it."

She squeezes my hand. "You weren't like that before. You were the class clown and the life of the party."

"Maybe it's time for a change."

Grace comes in carrying a white cup and packages of cheese and crackers. She scoots the table over my stomach, sticks a straw in the ice water, and picks up a remote control. "If you want your head higher or lower, use this. And press the red call button if you need help. I'll get the blankets and be right back."

She swishes out of the room, and Abby says, "They're efficient here, aren't they?"

I gaze at her. "Abby Love is a nice name."

"I'm your friend who will always be there for you, because I love you."

Tears trickle down my cheeks, and she hands me a tissue. "What's up?"

I say, "I can't believe you love me."

She leans over and gives me a gentle hug. "I do love you, Jack Fishbone, and I will always love you. You can count on that."

A smile spreads across my face. I'm bursting with joy at being found and named and loved in one fell swoop. I squeeze her hand. "I love you too. Will you kiss this fool?"

She kisses me. When she pulls away, I say, "Don't leave me again. Promise?"

She looks serious when she says, "I promise."

I say, "If we're not married, we should be. I love you, and you love me. Maybe we can find a Chaplin and get married in the hospital. We can do it tonight or first thing in the morning."

Abby's eyes fill with tears. "I don't want to take advantage of you, Jack. You just got out of an operation and probably don't have a clear head."

"I must've been stupid not to propose before."

She says, "Do you remember anything?"

"I wish, but it's a blank slate."

"What do you want to do for work?"

I make a face. "I don't know, but I feel like I want to help people who are sick. The people here are treating me so well, I want to pass it on."

She says, "This is a new side of you. Are you really sure you want to marry me?"

I take her hand and place it over my heart. My pulse picks up, and I say, "Will you marry me, Abby Love? Please say yes."

She grins and says, "Yes, I say yes, for the rest of our lives."

We kiss and pull apart when Grace bustles in, setting a blanket and pillow on the recliner. She drapes a warm blanket over me, pulling it up to my chin. My body relaxes in the warmth.

I say, "Thank you. Grace. We just decided to get married."

Her eyebrows shoot up. "I thought you were married?"

I say, "We put it off for some reason. Can you arrange for the hospital Chaplin to marry us first thing tomorrow morning? We'd really appreciate it."

Grace beams. "I'll get right on it." She stops at the door. "What about the marriage certificate?"

Abby grins. "I have my computer with me. We'll do it online."

Grace says, "I'll leave you lovebirds alone." She closes the door behind her.

I say, "Kiss me again, Abby, and don't pull away so fast. You're my medicine, and you'll make me well."

She leans over, pressing soft lips to mine, and her scent reminds me of a rose garden. Someone knocks on the door and opens it. Abby pulls away and stands at attention, as if we're in trouble.

Dr. Rhodes, the neurosurgeon, comes in accompanied by a middle-aged woman with blond shoulder length hair. They're wearing white lab coats. He says, "I understand congratulations are in order."

Abby and I smile at each other. Dr. Rhodes says, "Let's go over what our team did during surgery. We removed a piece of your skull and drained the hematoma. When the swelling in your brain goes down, we'll screw part of your skull back in place. You'll stay in the hospital and be monitored until we release you. Any questions?"

I say, "Will my headaches go away? And will my memory come back?"

He says, "It's difficult to predict with any degree of accuracy about your headaches or memory at this point. You might live with persistent headaches. We'll know more in the coming days. How's your pain level?"

I shrug. "It's bearable."

"Let your nurse know if it gets worse. It's best to stay ahead of the pain."

Abby says, "What about hospital costs? Will he have to pay for those?"

He says, "I don't handle that end of things. Billing would be the place to ask questions like that."

The woman says, "We have a foundation that covers bills for indigent patients."

I say to Abby, "Do I have much money?"

She winces. "You're deep in debt."

I blow out a breath. "I guess I didn't handle money very well."

Abby squeezes my hand and says, "How soon can he leave the hospital?"

"Let's see how he does before I answer that. I'll be back tomorrow to check."

I say, "I don't know where I live. Do I have a place?"

Abby says, "You're coming home with me."

"I don't want to be a mooch. I hope to get back on my feet soon and work."

The blond woman says, "You'll need to take it easy for a while."

Dr. Rhodes nods and says, "I'll see you tomorrow."

They leave, and Grace knocks and comes in. She smiles and says, "The Chaplin is here, and we can do the service tonight."

I say, "Thank you, Grace."

Abby kisses me. I pat her perfect back and whisper in her ear, "I'm so glad you found me. I love you." She breaks down, sobbing in my arms, and I cry tears of joy. Bitter despair and sorrow are left behind, and I'm not alone.

## 61

## BUZZ

I drum my fingers on my desk in my office at work and watch auction bids for the gold sneakers climb minute by minute. Jack being gone is a boon for me. I'll bring Irena flowers and scones until she agrees to marry me. The auction closes, and I jump up and yell, "All right!"

I print out the winner's name and address, grab the shoes and tell my staff I'm running a quick errand. I ship them insured, in case anything happens along the way, and hurry back to work, grinning from ear to ear. Now I'll be able to pay back the loan for Irena's diamond ring. Everything is going my way.

Back at the store, I take a minute to text Abby and see how she's doing. I want to find out if she learned anything from posting Jack's photo on socials. Did anyone say he's dead? If so, I'd like to get ahead of that news and be with

Irena when she hears the devastating truth. I was sure Jack was dead when I left him with blood oozing from his skull.

I shake my head. If only Jack hadn't insisted on going back for Irena and Kelly before he disappeared, I wouldn't have lost my temper and hit him. It was the final straw, where everything revolved around what Jack wanted. Irena and Kelly will fall apart when they hear the news, and I'll be there to comfort them.

I'm sipping coffee when my phone dings with a text. Abby says, "I found Jack."

I spew out a mouthful of coffee, spraying the window pane and papers on my desk. Gasping for air, I peer out into the dark night. I hope I didn't leave incriminating evidence when I left Jack with blood pooling around his head.

I text, "Is he alive? Or at a funeral home?"

She texts back, "He's at Riverside Hospital."

I slam my fist down on the desk, and my heart hammers hard. My thumbs fly as I text back, "Where are you? I'll join you."

She replies, "Room 801. We have a surprise. You won't believe it."

My palms are slick with sweat, and I wipe them on my jeans. My pulse races. I've got to get to the hospital and find out what's going on.

I pull on my rain coat. With inventory going on at the store tonight, and Irena wrecking my personal life, I took my dog over to a neighbor's house for the evening. I glance at my computer and see a message fly past. "Contact us for remote service. Your device is in danger of having a virus."

I perch in my chair and squint, unsure if I'm reading the computer screen correctly. But when I try to open a file, I can't. I'm locked out of my own device. I slam my fist on the desk top and yelp, rubbing my hand.

Paola, my assistant manager, knocks and cracks open the door. "Everything all right? I was passing by your office, and it sounded like you're upset."

I frown and point to my laptop. "I'm locked out of my computer. You're good with technology. Can you figure out what's going on?"

She slides into my seat, tapping on the keyboard. A few minutes later, she swivels to face me, shakes her head and stands. "I'm afraid you've got a computer virus. Someone got into your system."

I clap a hand over my mouth. "Oh, man."

She reaches around, yanks out the power cord, and the computer shuts down. "I'm not sure if they had time to get into your system. Do you have banking information on your computer that they could use to access your accounts?"

I run a hand over my face. "Yeah, I do."

She purses her lips. "What sites were you on when it crashed and you got the message?"

"I was on Flootbay, the online auction site. I was selling something."

She tilts her head. "They might've gotten in through there. Hackers are smart, smarter than we give them credit for. Did you click on anything in the last hour?"

I nod. "An email came saying the bookstore ad account on Meadow Book was in danger of being closed. It said to protest, click the link. So, I clicked." My face heats, and it dawns on me how screwed I am. "I fell for a scam, didn't I?"

"Those emails look real. You're not alone in falling for it. They can drain your bank accounts, take over your Meadow Book and Flootbay accounts, and send the proceeds from whatever you were selling to themselves. You might never see the money."

My mouth goes dry. I say in a tight voice, "I screwed up. What should I do?"

"Call Outrigger Services? I've heard they know how to deal with hackers."

I grab my phone. "Thanks, I'll do that. Sorry I'm not out there helping with inventory. A few things came up."

She smiles, drawing my eyes to her bright red lipstick and her generous mouth. But I prefer Irena's natural beauty to a woman who wears makeup. She says, "We're doing fine. We'll close the bookstore and finish inventory. Go deal with what you need to do."

I text Violet at Outrigger Services, who I know through

Gigi's Café and the Chamber of Commerce, because we're both business owners. I tell her I need her help and it's urgent. While I wait for her reply, I pace back and forth in my small office where the walls feel like they are closing in.

My phone dings with a message, and my hands tremble when I look at the screen. Violet texted, "I'll call you in a minute."

I grit my teeth and think about how I must get to the hospital. It'll take me at least thirty minutes to drive there. How could Jack be alive? Whatever his condition is, but it can't be good, given what I saw before I took off in my boat. I didn't want to hurt him, but he planned to take Irena and Kelly with him, and I flew into a rage and hit him on impulse. What I did to my best friend was wrong, but it's too late to change that.

My phone rings, and I say, "Hi, Violet, thanks for calling. Sorry to bother you so late."

She says, "No problem. Tell me what's going on."

I tell her how my computer locked up and someone took over. She says, "I'll be right there. Don't do anything." She muffles the phone and says, "Mimi, can you go with me to the bookstore? Buzz got hacked." She comes back on and says, "We'll be right there. Hang tight."

I wander through the bookstore in a daze and stumble over a stack of books on the floor. Paola says, "Sorry, boss, just doing inventory. You know how it is."

It crosses my mind that I should give her a raise. She's good with customers and the business side of things.

Violet and Mimi burst through the door, and I usher them into my office. I say, "Thanks for coming on short notice." I review what happened, and Mimi sits down at my computer.

She says, "Uh oh."

My stomach sinks. I wait for what I'll hear.

Violet nods to Mimi, who stands. "We need to take this back to our office, and we'll need your passwords. Is that okay with you?"

"Definitely, yes. Please, just take care of it. I hope you can stop the hackers." I tell them my passwords.

Mimi says, "Were you running an online auction tonight?"

My eyes open wide with surprise. "I am. How did you know?"

She looks at Violet. "We know more than we let on. Isn't that right, boss?"

Violet holds out her hand. "We need the engagement ring, while we're at it."

I cock my head. "I'm not giving you that. And how do you know about it?"

She taps a finger on her open palm. "Little birds talk around town. You were at the jewelers and spent a lot of money on an engagement ring, and then you proposed to Irena, didn't you?"

My hands fly up in the air. "Are there no secrets in this town? Does everyone know the inner goings on about each other?" I'm so rattled, I pull the red velvet-covered box with the ring out of my pocket and put it in her palm.

I blow out a breath. "Why in the heck do you want this?"

Violet slips the ring into her purse and points at me. "I don't completely trust you, Bud Wiser, and I'm keeping an eye on you. You covered up how you helped Jack disappear and lied to Irena. I'm on her side if she decides not to take you back."

I run my hands down my face. "I feel like you two are ganging up against me. Can't you just stop whoever is hacking into my computer and give me the ring back?"

Mimi says, "They may have already drained your accounts."

My stomach knots. They move to the door, leaving behind the scent of grilled hamburgers and fries.

Violet says, "We'll get right on it. You're in good hands."

As they leave, I say, "How much will this cost me?"

Violet says, "We'll let you know. It's too soon to tell. You shouldn't use your store computers if they're hooked up to the internet until we sort this out. The hackers might come in through your network, given you are compromised, and take over your system."

I put my face in my hands and beat myself up for falling into a fool's trap. But now I fell for one, so I've joined the many. I need the money from selling the gold shoes to pay back the loan I took out for the diamond ring.

I look out the door, wondering why Violet asked for the ring. So much is going on that I just handed it over, and I shouldn't have done that. I've got to get the ring back.

Striding over to the cash register, I say, "Let's close the bookstore early tonight. We've been hacked. Shut down the computers, and don't use them."

My two employees and I gently usher customers out the door, saying goodbye. I scrawl out a sign and tape it to the front door. "Cash only due to computer outage. Thanks for your patience."

"I've got to go," I say to my staff. "I need to visit a friend in the hospital."

I hurry out into the rain, pulling up the hood of my coat and running to my car. As I drive, I reflect that the hacking debacle is probably my fault for stealing the gold sneakers. In the wake of Jack's disappearance, my moral compass seems to have gone haywire, and I've done some horrific things.

I turn onto Highway 20 and head east. I've always been jealous of Jack, because he had the flash and pizazz that attracted people to crowd around him. But now I don't like who I've become. Maybe it was better to be dependable, boring Buzz, a bookstore owner.

Tightening my grip on the steering wheel, I question my recent decisions and release a sigh when the hospital appears ahead. I hope Abby is mistaken, and the person she thinks is Jack is a stranger to us. He can't be alive.

I pull up and park in the lot, hopping out of the car and hurrying to the hospital. I can't let Jack tell Irena how I hit him and left him for dead. She must never know that. She wouldn't understand my burst of insane jealousy. Even I was surprised by what happened. Maybe we all have a hidden murderer lurking deep inside, and mine let loose in a moment of impulsive hatred on a dark night at the wharf.

I could lose the love of my life and spend the rest of my days in jail.

## 62

## IRENA

When Kelly and I get home, I call Violet to hear who is selling the gold sneakers. She picks up and says, "I was waiting for your call."

I say, "Is it too late to talk?"

"It's never too late to call me."

I pace in the kitchen, and Kelly listens to every word I say. "Who is selling the shoes? What did you find out?"

She sucks in a slow breath. "I don't think you're going to like this. Are you sure you want to know?"

I scuff a sneakered shoe on the kitchen floor. "Yes, who is it?"

She says, "Someone created a new company the other day and registered it with the state. That company is selling the sneakers. And the registered agent for the company is none other than…"

In the background, someone says something to Violet, and she says to me, "Hold on. We've got a problem. I'll call you right back."

She hangs up, and I pocket the phone. "Why can't anything be simple? Since your dad disappeared, everything's complicated. This is driving me crazy."

Kelly says, "While we wait for her to call back, let's call the hospitals and check if Dad's there."

"It's late. I doubt the switchboard operator would know if he's there."

She looks at me with big brown eyes. "We might as well try, don't you think?"

I sit next to her at the table. "Let's use your phone in case Violet calls me back."

Soon, we're on the phone with the local hospital in Millersville, asking if they have Jack Fishbone. The operator says no, they don't. Kelly says, "One down, two more to go. Or three or four, depending on how big an area we'll check."

We call the second hospital and get the same answer. When we call the third one, Riverside Hospital, the person answering the phone says, "We don't have anyone by that name."

On impulse, I blurt out, "What about someone who didn't give a name? Do you have a patient like that?"

The operator pauses and says, "We do have a John Doe."

Kelly and I look at each other with open mouths. I say, "What room is he in?"

"I can't give that information to the public."

Kelly grabs the phone. "I could be his daughter. Please, tell me. I'm worried about my dad."

She says, "I'm sorry, I can't do that."

I say, "Let's go see if your dad is in that hospital."

She pulls on her coat. "Just what I was thinking."

We hurry out and hop in the car. I merge onto Highway 20, heading east, and say, "Don't get your hopes up. It's unlikely your dad is the John Doe."

"Okay, but I can still hope."

"I hope he's in that room too."

I drive in silence, swishing windshield wipers keeping us company. I park in the hospital visitor parking lot, and we jump out, slamming the doors. We hustle inside in Fishbone-style. My heart thumps, and my palms turn cold. I say, "No matter what happens, baby girl, I'm here for you. Don't you forget that."

She gives me a side glance while we walk up to the front desk. "It probably isn't Dad, so let's not make a big deal out of it. Everything doesn't have to be big drama. It's maybe an older confused man who got lost."

I let out a slow breath and say, "We'll see."

Approaching the receptionist, I say, "You have a John Doe here, and my ex-husband and my daughter's father is missing. Can you give us his room number?"

Her black hair shines, reflecting light. She smiles and says, "Let me call the nurse and see what she says." She turns away and speaks with someone on the phone. She turns back to us. "Is your last name Fishbone, by any chance?"

Kelly grins. "Yes, I'm Kelly Fishbone."

She says, "Take the elevator and go up to Room 801."

The elevator doors open, and we step onboard. My knees are trembling. Riding to the eighth floor, I take a deep breath and brace for whatever is coming. As a mother, I'm driven to protect Kelly from emotional hurt and physical harm. I'll keep her safe with my dying breath if it's the last thing I do.

The elevator doors open, and we step out, looking around. A sign points to Rooms 800-825, so we head that way. I say in a low voice, "I'm so nervous."

She grabs my hand, pulling me down a stark white hall. "I know, me too."

"We'll glance in and if it's not him, leave right away. No gaping or staring."

Kelly rolls her eyes. "Like I didn't know that? I'm not a toddler. Come on, let's see if Dad is here."

# JACK

I take Abby's hand in mine and say, "I'm so glad you found me." She whispers that she loves me. My chest is a warm puddle of sunshine, and tears wet my face.

She says, "I never gave up looking for you."

She exudes calm, and I'm safe with her by my side, ready to face anything coming my way. Someone knocks on the door, and it opens slowly. I say in a quiet voice, "Maybe it's the Chaplin, coming to marry us."

She whispers, "I'm so ready to marry you, Jack Fishbone. You have no idea how long I've waited for this moment."

I melt in the warmth of her brown-eyed smile.

A tall, older woman with black hair wearing a white lab coat and a stethoscope around her neck comes in and stands by my bed. She smells of coffee and mint lozenges. "I'm Dr. Abbott, the hospitalist. Are you in pain?"

I start to nod, but the motion hurts too much. I'm amazed Abby isn't disgusted by my appearance. I say, "It hurts, but it helps that Abby is here."

The doctor touches her black-rimmed glasses. "On a scale of one to ten, how intense is your pain?"

I take a moment to consider and say, "A nine or ten."

She nods. "We'll get you something for that."

Abby says, "He threw up a few minutes ago from the last pain pill."

"We'll add an anti-nausea pill." The doctor studies us. "You've had a severe head injury and lost your memory. We need to caution you against making life-changing decisions so soon after a traumatic brain injury."

Abby's grip on my hand tightens, and my pulse picks up. I grin at Abby, and she beams, kissing my cheek. "We're in love, and this was meant to be."

The hospitalist says, "Tomorrow morning, our staff will process your paperwork so people will know you're Jack Fishbone, and you're in the hospital. Do you have insurance?"

I look at Abby. "Do I have insurance? I'm not sure."

She shakes her head. "You don't. You lost your last job awhile ago. But now that we're married, you'll be on my health care insurance." A flicker of worry crosses her face, and she says to the doctor, "Is there a way we could keep Jack's name quiet for a while? He has some things to straighten out before he steps back into his life."

I spy a purple bruise on her neck and decide to ask her

about it when we're alone. We have so many things to talk about, and I have so much to learn.

The doctor says, "Of course. We'll discuss how to handle that in our staff meeting tomorrow morning. He'll be in this room recovering for the next several days, at minimum."

I say, "I'd like to leave as soon as possible to live with my new, beautiful wife."

Abby flashes a full wattage smile. I can't wait to spend hours kissing her. What a fool I was not to propose before this and ask her to be my partner. She's perfect.

The doctor says, "You need time to recover. It's too early to forecast when you might be discharged. We can't release you until you're ready.

I say, "I guess we'll spend our honeymoon in the hospital."

Abby grins at me, and I smile back.

The doctor says, "I'll be back to check on you tomorrow."

She walks out, and a gray-haired woman knocks and comes in. She smiles and says, "I'm the Chaplain. Would you two like to have a marriage service?"

Abby and I say yes at the same time. My stomach flutters, and in the back of my mind, I wonder if this is the right thing to do.

The Chaplain says, "Do you belong to a church or synagogue or mosque? Are you affiliated with any denomination?"

Abby and I glance at each other. Abby says, "No, we aren't. Not yet, anyways."

"Then I'll go ahead." The Chaplin opens a book and reads from it. My eyelids droop at her droning voice. She glances at me and says, "I'll make this quick. Do you two take each other to share your lives, through thick and thin, through sickness and health, to the end of your days? If you agree, say yes."

I look into Abby's eyes, and we both say, "Yes."

The Chaplin closes the book. "I now pronounce you wife and husband, partners in life. Go forth and enjoy a prosperous, joyous life. May peace be with you."

Abby wipes tears from her eyes and kisses me. I can't help but blubber like a baby. I say, "Thank you, Chaplain."

"Yes, thanks," Abby says.

We sign the marriage license, and the Chaplin says, "Have a wonderful honeymoon in the hospital. I wish you a speedy recovery."

She leaves, softly closing the door behind her, and Abby climbs into bed. She shifts around, avoiding my right wrist with the IV, finding space to snuggle on my left side, and I blink back tears. She knows me and wants to be with me, so maybe I'm not such a bad guy after all.

I put my left arm around her and pull her close. "Not much room, but we both fit."

I bend over to kiss the top of her head but stop short. Daggers of pain pierce my skull, blotting out happy thoughts, and a whimper escapes from my lips.

She says, "Am I hurting you? Should I get down?"

I grit my teeth. "Stay. It'll pass. I like you being here."

She nuzzles against my side and says, "I can't believe they cut into your skull. You must've been scared, all alone and not remembering a thing."

I let out a shaky breath. "I was terrified."

"Well, I'm here now, and I'm not leaving. You're what's most important."

My eyes fill with tears. The magnitude of what we've done sinks in, and I gaze out the window into the dark night, wondering what lies ahead. I squeeze her shoulder and say in a soft voice, "That's so good to hear. I'm lucky to be loved."

She looks up and smiles. "It goes both ways."

Just then, someone knocks, and Abby holds my hand and whispers she loves me.

Someone enters the room.

## 63

## FRANKIE

I press on the accelerator and floor it to the hospital. We found Fishbone, but it sounds like he's in bad shape. The police told us a John Doe turned out to be the man we were looking for.

I say to Brick, who is riding shotgun, "Someone roughed Jack up and cracked his skull to stop him from meeting us. They left him bleeding on a dead-end dirt road."

He nods. "We're up against hard core criminals who know what they're doing. They left him on the dock to die. It might've been a mob hit to prove a point. If you can't pay back what you owe, here's what happens to you."

I nod. "Yeah, or Jack could've been hurt to stop him from testifying against Craig. Craig could've hired someone from jail to take out his friend before the trial."

Brick says, "That's a possibility, but he's a first-time

offender and looks scared, caught with his hands dirty in a white-collar crime. We need to broaden the scope beyond Craig for attempted murder and witness-tampering and look at who else has a stake. There's a lot in play here."

Rain drums down on the car roof. We've got a break in the case, but we still have a lot to do. I say, "We'll ask Fishbone what happened when he was supposed to meet us."

"It'll be interesting to see what he has to say."

I say, "He was broken up about leaving his daughter and his ex-wife. I guess they're close. He had a hard time accepting he'd get a new identity and never come back."

Bricks grunts. "It'd be tough for anyone, to leave it all behind."

I follow signs to the hospital and pull into the parking lot. We hop out, making our way through rain to a ten-story building. I say, "We'd better get what we want tonight, so we can wrap up the case and move on."

Brick says, "I hope so. I'd rather be working out of the city."

I say with a smile, "You just miss your meatball sandwiches."

We chuckle and get on the elevator. I jab the button for the eighth floor. I say, "Too bad we haven't had time to dive into who Mother Mercy is, if she exists. Maybe he made her up to distract us. It'll wait for another day."

Brick says, "I wanted to belt that creep who was shot with the arrow. He was such an ass."

"My fingers were itching too. Nothing was his fault, despite his breaking in and choking the cleaning lady. If he thinks he's Teflon, he's got a lot to learn, and I'll be glad to teach him."

Brick nods. "I know what you mean."

We step off the elevator and stride down the hall to Room 801. I'm about to open the door when a nurse with gray streaks in her hair hurries over. She frowns and says, "The patient in that room needs to rest, so you'll have to wait until tomorrow. They're celebrating their wedding, and I'm about to ask everyone except for his wife to leave."

I say to Brick, "Jack Fishbone isn't married. Maybe we have the wrong guy."

"Could be. Let's go in that room and make sure."

We flash our badges at the nurse, and I say, "FBI, Special Agents McNalley and Brick. It's important we speak with Jack Fishbone now."

Her eyebrows arch, and she gestures to the room. "Go on in. Tell the others they have to leave."

# KELLY

My hand trembles on the door handle to Room 801, and I step inside before anyone can stop me. My heart pounds. The man in bed is older than my dad. His face is bruised, and he has a black eye. His short brown hair is chopped off with uneven edges. I stare, just to be sure he's not my father.

A woman is lying in bed next to him. They're holding hands, gazing into each other's eyes. My face feels hot, and I want to run from the room. We barged in and interrupted a private moment between two people. This can't be my dad.

I turn to leave and bump into my mom. She's standing with her mouth hanging open, her hands hanging at her sides. I pull her toward the door and say in a low voice, "Dad's not here. Let's go."

She points to the bed, and her armpit is dark with

sweat. She says in a shaking voice, "I think that's your father."

The couple turns to us, and I gape at Abby. She gets out of bed and says with a smile, "Look who's here. You're just in time to congratulate us."

My mom's face is pale, and her fists clench. "Congratulate you for what?"

Abby meets my gaze, and I've never seen her this beautiful. She's glowing with happiness. But I've never seen my dad look this bad. My toes curl, and my stomach twists. I blurt out, "What happened to you, Dad?"

He says, "Hello, who are you?" He puts a hand to his head, grimacing.

I burst into tears. "I'm Kelly, your daughter. Don't you remember me?"

He fiddles with a hospital bracelet around his wrist and says in a soft voice, "I'm sorry if I upset you. I don't remember anything about the past, except for Abby. She found me and told me my name. I was lost before she arrived, but I knew as soon as I saw her that I've always loved the woman with the heart-shaped face."

I cry in great gulps and through my tears see my mom march over to him. He blinks and says, "Do we know each other? I'm sorry, but I don't recognize you."

My mom says, "Kelly has been devastated by your disappearance. She was nearly frightened to death. You can come home with us."

He looks puzzled. I double over with a hand on my

churning stomach, and a whimper escapes from my mouth. This man is an imposter. He's not my father. And what is Abby doing by his side?

Abby kisses his cheek and says to us, "He can't go home with you when he's discharged. Tell her why."

My dad grins. "Because we're married. Abby Love and I just got married. I'm in love with Abby Love."

My mom says, "That isn't possible. You always said if you were going to marry anyone, it would be me for the second time."

He says, "I wish I remembered you, but I don't. I recognized Abby right off."

Abby leans over, and they kiss. Why doesn't he remember me? My stomach clenches, my mouth fills with water, and I whip open the door to the bathroom and stand over the toilet, retching.

I wipe my mouth and flush the toilet, coming out just in time to hear my dad say, "Please don't fight over me. I didn't even know my name."

I tilt my head. He's not acting like my father. Something's wrong with my dad.

My mom says, "I bet your marriage isn't even legal."

I give her a nudge to tone it down and take the bitterness out of her voice. She'll push them away if she keeps being this mean.

My dad smiles and looks at Abby, who says, "It's legal. We love each other, so you'd better get over it." His face is pale, except for purple and black bruises around his eyes. He says, "I'm tired. I need to rest." He closes his eyes.

Abby comes over and opens her arms, giving me a hug. "Oh, sweetie, we didn't mean to upset you. There's a chance his memory will come back and he'll recognize you, but the doctors don't know if or when that'll happen. I love you, and I'm sorry to see you this upset."

I wrap my arms around her waist and lean into her chest, weeping with shuddering breaths. In a muffled voice, I say, "How could he do this to me?"

She rubs my back. "He didn't mean to. It's not his fault. He got hit in the head."

My mom says, "Why didn't you call us? Why didn't you let us know?"

Abby lets go of me, and I step back, wiping my eyes. She hands me a tissue, and I blow my nose. Abby says, "It all happened so fast. He lost his memory and doesn't know how he got hurt."

The FBI agents walk in, closing the door behind them. They flash their badges and the woman says, "FBI. I'm Agent McNalley and this is Agent Brick. We're here to talk with Jack Fishbone, and we'd like a few moments alone with him."

The woman from the FBI opens the door, gesturing for us to go. Before my mom and I file out, my mom turns to my dad, "Take care, Jack."

Abby holds his hand, and I wrinkle my nose, tasting bitter bile. We step into the hall, and I lean against a wall for support. What happened in that room made me light-headed.

Tears streak my mom's cheeks. "Abby stole your dad."

I say, "I guess if he wants her as his wife, we have to respect it."

My mom taps a toe and frowns. When Abby doesn't come out of the room, my mom opens the door and says, "Abby, aren't you coming out with us?"

The FBI agents shake their heads. The female agent, who appears to be in charge, says, "She's staying, and we have questions for her too."

My heart sinks as we head to the elevator. I say, "I can't believe Dad didn't recognize me."

My mom says, "I can't believe it either. You're his own daughter. But I know he loves you deep down, no matter what."

I step on the elevator in a daze. The elevator doors open, and I shuffle out to the car and sink into the passenger seat with a sigh.

She starts the car and says, "I'm so sorry, hon. If I could make this right for you, I would. He must have really hit his head hard for him to forget us."

A sob escapes my mouth. I weep with a high-pitched wail, gulping for air. My own dad doesn't know me.

She drives and says, "He'll snap out of it and recognize you. I'm sure he will."

But I'm not so sure. The way he and Abby looked at each other with love was for real. I slump against the window, tears rolling down my cheeks. Rain splatters the windshield, and wipers groan, moving back and forth. I'll never stop crying for what I lost tonight.

My mom turns down our street and says, "I'll call the hospital tomorrow to ask your dad's doctor when his memory will come back."

"But you're not married to him. Abby is his wife. Will the doctor talk to you?"

She parks in the driveway, turns off the engine, and blows out a breath. "But as his daughter, you could. Call the hospital first thing tomorrow."

"Maybe he'll never know who I am. All I want to do is crawl into bed and hide."

I open the car door and climb out. My feet are heavy as I make my way to the front porch. I found my dad, but he's not my father. He doesn't know me or love me. He's a stranger who looks like an old worn-out man.

## 64

## IRENA

We trudge inside, and Kelly says, "I'm tired. I'm going to bed." I hug her tight and say, "I love you. I'm sorry this happened. His memory's got to come back."

She doesn't meet my eyes. "Night."

I say, "Don't worry about your dad. I bet he'll recognize you soon."

She shuffles down the hall, shoulders sagging. "He looked at me like I was a stranger."

I say, "Do you want me to make you some hot cocoa?"

"This is bigger than cheering up a kid with cocoa, so no thanks. Night, Mom."

She closes her bedroom door. I perch on the sofa and chew on a fingernail, worrying about Kelly. Then I text Violet. "Do you have time to talk?"

She replies a minute later. "Yes, call you soon."

My phone rings, and I answer. Buzz says, "I went to see Jack at Riverside Hospital, but they wouldn't let me see him. Did you know he was in the hospital?"

"Yeah, I did. Kelly and I saw him, but he's in rough shape. Abby was there."

"That's odd. She was in the room, but they wouldn't let me in."

"Abby and Jack got married. They probably let her stay because she is his wife."

Buzz's voice blasts in my ear. "They're married?"

"Yep."

"That was fast. Did he say how he hit his head?"

"He doesn't remember. He knows Abby, but he didn't recognize Kelly or me. It's breaking Kelly's heart."

"I'm sorry to hear that. Want me to come over for support?"

I sigh and consider what a relief it would be to have a friend by my side. Buzz had been a close friend for years, bringing a smile to my face no matter what we were going through at work and home. I say, "I'm tired, but sure, come over for a while."

Another call comes in, and I say, "Violet's calling. See you when you get here."

"Violet's calling? Ask her about my computer. Are my bank accounts safe?"

"Got to go." I hang up and answer Violet's call.

She says, "We've got to meet. Can I come over?"

My eyes grow wide. "Buzz is on his way over, but sure."

"Suits me fine. I have things to tell him too."

I hang up, and Kelly comes around the corner. "What's going on?"

"Violet's coming over, and Buzz is on his way to commiserate about your dad."

"I can't sleep. I'll make us tea." She goes in the kitchen, and I wonder how I can get Jack to recognize Kelly. Maybe I'll show him baby pictures of him holding Kelly to prod his memory. Kelly carries in mugs of peppermint tea and hands me one. She sinks into the sofa and says, "I wonder what Violet's going to say."

Someone raps hard on the door three times, and I say, "Who is it?"

"It's Violet, open up. It's wet out here."

She comes inside and glances around. "Buzz isn't here yet?" I shake my head, and she says, "Good. Let me tell you what's going on before he arrives."

Kelly says, "Can I get you some tea?"

Violet waves a hand in front of her face. "No, thanks. We don't have much time, and I need to say this. The seller of the gold sneakers is none other than Buzzard Solutions."

I cock my head. "I don't know that company. Who owns it?"

"Mom, it's got to be Buzz, doesn't it?"

Violet smiles. "Right you are. He recently opened a new LLC and was using it as a cover to sell the stolen shoes."

I say, "I was starting to trust him again. What a fool I was."

Violet touches my knee. "He did it for a good cause. He loves you and bought an expensive engagement ring to give you. He did the wrong thing for the right reasons with good intentions."

I huff out a breath. "Fat chance of us getting back together with him doing things like that behind my back." I sip tea and set it on the coffee table.

Violet says, "By the way, I heard from one of my contacts that Jack is in the hospital, and he and Abby were married."

I lean in and say, "He doesn't remember Kelly, and it's breaking our hearts."

Violet looks at Kelly. "I'm sorry to hear that. Is there any hope of his recovering his memory?"

I say, "We're not sure."

A loud knock on the door makes me flinch. A dog barks and whines, scratching at the door. I open the door, and Buzz's dog Happy bounds inside, shaking off rain and flinging drops of water all over.

"Happy!" Kelly opens her arms, and the dog runs to her. His wagging tail knocks a vanilla-scented candle off the coffee table to the floor, but I ignore it. Kelly is feeling low, and Happy will cheer her up. She sits on the floor and wraps her arms around the dog.

Buzz sits on a chair opposite Violet and me. He says, "I

hate to barge in with questions, but did Jack say how he ended up in the hospital?"

I shake my head. "No. His memory is gone."

The dog nuzzles Kelly with his nose. She pats his head and says, "Good dog."

Buzz sits on his hands, and his Adam's apple bounces up and down. "Violet, do I need to be worried about my money? What did you find out?"

I cock my head. "What's going on?"

Violet says, "Someone hacked into Buzz's computer when he clicked on a scam email." Kelly and I glance at each other with raised eyebrows. It reminds me of Craig's scam preying on the elderly. I wonder what the FBI agents are saying to Jack right now.

Violet says, "I'm sorry to report this, but they stole the money from the online auction you were running and redirected the funds to an offshore account. I don't think you'll ever see that money."

Buzz puts his head in his hands and moans. "The auction closed, and I shipped off the gold sneakers right before I got hacked and they stole my money. Irena, I took out a loan to buy you the ring. I thought if it was a bigger, better stone in the ring, you'd say yes. There's no way I can pay it back without money from the auction."

I say, "You know I don't care about rings. My hands get dirty at work, so I wouldn't wear it much. You shouldn't have gone into debt to buy a ring, but I guess I appreciate the thought behind it. But stealing the gold sneakers from me was just plain wrong."

He opens his hands, and his eyes are red. "I shouldn't have done it, and I'm sorry. I did it out of love for you. Is it so wrong to love someone for years despite not being noticed? I hoped if I bought the biggest ring with the shiniest stone you'd say yes."

I say, "I've always loved you as a friend. There's no question about that. And one day, we might have gotten married. But what you did puts a full stop to it for me now."

He clenches his fists and looks at the ceiling, gritting his teeth. He takes a deep breath and says, "I waited for years to propose to you, biding my time until the timing was right. But I'm done waiting in the wings. Violet, do you have that ring? Because I'm going to throw it off my boat and never propose to anyone ever again."

Violet says, "At Outrigger Services, we noticed that you took out a home equity line of credit before you bought the ring. When we learned your money from the auction was gone, I took the opportunity to ask a favor of Gus Griswold, the owner of the jewelry store, to see if he'd take the ring back and refund your money. I explained it was a very rough time for your group of friends, given Jack disappeared, and how Irena was upset and the timing was off for a proposal. I gave him the ring back, and he wrote you a refund check." She leans over and hands Buzz a check, which he pockets.

"Thanks, Violet. I really appreciate it."

I say, "Buzz, you've been such a good friend. You can be a great guy."

He rolls his eyes. "This is where you say you just want to be friends. I've heard that from you before. We'll leave it for now and see what happens. That's fine, for now, we're friends."

Kelly says, "The best of friends, I hope."

He says to her, "I'm here for you. Whenever you need something, just ask." He turns to Violet. "What about my bank accounts and the store? Can we open for business tomorrow?"

"We shut the hackers down. Vincent and Mimi love tackling projects like that, and they really dove into it to get revenge for you. You won't have problems from them unless you click on one of those scam emails again."

I stare at Buzz. "You took the gold sneakers. A friend doesn't do that to a friend."

He shrugs. "Jack sent them to me, and I was doing what I thought he would want, using the proceeds to make you happy. My intentions were good. Does that make sense?"

I bite my lip. "It almost does."

Kelly says, "Mom, Buzz is right. Dad sent the gold sneakers to him, not us. In a way, you stole them from Buzz when you kicked him out and kept his gold sneakers. It's his right to do what he wants with them."

I massage my temples. "From the sound of it, I'm the one who was wrong."

Violet says, "None of us like being wrong, do we?"

Kelly says, "I hate it."

Buzz opens his hands. "Who me? I'm always right. That never happens to me."

I say, "How about some drinks and pizza? We could celebrate that Abby found your dad, and one day, I hope he'll recognize us."

Buzz lowers his head. "I hope they have a long, happy life together."

We go in the kitchen, and I heat up a frozen pizza, pour beverages, and we sit around the table sharing stories. I frown as a thought crosses my mind and say, "I guess we should give the safe deposit box that Kelly found to Jack, now that he's back."

Kelly nods. "Sounds right to me. It was his."

Recalling how happy Abby and Jack were, I raise a glass of beer and say, "Here's to Abby and Jack. I hope they have a great future. And may Craig stay in jail for a long time."

We toast and set our glasses down. Violet says, "I wonder how Craig's doing in jail."

# CRAIG

I close my eyes. The hard bunk hurts my back. A stench of body odor hangs heavy in the jail cell. I grit my teeth and think of how to get back at Jack for betraying me. You don't rat out a friend to the Feds.

Springs creak on the lower bunk. My beefy cell mate stands and pokes me in the ribs. "Wake up, rich boy. I heard you were running a scam."

I barely breathe and hope he won't hurt me like he did earlier today when the guards weren't looking. The FBI called it a scam, but I don't think I did anything wrong. I should be congratulated for being an entrepreneur and starting a business.

My cellmate hisses at me. The sour smell of his pungent breath makes me wince. He says, "I'm looking forward to being a rich man, learning about your scam."

My right eye throbs where he hit me before dinner. I stare in the dark at the wall and blink back tears. But then a thought occurs to me. Maybe I could use this guy to get back at Jack. This cretin could be a conduit for revenge.

# 65

## FRANKIE

Agent Brick and I stand at Fishbone's bedside. We introduce ourselves and flash our badges after his ex-wife and daughter leave the hospital room. I cross my arms and resist the urge to wrinkle my nose, smelling body fluids and bleach.

I say, "What happened the night you were supposed to meet me? Why didn't you show up? Who hurt you?"

He frowns. "I don't know. I can't remember."

My partner gives me a side glance, and we raise our eyebrows. My pulse quickens. "It's important that you tell us who hurt you at the wharf. Was it a man or a woman?"

Abby holds his hand and says, "He doesn't remember anything. He lost his memory because of the head injury."

I nod to Brick to take over and step to the window to mull over this information.

Brick says, "Jack, do you have a faint memory of how you hit your head?"

Fishbone says in a hoarse voice, "I woke up when the ambulance came. That's all I know."

I release a breath and turn back to the man in bed. Monitors by his bedside beep. Fluids flow into the IV in his arm. I say, "We can see you're in rough shape. We'll come back later and see if your memory is returning. Any small bits you recall will help us track down who tried to kill you and stop you from testifying."

Brick says, "You remember your friend Craig, don't you? And the scam you were running?"

Fishbone gives us a blank stare. "I don't know what you're talking about." He closes his eyes, and Abby says, "He needs to rest."

I look at Brick and swallow hard. We're screwed without this key witness. Fishbone was the cornerstone in a case that could make my career. As we turn to go, I say to Abby, "One quick last question. Abby, were you his elusive girlfriend?"

A wide smile spreads across her face. "Yeah, that was me. We've been secretly going out, but no one knew. We didn't tell our friends because we wanted it to be a secret until we were sure it'd work out. We were about to break the news to his daughter, but then all this happened."

I nod and wonder if that's the whole truth as we file into the hall. I say to Brick under my breath, "Seems to me he was playing both women before he hurt his head, given how his ex-wife was sure he still loved her."

Brick punches the elevator button. "Love is a game with rules I'll never understand. That's why I'm seriously single."

"Me too."

We stride out to the car, and I say, "It looks like someone hit Jack to stop him from talking about the scam Craig was running. They wanted him silenced for good. Maybe that guy who was shot with the arrow told the Mother Mercy story to lead us off track. He could be the one who tried to kill Jack."

Brick says, "We should go back and interview that guy."

Jack closes his eyes, and I lean over and kiss his stubbled cheek. He's been through so much. I pat his hand and pick up my purse to grab something from the hospital cafeteria.

Jack opens his eyes. "Where are you going?"

"To get something to eat. I'll be back in a few minutes."

He says, "Leave the door open. It's stuffy in here."

I prop open the door and go out, just as the thug who choked me is being wheeled in a hospital bed down the hall. Our eyes connect, and I glance back at Jack to make sure he's okay.

The thug says, "Stop for a minute. I need to talk to her." He looks in Jack's room and says, "That's the guy I was looking for, isn't it? That's Jack Fishbone."

I pull the door closed, but it's too late. My body breaks out in a cold sweat. I've exposed the man I love to danger and possible death. I cross my arms and stand in front of the door. "You'd better stay away from him."

A nurse hurries over. "Keep your voice down. There will be no violence in this hospital. I'll call security if I have to. And take this patient to his room."

My body trembles as the big, broad-shouldered man in the hospital bed scowls at me with furrowed dark brows. Aides push his bed down the hall, and he says, "I'm sure we'll meet again. I'll come over when you least expect it."

I blow out a breath and stand guard at the door until the creep is wheeled out of sight. I slip into Jack's room and take his hand in mine. While he sleeps, I say, "I love you, and I'll protect you with my last breath."

Up next is *By Midnight!*

A debt-collecting thug threatens family and friends. They must come up with the money by midnight.
But the clock is ticking down...
**Read By Midnight!**

Sign up for my author newsletter to hear about new releases and book deals.

Follow me on BookBub for updates

Thank you for reading *Missing Man*. Please let other readers know what to expect by posting ratings and reviews on Goodreads, Amazon and BookBub.

My YouTube channel shows the setting for my novels

Thank you for reading my books!

# ABOUT THE AUTHOR

Susan Specht Oram writes mysteries-thrillers with high stakes and heart set in a small Pacific Northwest town. Previously, she served as senior director of corporate communications for biotechnology companies. Susan worked as an activity aide in an upscale nursing home's psychiatric unit. She was a potter and painter with an art studio in Seattle and has also worked as a market researcher, a nurse's aide, a waitress, and a library page. Her essays have been published in Mothering Magazine, Twins Magazine and Utne Reader.

Susan grew up near Detroit, Michigan and received a BFA with Honors from University of Oregon and a MBA in Marketing from Seattle University. She lives in a windy part of the Pacific Northwest with her husband and their rescue dog.

# BOOKS BY SUSAN SPECHT ORAM

**Novels by Susan Specht Oram**

Shore Lodge

The Thieves

Cabin Eight

The Mother's Threat

Secrets at the Cafe

Under Jackson Bridge

Missing Man

By Midnight

The Winter Storm

The Cold Night

Avalanche

These Lies

The Gas Station Motel

A Chilling Christmas Eve

**Humorous fiction**

Boating with Buddy, a report from a canine correspondent

**Nonfiction**

Personal memoir series: Strangers on a Train

Brief business books on investor relations, crisis communication and public relations

**Strangers on a Train Memoir Series**

Green Light

The Train

Canoe

Soup Kettle

Bathtub

Phone Call

Watering Can

Waterfall